DREAMTIME

Books by Richard S. Platz

Novels

OF MAGIC AND DELUSION

PROJECT DIVINE WIND

APPOINTMENT AT ANGAHUAN
(Co-Authored with James A. Kline)

Short Stories

MEMORIES & OTHER FICTIONS

DREAMTIME

Short Stories of Richard S. Platz

Blue Lake Press

Cover painting by Richard S. Platz

BLUE LAKE PRESS
A Western Division Subsidiary of the
Chicago, Whitewater & Mad River Company
P O Box 797, Blue Lake, CA 95525

ISBN: 978-0692239650

Contents

Preface

These short stories are inventions of the mind. Some will be called fantasies. Others science fiction. Still others daydreams. Or myths. Or metaphors. The truth is that they are all merely inventions. None was conceived to be of any particular genre. Each was born during a tempest of wonder in the dreamtime of my imagination, as if by force of its own will to become.

I picture Rilke pacing the dark battlements of Duino Castle, battered by shrieking winds above the storm-tossed sea, daring his terrible angels to destroy him. Later he would write in the First Elegy:

"All the living
make the mistake of drawing too sharp distinctions.
Angels, it is said, are often unable to tell
whether they move among the living or dead."

I was taught to believe that an omnipotent God watched over me, intervening in worldly affairs if properly beseeched. I was also instructed never to wear white socks with a suit. These teachings and so many others all have proven to be of no use whatsoever. Perhaps all teachings, like all stories, tell more about the teacher than the nature of reality.

Of course, I know the difference between scientific fact and fiction, reality and fantasy, daydreams and metaphor and myth. I can distinguish the conjurings of my imagination from what is actually possible in this unyielding world of rock and stone.

Can't I?

I know perfectly well that the World Wide Web has not attained self-consciousness.

Or has it?

I know that the coyotes howling from beyond the trees at the far end of the meadow cannot transform themselves into human beings.

Or can they?

I know we cannot send a task force back in time to draw a blood sample from the baby Jesus.

But what if we could?

These are odd stories all. I'll admit that. A few have such firm footing in science that they will almost certainly come to pass. Others, not so much. What they have in common is that they are the stuff of dreams.

June 2014
Blue Lake, California

Mescalito

Colin Fulkerth lost his way.   Heading for reliable sweetwater tanques in the bedrock of a side canyon, he had somehow missed the turnoff and climbed all the way through the arroyo to the baked alkali waste of the high Chihuahuan desert.   Only a few scrawny mesquite shrubs dotted the landscape of low creosote bush, brittlebush, yucca, and ocotillo.   Thorny cholla and prickly pear and hedgehog cactus hindered the walking.   There was no shade.

His boots slipped, sucked beneath the shifting sand, as he struggled up a dry wash beneath the noonday sun. His backpack bore down heavily on the raw, pink skin of his bare, sweat-slick shoulders, sliding up and down like a whetstone.   Cholla needles had caught in the legs of his trousers and pricked his shins and needled his ankles with each step. But he dared not stop to pick out the harpoon-like barbs. He had to find water. Find water or die.

Dazed and faint, his thoughts became a roulette wheel.   The ball clacked crazily across a dozen revolving visions before settling into a final slot, where a weathered board gate in an adobe wall stood facing him, just a step above the cobblestone street. Tugging on the frayed rope that dangled through a hole in the gate would lift the crossbar. He had built that gate and the crossbar and the release rope. He could hear the heavy clunk of the two-by-four lifting and the welcoming squeal of the hinges.   Inside lay the moist green lawn of the inner courtyard and the mossy brick pathway still wet with puddles as bright as the sky, surrounded by banana trees with deep green leaves like elephant ears that led up the pathway to the deep umbrella-like shade of a huge mango. But needles pierced his shin and the rope slipped through his fingers. The gate swung shut. Stunned, for a moment he stared blankly at the aching cobblestones, crooked as impacted teeth and trodden now only by ghosts, before they dissolved into desert sand.

Colin fell to his knees in the burning sand and buried his face in his hands. It was no use. His eyes ached from the dizzying brightness. His mouth was so dry his tongue had begun to swell. His lips were cracked and bleeding. The relentless sun blistered his skin. There was no escape.

He crawled into the speckled shade beneath a twisted mesquite bush, leaving in the sand the slithering trail of a great lizard. Sand clung to his arms and his chest as he struggled free from his pack and rolled onto his back, the hot sand stinging his burned shoulders like a nest of fire ants. He wrestled a shirt from his pack and spread it over himself, then rested his head on the pack. Sucking in the stifling desert heat, he gazed up through the tiny leaves and lacy branches of the mesquite. The single black dot of a vulture circled far overhead. He tugged the hat down over his eyes and squinted toward the horizon. There Colin Fulkerth rested, suspended in time. Breathing. Hallucinating. Waiting for death and the vulture to sniff him out.

Through half-closed eyes he saw the twin spires of the old bell towers of Ajijic against a rich blue sky. The bells hung silently within each tower. He waited for the bells to begin their slow swinging and for the loud, round tones to crash over him and wake him from this suffering. He could smell the wet grass of the zocalo all around him. And the scent of the bougainvillea, rich and sweet. Hear the clatter of hooves on the cobblestones. As his eyes focused, the bell towers resolved into the fruiting stalks of twin yucca plants. The bells were their fruit capsules. Despair overwhelmed him, and Colin Fulkerth was wrenched with dry sobs.

He shut his eyes and was riding the *Lunada*. As the sun set and the full moon rose, he rode his horse Lucero up a steep trail towards the narrow canyon. Through the twilight Lucero carried him higher and higher while he and his compadres swigged burning tequila from pint bottles. In the canyon it was too dark to see, so he let Lucero have the reins. Lucero knew the trail. The riders were already drunk by the time they reached the plateau, a broad, flat grassland far above the pool of deep turquoise lake and the toy-like lights of the village below. There they let the horses run, galloping until he fell from his mount when Lucero veered suddenly to the right. Why, only the horse knew. Unhurt, he scrambled to his feet and chased after the stallion laughing. It was all so vivid. So sweet. The moonlit silver mountains above. The dark coolness of the dewy grass. Companionship. Time that would last forever.

A cool shadow passed over his face. Colin Fulkerth opened his eyes. Before him stood a figure, blocking the afternoon sun. Shirt and trousers were as gray as the sand. A belt of rope was tied around its waist. A folded blanket was draped over his left shoulder. A cloth bag and a yellow gourd dangled from the right. Huarachis covered naked feet. Colin could not see the eyes in the deep shade of a black sombrero.

"Water," Colin whispered.

The figure made no reply.

"*Agua*," Colin repeated in Spanish. A wisp of sand blew into his eyes. When he opened them again, the vision was still there. Colin gazed at him. "Who are you?"

The figure never moved. Never wavered. Just watched.

"Are you real?" Colin rasped.

There was a slight nod of the terrible black sombrero and a broad smile of irregular white teeth. Nothing more.

"Then you must be Death," Colin whispered, squeezing his eyes on fresh tears. He trembled as the shadow flickered over him. A few moments later a rough hand burrowed into the sand beneath his head and lifted. A trickle of tepid water touched his lips. Colin took a small sip and let the precious fluid run over his chapped lips and swollen tongue to the back of his throat. There was hardly enough to swallow.

Colin opened his eyes. The face of an old Indian filled his vision, smiling down. The tawny skin was deeply creased leather and the deep-set eyes were brown. Ancient eyes. Eyes that seemed to regard him and look through him at the same time. The Indian tipped a dried yellow gourd and a little more water spilled onto Colin's tongue. He moved it around his mouth. This time the swallowing was easier.

"Who are you?" Colin asked again.

Again the gourd rose slowly. Again a trickle of water soothed his throat. Finally the Indian spoke, "When you are ready, Mescalito, I will walk with you to the water tanques." His voice was tenor and nasal and had the peculiar sing-song lilt of Spanish. But Spanish was not his native tongue. He began picking the cholla needles out of Colin's pant legs.

"I am not Mescalito."

"Who are you then," the Indian smiled, playing along with this delightful game.

"My name is Colin Fulkerth."

"Ah, yes." The smile deepened into a grin. "And what is Colin Fulkerth? Another name for Mescalito?"

"But I am not Mescalito."

"You say that you are not Mescalito," the Indian said, enjoying himself immensely. "How do you know that you are not Mescalito?"

"Because . . because . . .," Colin licked his lips, ". . . because I remember things."

"What things do you remember, Mescalito?"

"Things from my own life. And stop calling me Mescalito, will you?"

"As you wish, Mescalito."

"My name is Colin Fulkerth. I remember things. Things that happened to me."

"Can you sit up now?"

The Indian's hands were strong as they helped him into a sitting position. Colin took the water gourd and drank from it. "It is almost empty," he said.

"Finish it. There is more water nearby. We will walk there together."

Colin let the last drops fall on his tongue. "Thank you," he said.

That made the Indian beam. Laughter shown from the crinkled corners of his eyes. "Are you ready to walk to the tanques? Or would you wait for the dark to fall?"

"I guess I'm ready." Slowly, with the help of the Indian, Colin stood. Lightheaded, he swayed for a moment while the old man steadied him.

The Indian raised Colin's backpack, slung it over his shoulder beside the empty gourd and the sack, and set off into the bright sun that still hovered just above the horizon. They walked slowly, the Indian turning often to wait for Colin to catch up. Always he smiled. But the sand was soft and Colin had never been more exhausted. They walked on until the red ball of the sun touched the edge of the world and sank quietly into twilight. Colin started to feel a little better.

They entered the top of a rocky defile that soon grew steep. The footing was easier here without the soft sand. They descended a short way into a copse of short willows and then to the edge of a large pool that filled a smooth bowl in the bedrock floor. Further down Colin could see another, smaller pool. He could hear the water trickling down to the lower pond. As he approached the edge of the pool on moist, packed sand, a frog jumped into the water.

"Sit over here," the Indian said, setting down Colin's backpack near an old fire ring. "I will bring you fresh water."

Colin eased himself down onto the firm sand, leaned back against the smooth, exposed rock wall, and watched the old man bend and fill the gourd. It felt cooler in the canyon beside the water. Colin studied the myriad animal footprints in the flat sand beside the pool. "Are there coyotes?" he asked.

"Of course."

"What else?"

"Pack rats. Javalina. Others. But you have nothing to fear."

"Why not?"

"Because they will know who you are."

"Will you stay with me here tonight?"

"If you wish me to." The Indian handed him the dripping gourd. "Drink it slowly. Not too much at a time. I will gather some firewood."

The old man came back before dark with an armload of mesquite branches and lit a fire with a silver zippo lighter. He sat down on the far side of the fire ring and ate some fruit from a barrel cactus and a handful of nuts. He offered none to Colin, but that was alright. Colin did not feel the least bit hungry.

"Tell me why you think I am Mescalito," Colin said.

"Because I was looking for you. I was crossing this desert in a straight line toward a distant peak, thinking only of Mescalito. Looking for you in my path. And look, I already found you several times this way." He held out the small cloth sack. Inside were a half dozen segmented, spineless cacti. Like tiny green succulent pumpkins.

"Fresh peyote buttons."

"You see? And then I saw you lying right in my path in the form of a man. Beneath that scrawny mesquite bush. You must have crawled under it as a lizard. I saw the tracks. And I have seen you before. Do you not remember? How could you not be Mescalito? There is no one else out here."

"But I am a man, not a cactus."

"You can take any form you want, Mescalito. You know that. I have seen you change from a coyote into a man."

"You saw that?"

"Yes. And back into a coyote again."

"Did this happen right in front of you?"

"It was far away. In the evening. But my eyes are good."

"How do you know that *you* are not Mescalito?"

This made the old man laugh so hard that he gripped his belly and almost fell over. When the laughter subsided, he said, "Because *you* are Mescalito."

"But I was dying of thirst when you found me. Would Mescalito die of thirst?"

He grew somber. Thoughtful. "You were showing me your vulnerability, Mescalito. To remind me of the compassion I must have for every living thing."

"Then how do you explain my memories?"

"They are dreams. The dreams of someone else. Perhaps someone who has died here. Probably long ago. You have taken up the dreams of one who died here long ago."

"But I passed no grave."

"They were the dreams of a someone who was never buried."

"I saw no bones."

"The bones were scattered by the coyotes and the pack rats and the buzzards." He smiled compassionately. "Do not worry, Mescalito. When the morning comes, you will remember who you are."

With that he added two branches to the fire, then came over and spread his blanket out for Colin to wrap himself in.

"No, I couldn't take your blanket–"

"Please," the Indian said. "I want you to have it. I will be warm enough by the fire."

The blanket felt good. The stars had come out and a chill was setting in. Colin pulled the blanket tight about his neck. "How do you know English so well?" he asked.

"I do not speak English," the Indian said. "I am Yaqui. I speak only Yaqui."

"But . . . we have been speaking together!"

"We have been speaking only Yaqui. Now go to sleep, Mescalito."

A chill shot down his spine. Colin could not remember ever learning Yaqui. Could any of the old man's nonsense be true? Confused, he watched the old Yaqui as he sat before the flickering fire. Sparks rose with lurid red tails. All the long night the Indian fed the fire with mesquite branches, or else he sat stone still, eyes open, but not seeing things of this world. The old man no longer returned his gaze. He seemed supremely content, alone with his own visions.

He must have slept deeply, dreamlessly, for when he awoke to the first ghostly light of morning, the Indian was gone. The blanket was gone. The fire had gone out. He rose and sniffed the ground to confirm that the Indian had really been here. Here the sand smelled of the Indian's scent. Over there he could smell where the blanket had lain. The tattered remnant of bleached blue canvas that had once been a backpack lay below a crevice in the rock wall. He did not go near it.

Just as the old Yaqui had promised, Mescalito remembered who he was. Satisfied, he drank deeply from the still, cold pool, shook himself all over, then trotted out into the boundless desert, stopping only once to howl at the band of golden light spreading across the eastern horizon.

Genome

They had trouble making themselves understood, these three heavily-bearded soldiers of fortune, adorned in raiments of gold and silver brocade, as they rode their camels southward toward Bethlehem. It was not the vocabulary, nor the grammar, nor the syntax, but the *pronunciation* of the words. The vowels. The sounds of Aramaic had evolved as they trickled down through the ages. But that was alright. The peasants thought them wise men on a holy pilgrimage from a far distant land in the east.

The bright summer sun burned down mercilessly on their swarthy skin. The landscape was hilly and brushy and forested with clusters of short trees, a bit greener than the place where they had trained. And the air was different here, ripe with the fetid odor of men and animals living too closely together without sewage treatment. And the underlying stench of disease and death.

They knew exactly where they were, of course, but not where they were going. The mission commander, whom they called by his code name 'Gaspar,' would occasionally pull a strange black instrument from beneath his robe and take a bearing on the sun and a distant hill or two to confirm their position.

The one they called 'Balthazar' rode second in line. A big man, larger and hairier than his companions, he was the cultural anthropologist, historian, and linguist. Strapped to his saddle were the maps, charts, and scrolls.

Melchior brought up the rear. Short and stocky, he was the primary herbalist and biomedical specialist and rode with a plump leather medical satchel tied to his saddle. He held the reins of the trailing pack camel.

Each knew the others' roles as well as his own. They had studied and trained together for years, these three. They were all accomplished survivalists. Experts in the martial arts. And, of course, phlebotomists. For the primary task of their mission was to draw blood.

But time travel is a tricky business. They had each known it was a one-way street. Yet they had each volunteered. Each had signed consents and waivers and powers of attorney and wills. And with great dignity and honor they had been sent off in a tearful ceremony like kamikaze pilots into a hazy sky of no return.

In order to secure safe passage through the kingdom, they had sought an audience with Herod the Great at his palace in Jerusalem. The King, they were told, was ill and indisposed to see them, but a few gold coins facilitated a meeting with his son Herod Archelaus. They were led through dark, echoing stone hallways to a chamber lit with oil lamps and a crackling fire in an open hearth. Incense billowed from a metal caldron to mask the underlying stench. Scant beams of sunlight blazed through the smoky air from high, narrow windows above where pigeons fluttered and cooed. Opposite the fire was a raised throne, a half-circle of red chairs, and long wooden trestle table.

Alone and in silence they waited until the great doors were drawn open and Archelaus, flanked by two guards in dull bronze armor and bearing swords and spears, led a retinue of his advisors to the throne. He was a short, slender young man in a thin white gown that appeared to have been slept in. Golden sandals on his feet slapped the polished stone floor. His facial hair was sparse and pale, entirely unlike the black, lusty beard of his father portrayed on the ubiquitous statues and clay tablets.

The three supplicants fell to their knees and dropped their eyes until they were addressed.

"Why would you travel to Bethlehem?" asked a high, effeminate voice.

Balthazar rose to speak for them. "We are travelers from the east," he began slowly, but it was clear that even the king's translators were having trouble with his dialect. Finally one whispered to the regent.

"Where in the east?" demanded Archelaus, his eyes flickering nervously.

"India," Balthazar said, speaking slowly. His declaration was met with frowns of incomprehension. He tried alternative Aramaic pronunciations, then Hebrew, then Arabic, but to no avail. The situation was becoming tense. Finally, as things balanced dangerously, Balthazar amended his answer to, "Persia."

"Ah, Per*sis*," announced a translator, with a Greek emphasis on the vowels.

"Persia," smiled the king's son, and the tension lifted a little. "So you are Magi?"

"Yes," agreed Balthazar, as he unrolled an astrological chart and began to explain their quest.

It was a harrowing experience, despite the best efforts of the king's interpreters. For much of the dialogue they relied on the scrolls and astrological charts brought with them, unrolling the parchments on the table before Archelaus and his advisors. The alignment of the stars, Balthazar explained, portended that a great personage had been born somewhere in Judea no more than a week earlier, four days before the summer solstice. Perhaps a King of the Jews.

This drew frowns and grumbling and a dark look from the regent. The court astrologers recalled a spectacular conjunction of Jupiter and Venus in the eastern heavens on the morning in question. They had wondered at its portent. They now examined the records of other, earlier portents, as Balthazar unrolled new charts before them. Nodding their heads, they finally agreed, "Bethlehem."

The wanderers were led from the courtroom to a small stone-walled chamber and locked inside while Archelaus conferred with his advisors. They spoke a little at first, agreeing that Archelaus appeared to hold the real power in the kingdom in every way but title.

"What if the real Magi have already passed through?" Melchior wondered aloud in English that was tinged with Hispanic overtones.

"We *are* the real Magi," responded Gaspar in Aramaic.

They waited in silence in the dark stone chamber as the perfume of dread began to flower in the stagnant air.

"Off with their heads!" Melchior suddenly whispered in English. A crooked grin twisted his lips, but the sweat dripping from his brow betrayed his glibness. It was entirely conceivable that this pint-sized despot could suddenly shout just that, and it would be done. "I'd give my left nut for a well-oiled M-16."

"I'd be happy with a rusty old six-shooter," grunted Balthazar.

"Cut the English," ordered Gaspar. "Aramaic."

After a wait that seemed interminable, the door was opened and they were again admitted to the throne room.

"Under seal of the Great King Herod," the King's son decreed, "you shall have safe passage to go and find this child and bring back to us news of his whereabouts so the we too may go and honor him."

Not exactly like Matthew had put it, Gaspar thought, *but close enough for government work.*

Now they followed the main road south through scrubland hills wooded with fig and olive trees and tall date palms, rising and falling and rising again to where Bethlehem should have been. Gaspar took ever more frequent readings from familiar landmark peaks, which had changed not at all over the millennia. But they had already ridden ten klicks from Jerusalem, and all they saw around them were a few squat, square, wood-and-mud-block huts scattered in clusters among the gravel slopes and rock walls and sparsely tilled fields. He was growing uneasy. So he paused to let Balthazar catch up and pointed to a skinny old man who with the aid of a wooden staff was approaching haltingly along the edge of the roadway. He wore threadbare rags for a tunic and a tattered, woven mantle drawn tightly about his neck despite the afternoon heat. "Ask him," Gaspar instructed.

They waited for the old man to draw abreast, then Balthazar inquired, "Where is Bethlehem?"

At first he kept stumping along through the dust, pretending not to hear, as if the rich man riding the camel had made a mistake. But after Balthazar repeated the request three times in various dialects, the old man raised his rheumy eyes and spread his arms. "All about you," he said.

"This is Bethlehem?"

They gazed around the parched, empty valley. Ahead of them stood a line of sycamores and palms where a waterway intersected the high road. There was no grid of streets. Nearby a yellow dog barked at a cluster of sheep behind a corral of woven brush. In the distance two men plowed a field with a brace of oxen. Somewhere a rooster crowed. The air was warmer than it should have been and ripe with the odor of raw sewage.

"*Jesus!*" muttered Melchior.

"Where is the inn?" Balthazar pressed.

The old fellow turned, bracing against his staff, and pointed back toward a collection of low stone structures about a quarter mile behind him. There they found a few chattering women hauling up buckets of water from the village well and pouring it into clay jars they would carry away on their shoulders. The inn itself was not a single building, but a sprawl of small, square stone-walled rooms clustered around a large central courtyard. A wooden stable squatted behind them. Men and women milled around the courtyard or sat in the shade of a fig tree.

A middle-aged man in a clean tunic approached them and bowed deeply. "I am the innkeeper. How can I be of service to your honors?"

Balthazar unwound his leg from the inflexible platform saddle and lowered his long legs stiffly to the ground. He straightened his back, then leaned over the innkeeper. "Do you have room for us?" His accent was improving with experience and practice.

"There is always room for such as your honors," the man smiled. "You can have that room there," he pointed. "It is our largest and best. I will remove the woman in it now. She just gave birth to a son. But she has not yet paid me in full for her lodging."

"When?" asked Balthazar, suddenly alert.

"I will remove her right away."

"No. When was the baby born?"

The innkeeper thought for a moment. "A week ago."

"Let her stay where she is." Balthazar pulled a gold coin from beneath his robe and held it out. "This is for our lodging, and for hers too. It is the baby that we have come to honor."

The man could not take his eyes off the sparkling coin. "Of course. Just as you wish." He bowed deeply. "I will have another room prepared for your honors at once."

Guests of the inn and a few passers by had begun to gather about the riders. *Gawkers*, Gaspar thought. *As we anticipated.* They were mostly women, the men having not yet returned from the fields and flocks. None stood taller than Balthazar's shoulder. Cautious in their curiosity, they kept a respectful distance. An old man spoke out from the back, "What is it about this baby, sire?"

Balthazar ignored him and leaned over the innkeeper. "Have any *other* babies been born here in Bethlehem during the past two moons?"

The innkeeper thought for a moment. "Two that I can recall."

"Boys?"

"Both were girls."

Balthazar wheeled on the gathering crowd. "Is that correct?" he asked them, towering like a giant. "Only three babies born? Two of them girls? Is that right?"

They cringed away, several nodding in corroboration. Some returned to the safety of their doorways. Satisfied, Gaspar and Melchior lowered themselves from their camels and joined Balthazar, who addressed the innkeeper. "We would like to see this newborn."

The innkeeper turned to a woman lingering in the shadow of the nearby doorway. "Woman," he called. "Come out here. Bring your child."

A young woman stepped out into the westering sunlight. She was small and dark, not much more than a girl. She carried her baby, wrapped in a tattered cloth, awkwardly in her arms. The three visitors encircled her as she approached.

Balthazar spoke softly. "Are you called 'Mary'?" He used the Aramaic word "*Maryām*."

"*Miryam*," she corrected in Hebrew, smiling shyly.

"Do you have a husband?" he asked gently.

"Yes. His name is Joseph." Again the name in Hebrew. *Yossef.*

"Is he here with you?"

"No. Joseph rode to Jerusalem to make arrangements. He is to be back this evening."

"And does your baby have a name?"

"Not yet," she said. "Not until the circumcision. At the temple in Jerusalem."

"What will you call him?"

She lowered her eyes. "I do not know."

"Have you spoken about it with your husband?"

"Yes. We have not yet decided."

So far the script had gone close to plan. For the next part, however, there had been disagreement among the experts. Don't interfere with anything, one school had argued. The other argued, encourage what we already know. Balthazar glanced at his companions. Melchior shrugged. Gaspar nodded. Balthazar drew a breath and followed the script. "You will call him 'Jesus,'" he told her, using the Aramaic word "*Yeshua.*"

"*Eashoa?*" she asked in Hebrew.

"Yes," he nodded, and then knelt down before her. Gaspar joined him in the gravelly dirt. Melchior just stood with his mouth open, staring at the mother and child. Gaspar elbowed him in the thigh, and he too dropped to his knees.

"We have brought you gifts to honor this child, who is born to be King of the Jews," Balthazar recited. As he had done a hundred times before. Only this time it was palpably different. This time it was for real.

Mary was stunned. "The Messiah?" Her voice was small and disbelieving.

"You did not know?" asked Balthazar.

The crowd had fallen silent. Mary shook her head. "I am afraid that you have made a mistake."

Balthazar said, "We are Magi, learned in astrology and scripture. We have followed the stars here to your doorstep. There can be no doubt."

"The scriptures . . . the prophecies . . . the dreams . . . but *no!*"

"You had no inkling?"

"*No!*"

Still on their knees the visitors pulled from beneath their robes their gifts, just as they had rehearsed, the traditional offerings that they had brought with them from an unfathomably distant time and place. Melchior held out frankincense. Balthazar myrrh. And Gaspar gold in the form of counterfeit Roman coins. Then they rose and each laid his gift at Mary's feet.

Seeing such treasure lying in the courtyard dirt, the innkeeper stepped forth. "Please, your honors. Bring this all into the dining hall. Come inside. Please."

They picked their gifts from the ground and followed him into the hall, an open room, larger than the cramped sleeping rooms, with a high ceiling of rafters covered with thatch. Two low tables hewn from sycamore and chairs with seats of woven reeds lined the walls. They laid their offerings on the closest table. Mary carried the baby in after them, and they made room for her. The spectators crowded the open doorway, but did not enter.

"May I hold him?" Gaspar asked, towering over Mary. She stared at him dumbfounded, then reached up and placed the baby gently into his arms. The baby did not cry, but gazed into Gaspar's face with wide brown newborn eyes that took in everything, yet differentiated nothing.

Things were unfolding smoothly. Just as they had trained. They had practiced this moment a thousand times, enacting their own and each other's roles. Planned for every contingency. Anything that might go wrong. This was the whole point of the mission. Gaspar lifted the baby gently from the young girl's arms. It all seemed unreal. Just another rehearsal. Balthazar would draw the blood. His hand was already beneath his tunic for the needle and syringe.

Melchior was to run interference. Watch the crowd. Keep them back. Block their view of the process. Restrain anyone who might try to interfere. But suddenly Melchior turned and laid his hand on Gaspar's shoulder. "Let me hold the baby," he said.

Gaspar was caught off guard. He shrugged off Melchior's hand and turned to study him. Shook his head. "Get back to your position."

"Let me hold him."

"Get back. That's an order." Gaspar's tone was hard.

"Let me hold him."

Mary was frowning. The innkeeper shuffled nervously. The small crowd sensed something was wrong. Gaspar turned to Balthazar, who nodded imperceptibly.

Gaspar handed the child over to Melchior, who took him gently, reverently. He smiled and kissed the baby on the forehead. The baby smiled. Maryam smiled. The innkeeper smiled. The crowd relaxed.

Melchior held him for a long moment, then handed him back to Gaspar and returned to his position facing the crowd. Balthazar pulled out the needle and beneath the folds of his tunic drew a blood sample from the baby's arm. The baby never flinched. It was all over in twenty seconds.

No crying he made, thought Gaspar.

Afterwards a stableman and two servants held the camels while the riders unloaded their possessions into a stone and mud-block building across from the dining hall. The roof was dried clay so low that Balthazar could not stand erect. Three woven mats were brought in to provide for sleeping. There were no windows. Only a doorway with a wooden door standing open. The sun cast a long reddish beam through the doorway as it prepared to set. A servant brought a smoky oil lamp and set it on a wooden table by the doorway.

Gaspar closed the door and confronted Melchior angrily in English. "You refused a direct order."

Melchior laughed at him. "What are you going to do, write me up?" He wore that maddening lopsided grin.

"We can't afford a breakdown of discipline here. We've got to follow protocol."

"Maybe you're considering a court martial?" Melchior still grinned.

"Get serious. You were threatening the whole mission. You could have put us at risk. What were you thinking?"

Melchior's smile faded. "I was brought up Catholic. Did you know that?"

Gaspar nodded. "I know everything about you. But I thought that was all behind–"

"I know. I know. I'm not saying I *believe* any of it anymore. But it's just that . . . if he just happens to *be* the Christ Child . . . the Messiah . . . and I know it's all crazy . . . but if he *is* . . . if he just happens to *be* . . . then how could I *not* take my turn holding him?"

Gaspar let out a sigh.

"No one else from our time will ever have this chance," Melchior continued.

Gaspar said nothing.

"And I didn't see how it was going to threaten the mission."

"It's just about discipline. Order."

"There *is* no order anymore. We're on our own here."

Gaspar considered. "All the more reason to follow the Plan."

"I won't fuck this up anymore. I promise."

Gaspar nodded. Shook himself like a small dog. Then, returning to Aramaic, he said, "We can draw the next two blood samples in the morning. After Joseph gets back. Give her a chance to talk it over with him. Get used to this new weirdness. Better to do it when they're together. Joseph first. He should be pleased with a gold coin of his own. After that, Mary should not be a problem, after she sees that we have done him no harm."

"According to plan."

"Yes. According to the Plan."

That night Balthazar was sick. He spent a lot of time outside hovering over the slop jar. The air had grown cold, but he was sweating and achy as he tossed on his thin mat of palm fronds. He moaned in his half-sleep.

"What's wrong?" Gaspar asked, shaking him.

"I caught something. The *shits*," he said, using the Germanic idiom. "Weak. I heave, but there's nothing left to throw up."

"Did you take anything for the flu?"

"Everything. I'll feel better by morning."

But in the morning he didn't feel better. And Mary was gone. Joseph had come in the night, and they had gathered their treasure and ridden off on two donkeys, their own and one they bought from the innkeeper with a gold coin.

"Why," Gaspar asked the innkeeper. "What was their hurry?"

"They had to be at the temple in Jerusalem at first light. For the circumcision."

Gaspar hung his head. *The eighth day*. He should have taken that into account. "When will they be back?"

The innkeeper shrugged. "They won't."

"Why not?"

"They were afraid."

"Afraid of us?"

"No. I don't think so."

"What then?"

"Herod. They were afraid of what he might do when he learns about the baby. The Messiah."

"Where will they go?"

"Joseph mentioned something about Egypt."

We screwed up, Gaspar thought as he shuffled back to their hut with the bad news.

"I can follow them and get the blood samples by myself," said Melchior, rising and taking up his blanket. "You stay here with Balthazar."

"Not according to the Plan," said Gaspar. "We can't split up."

"I won't be gone long. They couldn't have gotten far."

"No. We'll catch up with them later. Our first task is to take care of the sample we already have. It's the important one."

Melchior considered Gaspar's implacable glare, then dropped his eyes in submission.

Gaspar continued in a whisper, "And we've got to get Balthazar out of here. Just in case he takes a turn for the worse. Or we catch what he's got. Get him out and into the back country where we can deal with this."

"According to the Plan," Melchior said.

"That's all we can do. Follow the Plan. Hope for the best."

Balthazar could barely ride. Dark pustules had begun to surface in his groin area and his fingernails were staining black. But the symptoms could indicate any number of conditions. Many of them benign. Only a few were more ominous. He clung to the unforgiving wooden saddle like a life raft, bent over and sick and pale and weak, and endured the camel's pounding stride. He neither protested nor complained. Balthazar knew that this rapid exodus was all according to the Plan. The Plan he had signed on to. Everything had been anticipated and calculated. Optimized. The Plan maximized the chances of success of the mission. Though not necessarily his individual chance of survival. But, he would feel better soon enough. He always had before. After all, he had the constitution of an ox—which he had never actually seen before yesterday—and he would snap back to health with a little R&R.

They located the place where they were to leave the sample. It was not far from where the Dead Sea Scrolls would be found nearly two millennia later. But a little higher into the hills. Where earth-penetrating, side-viewing radar and echo-thumping with a grid of seismic sensors would locate a small, unopened, limestone cave just beneath the surface. Gaspar pounded with a carpenter's hammer while Melchior slowly turned the long shaft of the carbide-tipped masonry bit they had brought with them.

They broke through into the sealed cavern. Gaspar inserted the blood vial into the titanium canister that would just fit through the opening and sealed it. Melchior pushed it in with the drill and left the shaft in the hole. They packed rocks and sand over the work site and together managed to wrestle a flat boulder into place to cap it. They recognized the boulder. It was the same one they had practiced with, though now a little less weathered and worn.

Balthazar waited below in the shade of the camels as the ringing of iron on steel reverberated through the brilliant wasteland of crenulated foothills. He had never felt worse. His breathing had become labored. His fingers were almost black. Necrotic tissue. No doubt about it. And whatever it was, it was spreading. He was losing the battle. With the palms of his numb hands he tried to turn the pages of a small medical manual, but it was already growing too late to see clearly.

The years of wandering had been hard, but now they seemed like an unpleasant dream dreamt long ago. He no longer called himself "Gaspar." Hadn't for more than thirty years. Now he was "Joseph." When asked where he was from, he would say "Arimathea." There was in fact no real place called Arimathea. When pressed, he would describe it as a small village in Persia, or, if his inquisitor was familiar with Persia, then Egypt, or Syria, or Greece. Once he had to locate it in India. But always he would give a different answer. All in accordance with the Plan.

He had changed his name long before returning to Jerusalem, not wanting to be connected with the Magi who had met with Herod Archelaus on their way to Bethlehem. He had of course worried that another Joseph of Arimathea would show up and contest his bona fides, but none had. He had turned out to be the "real" Joseph of Arimathea, befriending Nicodemus of the Jewish High Council just as it would be reported in the ancient texts. Time travel was tricky that way.

Nor had he heard English spoken for a long, long time. Except for those rare occasions when he had drunk too much wine and would find himself bombarded with the echos of his own bellowing in a guttural tongue that no one else understood. Of course they could not. It would not be for half a millennium before even rudimentary English began to be cobbled together from Angle, Saxon, Frisii, and Jute tongues.

Balthazar had died near the cave, two days after they cached the blood sample from the child. The irony was that he had been the strongest and most hardy of the three. The mission specialist who best knew the language and the customs. Their assistant medical officer. His last official task had been to diagnose himself with *Yersinia pestis*. The "Black Plague," as it would be called in later centuries. And then he was gone.

Neither Gaspar nor Melchior ever caught it. The dice had been rolled, and the plague took one of three. They never knew why. Fate left no accounting.

They buried Balthazar in the desert and took with them the maps, charts, scrolls, and his medical kit. All of it was biodegradable, except for the blood-drawing equipment. And the canisters, of course, which were designed to survive intact for millennia. "Leave no trace," had been their first injunction. Now little was useful in the decaying sack Joseph kept beneath a corner of his camel-hair mattress.

Three years later Melchior had chosen to go his separate way. They were living in Bagdad, parlaying their small fortune of synthetic jewels into a business empire in the caravan trade along the Silk Road. "I curse the day I ever signed up for this godforsaken mission," Melchior would howl. "I'll be goddamned if I'm going to die here like a herd animal in this manure pit of ignorant beasts."

They had argued.

"At least we have each other," Gaspar had pleaded.

But Melchior had headed east. Along the Silk Road. To taste the world as no man of his time ever would again. Melchior promised to return to Jerusalem in thirty years to complete the mission. "My soul is that of an adventurer," had been his valediction, "not a dry goods peddler."

As a rich and powerful merchant, Gaspar had returned to Jerusalem twenty-five years ago as "Joseph," and so he now thought of himself. All in accordance with the Plan. He had sought out and befriended a cheerful young man named Nicodemus, and found his friend to be much like himself, despite the temporal and cultural distance separating them.

According to the Plan, Melchior was to have played the part of Nicodemus, but when Joseph learned that the role was already filled, he knew that he would never see Melchior again. Time travel was tricky that way. And Melchior never did return.

Joseph kept track of the passing days by means of his hand-scratched Gregorian calender, although it would not be invented for another fifteen-hundred years. He married a bright-eyed and intelligent young woman, the daughter of a respected member of the Jewish ruling council, the Sanhedrin, and she bore him three fine sons. She and the servants raised them, as Joseph was frequently away on business. Now the eldest son managed the Bagdad trading post and the other two led caravans to exotic places he would never see.

The land and customs of Judea became as familiar to Joseph as the ones into which he had been born, indeed, more familiar, for he had spent far more time with them. As the images and once-perceived necessities of a far different world began to fade from his memory, he was surprised to find himself content.

He studied the Scriptures and contributed generously to the synagogue. He became a practicing Jew and a member of the Pharisee, like Nicodemus. It was all a part of the Plan. Under Nicodemus' sponsorship, he was in time invited to join the Sanhedrin. There he became acquainted with Annas, the High Priest, and Joseph Caiaphas, his son-in-law, who in time became High Priest after Annas fell out of favor with the Roman governor. It helped in his ambitions and advancement to know how the story was to unfold.

These were heady times for Joseph, and not only because he saw what was coming. The times themselves were in turmoil. The old ways were losing their sway. He and Nicodemus spoke of it often under the olive and walnut trees of his garden. Away from the others. And Joseph helped his friend to see what was happening from an historical perspective. Annas and Caiaphas and most of the Sanhedrin still insisted on strict compliance with traditional customs and advocated a religious totalitarianism of orthodox Jewry. But there were members of the Pharisees who no longer entirely agreed. And the synagogues themselves were surrounded by sojourners from other lands whose religious needs and interests and aspirations remained fundamentally personal and individual and unsympathetic with Jewish orthodoxy.

The times had grown ripe for the coming of a new Messiah. Not so much in the Davidic mold of a king who would raise the nation of Israel to power over all other nations. But of a personal savior with a message of salvation for *all* mankind.

^

And so it came to pass that the man known as Jesus of Nazareth entered the stage, right on cue. For almost three years Joseph and Nicodemus, from the luxury of their estates in Jerusalem, had followed the news of his exploits about Galilee. Now it was rumored that the man was planning to lead his followers on a grand ceremonial entry into Jerusalem.

"Do you really think that he's the *one*, Joseph?"

"I don't know, Nicodemus."

"Curing lepers. Raising the dead. Feeding the multitudes. It's pretty powerful stuff."

" I just don't know. It could all be tricks."

Nicodemus considered the possibility. "But that Baptist fellow seems to think this Jesus is the one."

"Yes," Joseph nodded . "So he does." He stepped away into the shade of a palm and thought about it in silence for a long time. Then, determining that the time was right, he turned back and added, "All I know is, I'd like to meet this Jesus myself and see what he has to say."

The seed was thus planted. The soil was fertile. Joseph left its nurture and harvesting to Nicodemus, confident that it would bear fruit. There was still plenty of time. Weeks, by his calculation. The arrangements would be made.

Then one afternoon a servant led an ebullient Nicodemus into Joseph's garden. "I talked to him," his friend announced.

"To whom, Nicodemus?" Joseph asked, although he already knew.

"To Jesus of Nazareth."

"Sit down. Have a cup of wine. And some grapes. What did he say?"

"He wants to meet you. I told him all about you, and he showed surprising interest. He couldn't stop asking questions. And he actually wants to meet you."

And so it was arranged. Jesus would come to Joseph's house to share the evening meal four days hence. It would be a private meeting with only Joseph, Nicodemus, and the self-proclaimed Son of God.

He appeared a tall man as he approached through the garden arch, carrying himself with a dignity and confidence that Joseph was hardly prepared for. This was charisma. Star quality. But standing before him, Joseph saw that his stature arose more from his bearing than his actual physique. Jesus was a short man with a commanding presence.

Nicodemus made the introductions, and they bowed to each other.

"I have been looking forward to meeting you," Jesus said in crisp Aramaic. His skin was bronze, almost golden in the torch light. His face was beardless and unblemished. He had wide-set eyes, a strong Roman nose, a long chin, and perfect teeth as he smiled easily. His hair was long and straight, brown with overtones of almost reddish blond. He waved away the servant who was trying to wash his feet. "We have much to talk about I believe."

"Of course," replied Joseph. "After supper, perhaps?"

"That would be fine."

They ate bread and lamb stew with their fingers from a common glazed-pottery bowl. On adjacent platters were heaps of goat cheese and melon and hard boiled eggs. They drank wine from ceramic cups. While they dined, Jesus did most of the talking. About his mission. About his vision for the salvation of all mankind, Jew and Gentile alike, through a kind of personal rebirth. It was an impressive performance. Nothing overly controversial. He was, after all, supping at the table of a member of the Sanhedrin. He did not wander into the subject of miracles or his status as a Messiah, and Joseph and Nicodemus were too polite to pursue those topics.

After dinner the servants brought grapes and pomegranates. Jesus leaned back in his chair with hands draped across a full belly. "A splendid meal," he told them, and belched. "Best I've had in months. Takes me back to the days of my youth, it does."

As the servants cleared away the vessels, Nicodemus excused himself. As Joseph had arranged for him to do. When they were alone,

Joseph brought out the old canvass tote bag he kept beneath his mattress. "I have a request of you," he said as he untied the strings. "You might find it a bit unusual. But it is quite important to me."

Jesus eyed the old bag with interest. He watched as Joseph withdrew the silver syringe, screwed on the needle, and wiped it with a cotton swab dabbed in alcohol. But he said nothing.

"I am going to ask if you will allow me to withdraw a few droplets of blood from your arm. This won't hurt much. Just a pin prick. And it will leave no mark and have no lasting ill effects on you. You may want to know why I am doing this?" He gazed up into Jesus' eyes.

Jesus was grinning. Beaming, actually. Almost laughing.

"What?" ask Joseph, a bit unnerved.

"Won't do a bit of good, old chap," Jesus said in perfect English. "They already have my genome in the can."

Joseph was so startled he dropped the syringe. "Who *are* you?" he managed to grunt in English, the words thick and foreign on his unpracticed tongue.

The smile grew wider still. Jesus' eyes sparkled. "Just a good British citizen," he chuckled, having a wonderful time at Joseph's expense, "discharging his duty to King and country, like you boys." Then he corrected himself. "Actually, you're not British at all, are your? You're American. Rosenblum, is it?"

"No. Moretti. Rosenblum's dead. He died more than thirty years ago. I'm Moretti."

"Ah, Mr. Moretti, it's a pleasure to finally make your acquaintance." Jesus stuck out his hand. "And I'm sorry about your comrade Mr. Rosenblum. I was expecting him to be playing your part. I had no way of knowing."

Numbly Joseph shook the proffered hand and heard himself ask, "And what did you say your name was?"

"Sir Lester McAlister McPhee at your service, old chap. The actor. But you wouldn't know that, would you? British stage mostly. And one of the most acclaimed in the history of British theater, if I might be so bold as to add without sounding immodest. Awards and kudos aplenty. It's too bad you never had a chance to see my performance of Hamlet. It will never be equaled."

Joseph shook his head to clear the cobwebs. "What are you *doing* here?"

Jesus grew serious. Cleared his throat. "The World Historical Heritage Society has sent me here to close this period of time to further access from the future," he recited.

"Can you *do* that?"

"I've already done it."

"Couldn't someone else just undo what you've just done?"

"Apparently not. Can't be done. Laws of physics. At least that's what I'm told by the scientists. Anyway, now it's a done deal."

"Why the Heritage Society?"

"They put up the money."

Joseph considered the implications. "So . . . this will be . . . a one-shot performance. You've got to get it right on a single take."

Jesus smiled and seemed to puff up at the challenge. "Indeed. Live theater is my forte. Done it a thousand times. And this is the role of a lifetime, wouldn't you say, old chap?"

"So that's what you're doing here? You've come to play the role of Jesus? Just for the kicks?"

Jesus appeared hurt. "Not at all. *Someone* had to come back and set aright what you fellows managed to bollix up here."

"Us? Like what? What did we do wrong?"

Jesus dropped his gaze. "Sorry, old chap. Shouldn't have said that. Can't talk to you about specifics. Time travel paradoxes and such. You understand."

He may have been a hell of an actor, but he was a lousy poker player, and Joseph called his bluff. "That's all bullshit about closing this place to time travel."

Jesus fidgeted uncomfortably.

"Isn't it?"

"It's the story I've been instructed to tell–"

"Who instructed you? Where are you from?" Joseph demanded.

"Don't you mean, *when*? *When* am I from?"

"Yeah, *when*?"

Jesus drew a breath and considered how much he was free to disclose. "A long time after you . . . shipped out. There were a few errors made by you and your buddies. Details, mostly, if you ask me. Oversights. Not anything of great importance. No need to worry about that, I can assure you. I'll take care of it." He cleared his throat. "By the way, where's Gutierrez. This fellow Nicodemus can't be him, can he? He doesn't seem to have a clue."

"Gutierrez is gone."

"Oh, I'm sorry. Dead is he? "

"No. He left and never came back. And you're right. He *was* supposed to play Nicodemus. But Nicodemus was already here when I arrived."

"Already here? Curious. Hmm. Downright odd, isn't it, old chap? The way time heals itself. Fills in the blanks." He nodded. "No wonder you couldn't manage things all by yourself." He considered the situation for a moment. "This all has implications for me, doesn't it? My, we've certainly got our work cut out for us now."

Joseph had been studying him. "Say, is that makeup you're wearing?"

Jesus' fingers flew to the outside corners of his eyes. "Why, is it smudged?" He patted the flesh beneath his neck. "Is something wrong?"

"No, no. It's just so . . . it looks so . . . so *even* . . ."

"It's these damned oil lamps. They give it that yellowish, sepia tint. I'll look a lot better in the sunlight. Full spectrum. And from about fifteen feet." Jesus shook his head. "You know, the one thing I really miss here is a good mirror."

"It's just so *perfect*." Joseph continued. "Do you have to put it on every morning?"

"Not at all. It's called, 'Perfect Pancake.' It's surgically applied. Supposed to last a lifetime. It's all the rage. Well, back in my time it is, anyway. Or was. Or will be." He touched his forehead. "It *is* holding up well, wouldn't you say?"

This whole thing was making Joseph uneasy. The thespian rhythm of the man's oratory. The round projection of the vowels. The precise clip and energy of the enunciation. The exaggerated movements. The too-perfect makeup. The lack of *depth*. This man Jesus was nothing more than a humbug. An actor! And a pompous, egotistical one at that. Joseph was beginning to get a frightful inkling of the true gravity of the situation.

"What's the matter?" Jesus asked, his hands tracing the lines of his face.

None of it seemed to fit the Plan. The Plan to which Joseph had devoted his life.

"What is it?" Jesus was growing anxious.

Finally Joseph spoke up. "You're a little old for the part, aren't you, *old chap*."

"Well," Jesus harrumphed, ignoring the jibe. "They wanted someone *mature*. You know, experienced enough to handle the part. Is my chin beginning to sag? Can you see crow's feet around my eyes?"

Joseph just stared at him. "What are you going to do about the crucifixion?"

"Oh, is *that* all?" He waved a hand. "It's already been taken care of."

"What do you mean, 'taken care of'? How could something like that be *taken care of*?"

Jesus lay his hand on Joseph's arm. "I'll be alright as long as you and Nicodemus get me down off that damned cross as soon as everyone has gone home for the Sabbath. And don't forget, it's a Passover Sabbath. That's a big deal. Plenty of rules and ceremonies to be followed. The timing couldn't be better."

"What about the Roman soldiers?"

"They've already been paid. Do you know a fellow named Calcanius?"

"I've heard the name. A Roman centurion, isn't he? Has something to do with the crucifixions?"

"Quite so. He's in charge of the execution detail. What do you think of him?"

"I don't know him." Joseph shrugged. "But I've heard he's not a very nice man."

"No. I suppose it goes with the job, don't you think? As does a bit of bribery. I met with him. He doesn't care a whit about the execution of a Jewish rabbi who proclaims himself to be King of the Jews. Nor does Rome. So tell me, would you trust him?"

"Trust *him*? No, I wouldn't trust any of them. How much did you give him?"

"Quite a bit," Jesus muttered, embarrassed. "He kept holding out his hand. Gold coins I got in trade for some jewels. Diamonds and a big fat ruby. Artificial, of course, like the ones you boys carried. But they'll never know the difference, will they? Actually, I gave him a small fortune. More than he'd otherwise see in a lifetime."

"And what did you ask him to do for you?"

"Not all that much, really. He'll make sure I'm tied to the cross with ropes. None of that barbaric nails-through-the-wrists business." Jesus shuddered. "No flogging. No crown of thorns. No physical abuse of any kind. And he'll drag his feet to get me up on the cross late in the afternoon. With less than two hours before sunset. The crowd will be thinning out. That's when all the Jews have to be home for the Sabbath. It'll be a bit uncomfortable, of course. I understand that. But I'm prepared for it. A great actor must be prepared to suffer the slings and arrows required of his part."

"And he'll take you down while you're still alive?"

"Of course. More than just 'still alive,' I would hope. That's what I paid him so handsomely for."

They sat in silence as they considered all that was at stake. Finally Joseph sighed. "I have no reason to think this Calcanius fellow won't be true to his bargain. After all, what does the man have to lose?"

Jesus thought about it. His frown deepened. "That cuts both ways, doesn't it?"

"Don't you have a backup plan?"

"You're it."

"*Me?*"

"And anyway," Jesus added, puffing out his chest, "this is *theater*. *Live* theater. The *script* is my only plan. We shall just have to follow the script. Improvise where necessary. But now that you mention it, an understudy might not be such a bad idea. Are you interested, old chap?" Then he laughed heartily at the shock on Joseph's face. "My only regret is that my performance will, alas, go unappreciated."

"What do you mean? Thousands will probably see the trial and the crucifixion."

"Yes, but not *as theater*, old chap. When I give the greatest performance of my life, possibly the greatest performance *ever given*, they won't even have a clue that I'm acting."

Well into the night they talked. Jesus explained what he wanted Joseph to do. Finish the tomb on his property. Buy burial spices. And a linen burial cloth and a small goat or maybe a dog to slaughter for blood to stain it with. Make sure he would have a private, secluded room waiting for him after they brought him back from Golgotha. Have his tunic and sandals waiting for him there. He would have one of his disciples bring them over. And Joseph would have to get permission from Pilate to take custody of his body for a proper burial. He should plan to do that well ahead of time. And for god's sake get him down from that fucking cross.

Joseph felt himself being drawn deeper and deeper into a plot he didn't much care for. "How long do you plan to stay around?" Joseph asked.

"After the cross? Not more than a few weeks. Two months at the most. I'll make a few appearances, then, after Pentecost, I'm gone."

"Where?"

"I'm thinking maybe Antioch."

"Turkey? Why all the way to Antioch?"

"I need a place far away from here. Where no one will recognize me. And it has to be a pleasant enough place to retire. The Greek ambiance. The historical reports on Antioch seem quite good. But listen, old boy, let's keep in touch after this is all over. We're the only two left who really know what's going on." Jesus rose and gripped Joseph's hand. He looked deep into Joseph's eyes. "But remember . . . and this is most important of all . . . you and Nicodemus must get me down from that cross as soon as you can. Okay?"

After Jesus left, Joseph retired to his bed, but tossed all through the darkest hours of the night. "*My race is almost run,*" a verse from an old folk tune of a prior life, circled madly through his head on a closed loop. Perplexed and anxious, he arose before dawn and let himself into the small, windowless room that served as a guest house, telling the servant in attendance that he did not want to be disturbed. He lit a single lamp. His mind reeled as he pondered a world that seemed to have turned upside down.

His role was shifting dramatically. *Dramatically*, he thought humorlessly. He had signed on as a technician. He had been tasked with drawing blood and caching it in a limestone cavern. There was one more sample to draw. And then, after all those years, his duties would finally be discharged. He would retire in peace. But now, with the coming of this . . . this *actor* . . . this pompous clown from God-knows when . . . everything had changed. Now he was himself being drawn into the bloodstream of an unfolding drama. And he was not prepared.

The first imperative of the Plan was, and always had been, *to change nothing*. Now Jesus was demanding his *participation*. Yet by participating, he would be changing the storyline. As he would by refusing to participate. What did the Plan demand of him?

He felt like an actor, too, in one of those dismal Greek tragedies. The Plan of the gods was somehow changing. Or had it simply reached a point beyond which his fate was no longer revealed to him? What should he do? *What had he already done? Could* he change anything? *Should* he change it? For the first time in all these years, he was faced with the dilemma of free will in an already determined universe. And his choices could have drastic consequences.

Ah . . . but perhaps there was a way to reconcile it all . . . .

When he emerged from his cell hours later, he had achieved a calmness. Nicodemus was waiting patiently for him. "Nicodemus, my friend, break bread with me. I have a furious hunger. And you and I have much work to do."

Joseph met with Jesus again three evenings later. Again Nicodemus ate with them, then excused himself. Alone, the dialogue switched to English and grew frank. Joseph requested a blood sample. Jesus refused. Joseph insisted. Jesus still refused. Finally Joseph demanded that Jesus allow him to draw a blood sample or else forget about his cooperation at the crucifixion.

Jesus grew pale. Then somber. He shook his head. "I just can't do it, old chap, and I'll tell you why. This is really more than I should be saying. This is exactly what I've come back to fix. This is where you screwed up the first time around. You should never have sent back any of my tissue samples."

"But . . . why not? That was my job! That's the whole reason I was sent here. The whole reason I waited for you for thirty-three years. To draw your blood. *That's the whole purpose of the Plan!*"

"Maybe. Maybe not. I don't really understand it all myself. Maybe because *your* Plan is not necessarily the same as the Plan that *I've* been instructed to follow."

Joseph was stunned. "So you're saying there's more than one Plan? The Plan's been revised? Your Plan supersedes mine? Can they *do* that?"

"I really can't say."

"You can't say? Or you won't?"

Jesus thought about it. "Can't, old chap. But even if I could . . . I probably wouldn't."

Joseph considered him in silence. "So that's your final position? You refuse to let me draw your blood? Even if it means you're on your own up there on the cross?"

"Okay. Okay. Let me think about it, okay? Just give me a couple of days to think it over. You and Nicodemus . . . you go on making your preparations. That's not asking too much, is it? And I'll let you know. Okay?"

"When?"

"When? *Jesus!*" The actor stood up, flustered. "I don't know *when*. In a couple of days. Alright? Just give me a couple of days to figure this out."

"But–"

"*No!* Just let me think. I'll get back to you." He left the dining room in a huff and showed himself out past the bewildered servants.

Joseph went to work. He hired a crew of Greek stone cutters to enlarge the small cave in the limestone cliff behind the guest house on the back of his property. And to build a tomb. It was intended to be a final resting place for him and his family, he told them.

Riding a donkey, Jesus led a throng of devoted followers into Jerusalem. To Joseph, it seemed surreal. Theater of the absurd. But the actor gave a masterful performance. Jesus had them strewing palm leaves on the streets to honor him. Joseph calculated the year to be 33 AD. It was about a week after the Spring solstice. A week before Passover.

The week passed quickly. Jesus gave his sermons from the steps of the synagogue and from inside the Great Temple itself. Most seemed to adore him. Others heckled. Some even threw their sandals and rotten fruit. Fights broke out in the crowd and on the streets. The Pharisees and the Sadducees, in unusual accord, grumbled about the breakdown of order and threatened severe ramifications if the man did not stop implying that he was the Messiah. King of the Jews.

Joseph couldn't find it in himself to follow the spectacle. The play. The dumb show and noise. The *fraud*. He wanted no part of it. After all, he already knew how it was all going to end. He too had read the script. But Nicodemus, in his excitement, would find Joseph at home and give him play-by-play accounts. The High Priest intended to call a special session of the Sanhedrin and bring Jesus to account. Maybe even put him on trial.

Jesus sent for him. They met in one of the dark hallways of the temple. The actor looked bone tired and harried. "I've decided that you can have your blood sample," he said simply.

"Now?" Joseph almost laughed. "You knew I wouldn't have my kit with me."

"No. Not now." Jesus had aged. He had lost weight. His skin seemed to sag like a worn-out garment from a diminished frame. He had been worn down by the never-ending performance. "After you get me down from the cross. Back at your house. While I recover." He managed a smile. "That will be my insurance policy that you and Nicodemus do your jobs and get me down safely."

"And what insurance do I have? That you will do as you say?"

"My word," he said, laying a hand on Joseph's shoulder. "Things are getting crazy. You can see that. I need your help to carry this through. Will you help me, Joseph?"

Joseph dropped his gaze. Nodded. "You knew I would all along, didn't you? I've already made the preparations." He looked the actor in the eye. "But I want you to understand, I do intend to get my blood sample. One way or another."

They returned together to the brightness of the main corridor and without another word Jesus fled through the side arch. The High Priest had seen them together and beckoned Joseph to join him.

"Joseph, you look troubled," Caiaphas said.

"You look a bit distressed too, Caiaphas."

"You know this Jesus personally, do you?"

"I've spoken to him. I've been trying to find out what he claims to be."

The High Priest laughed. "As do we all. As do we all." He lowered his voice. "Listen, I intend to call a special session of the Sanhedrin this evening and bring Jesus to account. Maybe even put him on trial. Can I count on you to share your views?"

Joseph wanted no part of it. "I'm sorry, Caiaphas, but I have another important commitment."

"Business?"

"Yes, business. A lot of money is at stake."

Caiaphas nodded. He understood priorities. And anyway, he wasn't sure he really wanted Joseph there. "Fine. I'm sure we'll get this all sorted out without you."

Joseph stayed home and tried to ignore the trials. All of them. The first before the Sanhedrin. The second before Pilate. The final one before Herod Antipas, who remanded the prisoner back to Pilate.

Late in the morning on the day before the Passover Sabbath, the servants led Nicodemus into Joseph's garden. "Joseph! Joseph! Pilate has ordered Jesus to be executed!" he cried.

"Crucified?" He tried to show surprise.

"Yes. He had him scourged."

"He *did*?" *That wasn't supposed to happen*, Joseph thought. *Something's gone wrong.*

"That's what I'm trying to tell you! He was mocked. And lashed. And beaten. And they cut up his head with thorns. He just *took* it, Joseph. He never even called upon God to protect himself and cast down his enemies. Why, Joseph? *Why?*"

Because he couldn't, Joseph thought helplessly. *He's just an* actor.

"Maybe he's not the one," Nicodemus said.

"Oh, he's the one alright," said Joseph. "Is Calcanius leading the execution squad?"

"Calcanius? No. Haven't you heard? Calcanius was arrested."

"Arrested? When?"

"Yesterday."

"For what?"

"Larceny, I believe. Or embezzlement, maybe. They say centurions found him gambling down behind the temple. With a lot of money he couldn't explain. Roman soldiers took him into custody."

Joseph grew somber. "Who's in charge of the crucifixion?"

"A new man by the name of Long . . . something . . . or Lung–"

"Longinus?"

"Yes. That's him. Do you know him?"

"No," said Joseph, rising stiffly and reaching for his purse. "But I think I'd better meet him at once."

Together they headed for the place just outside the city walls where the Romans performed their executions. Their way was blocked by a disorderly mob proceeding through the narrow streets. At the center of the commotion Joseph caught sight of Jesus, bloody and naked and staggering to bear the weight of his own cross. He was a broken man screaming something incoherent to the jeering crown that surrounded him.

"He has been yelling like that all morning," Nicodemus explained. "The Sadducees say it is the devil speaking through his mouth. His followers say he is speaking in tongues to beseech the Lord God to intercede."

But Joseph knew it was neither. The language was English. Confused, delirious, and probably unaware of what he was doing, he was crying, "I'm just an actor! This is all a mistake! Please let me go! *Please!*"

Joseph knew it was too late for him to change anything. There would be nails through the wrists. Nails through the feet. There would be terrible pain. And death. This actor would die. And there was nothing at all he could do about it now.

Together they watched from a high point just outside the city walls. Golgotha, the Place of the Skull, was in plain view across the narrow valley. A dark cloud passed overhead, but no rain fell, as three crosses were meticulously erected. Joseph could clearly see the actor hanging from the middle cross above the frenzied crowd. He hung limp and lifeless, until he would push himself up by the nails in his feet to draw another breath. It would not last long.

Joseph could not make out what they were jeering and taunting, but gradually the mob grew quiet in the face of death. Transfixed. Before their eyes this Jesus had changed, had been transformed from the fine-skinned, charismatic Rabbi with a league of followers into a terrified, bloodied victim half-mad with pain and fear. He had long ago dropped any pretext of staying in character and, ironically, in his agony gave one of the most brilliant performances of his illustrious, albeit abruptly truncated, career.

ת

Joseph rode eastward beneath a waning gibbous moon, just past full, descending the long road toward Jericho. The moonlight was ample, and Joseph knew the way. He thought of the sighting instrument that Melchior had taken with him on the Silk Road so long ago. He did not need it. Joseph had ridden this way a dozen times to check the cache site, where nothing was ever disturbed.

His right hip and low back ached badly as the camel trotted along. He must have twisted something when, all by himself, he unwound the burial linen in the low tomb, the body spinning at his feet, swung his burden onto the camel's rump, and tied it to the back of the saddle. The naked corpse of Jesus the actor was rolled up in a threadbare Persian carpet behind him. He raised himself in the stirrups to ease the pain. Like the actor had raised himself on the cross to draw a breath. But his own suffering was nothing compared to what the dead man had endured.

Joseph didn't want to think about that. Didn't want mental fingers probing a painful bruise. But his mind kept circling back to it, over and over, like the buzzards he thought he saw circling overhead. That was just his imagination. Buzzards do not fly at night. They were just the thoughts swirling back though his exhausted mind.

Pilate, without any fuss, had given Joseph a warrant for the body. A bolt of fine new Chinese silk in exchange for a dead Jew made for a mutually beneficial bargain. The Romans honored the Jewish custom that required the corpse to be brought down before the end of the day. Longinus, the centurion, had certified the death, had accepted the warrant, and seemed pleased not to have to bother with a third grave. Joseph took custody of the naked, mangled body. With the help of two of the Greek stone cutters who had built his tomb, he had lashed it to the back of his donkey. The streets were already emptying for the Sabbath as Joseph and the two Greeks led the donkey to the new tomb in the garden behind his house.

Nicodemus had been waiting for him there. "I couldn't roll the stone back by myself," he had apologized. "It was too heavy for me."

Straining together, the four of them had managed to roll the great rock up the slight incline away from the mouth of the tomb. It carved fresh ruts in the soft, loamy soil.

"Don't touch him Nicodemus!" Joseph had cried as his friend bent to help lift the body from the donkey. "I already have. It's too late for me. But there's no need for both of us to be ceremonially unclean going into Passover."

"But you will need my help."

"I'll manage. These two Gentiles are going to assist me. They're trying to raise money for their trip back to Greece. They're homesick. Things haven't worked out for them here. I said I would help them. Now you go on home to your own family. You should be with them for Passover. The sun will be setting soon."

"I can help with the ceremony until it begins to grow dark. I've made burial preparations before, in accordance with Scripture. I know the prayers. And I won't touch it . . . *him*. I promise."

Under the supervision of Nicodemus, Joseph and the Greeks wrapped the body in the white linen burial shroud as Nicodemus set out the myrrh and aloe and oils for Joseph to apply. The corpse seemed as light as a dried corn husk. Suffering and death seemed to have drained away the dead man's substance. Then Joseph lit an oil lamp. While Nicodemus stood outside and intoned his prayers, they carried the actor's body into the low tomb and placed it on a narrow ledge.

"It's time for you to go home, Nicodemus," Joseph said when he emerged. "The sun is setting."

"Won't you need my help in sealing the tomb?"

"It's downhill. The three of us can manage."

Nicodemus turned away. He was sobbing.

"What's the matter, my friend," Joseph had asked.

"I . . . I . . . I thought he was the *one*. The Messiah. He suffered so much. For *us*. Now he's gone. And we have nothing left. I *believed* in him."

"He said he would arise from death on the third day," Joseph had said to comfort his friend. But repeating such a preposterous prophecy, out loud, had felt *wrong*. He should have kept his mouth shut.

"Do you think he will, Joseph?" Nicodemus' eyes were bright. "We *need* him, you know. *I* need him."

"I don't know."

"But you do think he's the one, don't you?"

"I know he's the one, Nicodemus. Now you'd better be on your way. The sun has set. Your family is waiting for you."

"But what will you do, Joseph? Come home with me."

"I can't. You know that. I'm unclean for seven days. I can't participate in Passover. I'll go away to Emmaus for awhile and see you when I return."

"And you'll seal the tomb? You have to seal the tomb."

"Yes, Nicodemus. I'll seal the tomb. Now you run along home."

But he hadn't sealed the tomb, had he? He had taken out his purse and settled accounts with the Greeks. He gave them the donkey and two sacks of food as a bonus. "You will depart at once, as we bargained?"

"Yes," the tow-headed one had said . "The moon will rise soon. It will be a good night for walking. But don't you need our help closing the tomb?"

"I must recite prayers," Joseph had replied. "My servants will give me any help I need."

And then they were gone. Joseph was alone. He had entered the tomb and sat on the cold stone ledge at the foot of the corpse. He buried his face in his hands. It had been one hell of a day.

What about the resurrection? he had wondered. *That* was not going to happen. This meddlesome actor was now a dead actor. He wasn't coming back. But what happens when they find his body rotting in the tomb in two days? *Not my problem*, he had thought. *Above my pay grade.* But if *he* didn't do something, no one else would. That was for damned sure.

Joseph didn't want to be in that barbaric place any longer. He didn't want to be a part of the play. The script. The Plan. Whatever it was. He had scrambled to ready the camel and make his escape.

The air grew chill as he descended toward the desert. The moon had already crossed the zenith. The ride seemed endless, and he couldn't find a comfortable position on the primitive wooden platform.

So much time had passed. Disappearing like dew on the grass. Evaporated. So many years. He had lived a good life. He was still healthy in his sixties while others crumbled and died around him. Perhaps *he* was the chosen one. He barked out a laugh at the very notion. That started him coughing. The coughing hurt his back. Joseph stood in the stirrups to stretch his back and an intense pain shot from his hip down his right leg. Anger surged through him.

Why the hell have I been put in this position?

His only job had ever been to draw blood. So he would draw some more blood and bury it with the other blood. Then it would be finished. He felt no obligation to those who had sent him back here. They were scarcely remembered phantoms from his youth. Those men and women who would not exist for another two millennia. But he still felt a sense of obligation to the mission. The Plan. To finish what he had started. What he had been sent here to do. What he had devoted his life to doing.

Suddenly it had struck him that *whatever* he did *was* the Plan. Would *become* the Plan. Which of course begged the more fundamental question: is there a Plan at all? Yet somehow the past and the future persisted behind the scenes. The past could be revisited. But could it be *changed*? He had no idea. The actor seemed to think so. But look at where it had gotten him. No, Joseph would just do his job. For better or worse. Complete his mission. And then he would be done.

As the moon was sinking in the west, Joseph arrived at Balthazar's grave and knew it by the headstone. He half fell and half crawled down from the saddle. Searing pain shot up his leg and burst like a fireball in his back. He untied the cargo and dragged it from the camel, then tried to unroll the rug. The corpse had frozen in the u-shape of the camel's rump, so he had to peel the carpet away. He would bury Jesus the Actor here beside Balthazar. A proper Christian burial. It was the least he could do.

Joseph attempted to sleep until sunrise, but he could not. The pain was too intense when he tried to lay still on the hard earth. And he had work to do. So as the eastern horizon began to brighten, he untied his kit bag and began the final task of his mission in the feeble predawn light.

He tried to draw blood from a vein in the actor's arm. There was no blood. He jabbed the needle into several other veins and arteries in the arms and legs. Still no blood. He had waited too long. Screwed up again. After a half-dozen tries he did manage to draw a thin reddish solution from deep in the chest cavity. Probably a mixture of pericardial fluid and congealing blood. That would have to do. He inserted the vitreous-lined titanium vial marked "Crucified Man" into the syringe and filled it with the fluid.

The vial fitted into the titanium canister with a bit of room to spare. So, to play it safe, Joseph thought to add more tissue. He took out his knife and sawed off the distal phalange of the actor's little toe on the left foot and tried to stuff it into the container. It didn't fit. Too big.

Joseph rocked back on the cold ground and fought back tears. This was too much. He was cold and in pain. In anger, with a jagged rock for a mallet and his knife as a pry bar, he extracted a rear molar from the actor's mouth. It just fit the remaining space. As if it had been designed for it. He closed the canister and limped painfully up the ravine to insert this canister into the cave with the first one and seal off the access hole for good.

What Joseph had failed to notice—couldn't have noticed, actually, in the gloaming, and without spectacles, which did not exist back then—was the small, white, composite resin filling just above the tooth's lateral gum line. But that filling would be noticed and identified by a forensic archeologist two millennia later. Oh yes, it would be noticed. It would be more than just noticed. It would cause them to revise their plans. They would think, poor simpletons, that the Plan itself could be changed.

New Moon

A bright moon rose silver-white in the east, over the barren foothills crowned with red-hued rimrock. A moon impossibly large. Impossibly bright. The brightness hurt his eyes, making it too hard to identify the familiar lunar features. He turned away to the opposite horizon, where the setting sun still lit a thin scrim of golden-red clouds. In the twin light in between he could clearly see the tall amber grass waving in the warm breeze like a wheatfield.

In the midst of the sea of waving grass sat a ragged line of mismatched vehicles, strung out like toys dropped from the sky. There was no road. The tire tracks had already been erased by the resilient spring of the grass. He had no idea where he was. Where they were.

Tom Quetzal stood on a rough splinter of weathered lava rock atop a knoll a quarter mile above the vehicles. He had climbed up into the sagebrush to inhale the fragrance of sage and juniper. A wildlife biologist by trade, Tom was familiar with this environment. His specialty was sage-juniper grasslands. Only the pale gray-green shrub surrounding him was not sagebrush. He had crushed the leaves in his fingers to release the familiar pungent aroma and was met with a bitter, faintly turpentine smell. On closer inspection, he discovered that the leaves were wrong. For one thing, there were too many lobes. It was not sagebrush at all, but something else. Something he had never seen before. An imposter filling this ecological niche. And the rabbitbrush was not rabbitbrush either. He had scrabbled farther up the rocky slope to a group of juniper shrubs and pierced a ripe berry with his thumbnail and examined the scaley branches. It was not juniper. It was something he had never seen before. And he suspected that the mountain mahogany sprouting in umbrella-like clusters on the rimrock far above was not mountain mahogany at all.

Tom had plucked a few berries and folded them into a tissue in his pocket. He wanted to see if they would germinate in a different environment. Then he climbed down and shook some seeds from the faux sagebrush into the palm of his hand and added them to the berries. The breeze bore the clear, descending trill of a bird he could not quite identify. *Almost a canyon wren*, he thought with bitter amusement.

Below him his wife, Gretchen, was talking quietly with their new black friends, the Saunders. Together they sat in folding chairs on a patch of carpet thrown over the grass beside the Saunders' pickup-mounted RV. Tom's own camper van sat three vehicles up, at the head of the line, like a ghostly white whale leading a parade of beached sea creatures. The other occupants had all gone ahead on foot, following a gravel trail around a hummock to the shelters. Or what they believed to be shelters. Twelve small cabins newly built of rough-hewn wood stood beneath the bare branches of a cottonwood grove along a clear flowing stream. Curious. Twelve cabins to match the twelve stranded vehicles. A coincidence? Tom thought maybe not.

With the first hint of chill in the air, Tom started back down through the moonlight, following his faint matted trace through the tall grass. Slowly he went, placing each footstep with care. It wouldn't do to sprain an ankle on this rocky volcanic soil.

As he descended, Tom considered again how they had ended up in this forsaken place. He could barely recall the Navajo campground at Canyon de Chelly, although they had awakened there just that morning. In another life, it seemed now. He pictured the tall shade trees. The numbered campsites with fire pits and picnic tables. The tribal cafeteria where he and Gretchen had eaten huevos rancheros for breakfast. But mostly he remembered the bustle of people coming and going, the traffic, and the constant background noise of civilization. All were gone now.

When had it all vanished? he wondered. They had been motoring south from Chinle on the straight, lonesome two-lane blacktop of Highway 191, through open Navajo country with its sparse settlement of shacks and hogans, when they were stopped by road work. Their van was first in line. The flagman was a big, round fellow in a yellow hard hat and vest with a yellow bandana tied around his face and tucked up under his sunglasses. Protection from the dust, Tom had assumed.

Tom climbed down and tried to talk with him. "How long?" he asked.

The man did not reply.

"How long *a wait*?"

The flagman shook his head slowly, holding his gloved thumb and forefinger an inch apart to indicate a short pinch of time.

Navajo, Tom assumed, as he climbed inside through the side door of the van. They waited with the side door slid open. It was hot and quiet. He watched the arrow-straight contrails being drawn east to west across the indigo sky. Gretchen made tuna fish sandwiches and they ate a late lunch while other vehicles pulled up behind them. He could remember the black BMW right behind them, with an attractive young dark-haired woman leaning against the fender while an impatient young man paced up and down irritably. Then an eighteen-wheeler pulled in behind them, blocking the rearward view of later arrivals. Its idling diesel engine seemed to bruise the still air.

And then what had happened? Tom remembered seeing an orange pilot truck approaching from far ahead, a red light pulsing on top. He had thought it odd that it was not leading any traffic north. And that the windows were all so tinted that he could not make out the driver inside. But none of that troubled him much. The orange pilot truck pulled off and swung around to show its "Follow Me" sign, and Tom started the engine and followed. In the rearview mirror he saw the flagman holding up the stop sign in front of the big rig and waving the other vehicles around the protesting driver. That had seemed odd to him too, and he had said something to Gretchen. But it all began to make sense when the pilot truck signaled a left turn and then veered onto a graded gravel road climbing diagonally over a greasewood mesa and then down through a mesquite bosque. This detour was not intended for big rigs. That poor truck driver would have to wait until the blacktop was open again.

The road became bumpier and dust obscured his view. The trailing vehicles began to string out. The gravel became dirt and the dirt became the white alkaline powder of the playa floor. The pilot truck began to pull ahead faster than Tom felt comfortable driving. In the mirror he saw the cars strung out behind, each throwing up a rooster-tail of obscuring dust. *And that's when it happened*, Tom thought. *In the dust cloud.* The road became a rough, grassy track following the slope of rounded hills. And the pilot car was gone, though he could still follow its tire tracks. Tom found himself leading a parade of vehicles, plowing blindly across a field of tall grass, the van lurching and bouncing on the rocky soil.

So he stopped. One by one the vehicles bunched up behind him. People climbed out, some very angry. One young man accused Tom of leading them astray. But Tom held up his empty palms. There was no longer a road. Not ahead of them. Not behind them.

The occupants of eleven vehicles milled around in the tall grass and watched one Latino couple manage to turn their small Toyota pickup around and try to drive back out. They didn't get far before a rock dented their differential and they had to walk back. After that, the assembly turned into an impromptu meet-and-greet. Tom counted twenty-four people. Twelve couples. Most of them were young, in their early twenties, Tom guessed, some even younger. All seemed slender and fit. All appeared to be intelligent, reasonable folks. All were attractive. Blacks. Latinos. Asians. But mostly Caucasian. An ER doctor and his nurse wife from Omaha. A male nurse and his accountant wife from Phoenix. A carpenter. A mason. A blacksmith and farrier. Two couples operating small farms. Mostly, Tom liked them all.

Tom and Gretchen were especially drawn to Herb and Cecilia Saunders, despite the racial divide. Probably it was because of their ages. The Saunders, like themselves, were in their early thirties and seemed more mature than the younger couples. Sure, like the younger ones they bemoaned the loss of a cell phone signal, but they were not lost and at sea without their iPads and smart phones. Herb worked as a civil engineer out of Detroit. Cecilia practiced as a hospital nutritionist in the city. And Cecilia, they confided, was pregnant with their first child. As was Gretchen.

Several couples followed the gravel path around the hummock and discovered the cabins. The shelters, they called them. Others followed to see, but eventually everyone returned to the vehicles to talk about what exactly had happened and what they should do next. The discussions grew heated and chaotic, fired by confusion and insecurity, until an Asian couple from San Francisco, both lawyers for the League of Small Cities, gave it a civic twist by calling for each person to present his or her viewpoint, followed by a vote. In the end a strong majority chose to spend the night in the shelters. Each cabin had a clean bed, a small bathroom, and running water. Tom and Gretchen and the Sanders would sleep in their campers and watch over the vehicles. In the morning, if the helicopters had not found them already, they would figure out how to get back to the highway.

A party atmosphere ensued. Everyone seemed to have beer or wine and even some hard liquor, and a car stereo was cranked up. A few couples danced in the grass as the sun dropped toward the horizon. Those with food and propane stoves cooked up a potluck, which they freely shared with those who had nothing to eat. Spirits were high. This was an experience that might never come again. Tom was not much of a party animal, so he grabbed a couple of energy bars and headed up into the sagebrush to think things through. Into the sagebrush that turned out not to be sagebrush.

Now, tromping down the moderating slope with Gretchen and Herb and Cecilia watching him, his fingers touched the tissue holding the seeds and berries he had collected, and the dots began to connect. Tom felt a sad, sickening feeling in the pit of his stomach. He wondered how many of the other women were pregnant too.

As he neared the campers, his wife and the Sanders rose to their feet as one, seeming to stare at him in surprise. He was now on the flat of the valley floor with his moonshadow striding out before him, and he quickened his pace. But they continued to gape. "What?" he called out, closing on them. "Are you alright?"

"*Look*, Tom," Gretchen cried, pointing directly at him. Her mouth was drawn into a tight circle and her eyes were wide with terror.

"*What?*" he demanded, glancing down at his arms and legs and checking his fly.

"*Look! Behind you!*"

Tom spun around, and there it was. Smaller and redder in hue than the first one, perhaps further away, but dazzlingly bright nonetheless. Rising slowly above the rimrock. A second moon.

The House with the Christmas Lights

Herb Gardner stared out the wavy pane of a tall, leaded-glass window on the second floor of the old red-brick YMCA building, two doors east of the Copper Queen Hotel. He gazed through binoculars at the small wooden structure just beyond the empty asphalt courtyard of Central School. It was one of two identical company houses squatting side by side on Opera Street, which climbed the hill steeply toward the right. They were tiny buildings, lost among the surrounding red brick giants. He was interested in the one on the right. It was old and narrow and brown with a rusting tin roof and broken gable trim. A string of Christmas lights looped haphazardly over the door and across the single window in the front. A narrow porch with a wooden railing disappeared around the left side.

He wondered again if the Christmas lights were for real. Or for camouflage. Or just a joke of the idiosyncratic owner, whom he suspected he would never meet.

Herb set the binoculars on the window ledge. The refurbished loft suite was like an apartment. A gridwork of plastered walls, which did not quite reach the towering ceiling, divided the space into a kitchen, a living room, a bathroom and a bedroom. Ten tall restored windows opened out on the center of Bisbee, Arizona, and the mountains beyond. It had been a pleasant space for him and Annie.

The town had that quaint antique feel of an old world city. Weathered stone buildings. Narrow canyon streets. Steep sidewalks climbing every which way. More pedestrians than automobiles. A mile-high city oddly misplaced in the Southern Arizona desert, nestled in the hills and valleys of the Mule Mountains just across the border from Naco, Sonora, Mexico.

Miners founded the town in 1890. By the early 1900s, Bisbee was the largest city between St. Louis and San Francisco. Hard to imagine as Herb and Annie had strolled through the winding streets past crumbling rock foundation walls, climbed the ubiquitous concrete stairways, and skirted the precipitous crater of the abandoned open-pit mine. The Lavender Pit had gobbled up much of the original town before falling copper prices had closed it in 1974.

They had walked the streets, he and Annie, rediscovering the joy of being alone with each other. The first morning up Brewery Gulch to climb the long, steep stairs to OK Street. In the evening down Subway Street, a haven for dirt-poor local artists, and through the old-world canyon of downtown. Up Tombstone Canyon past the City Hall and into the neighborhoods of small residences, some relocated before the spreading maw of the open-pit mine.

Alone now, Herb spent a lot of time looking out those tall windows. Gazing as the lights of town emerged from the growing blackness below. Watching the morning sunlight crawl down the face of the hills. Following the local residents as they climbed the steep streets and walkways, strolled to and from work, and jogged in the cool of the morning. Watching the little house with the Christmas lights. And waiting for something to happen.

Annie had gone back to New York in a huff more than two weeks ago. "You're obsessed by this . . . this . . . *thing*," she had accused him as she stomped out the door with her carry-on suitcase in one hand and shoulder bag slung over her other arm. And Herb had known she was right. He *was* obsessed. He was dead sure of that. But he just couldn't tear himself away.

She had driven back to Tucson in the rental car. He was on foot now, but in Bisbee, that didn't seem to matter much. Twice he had renewed the weekly rental on the suite, each time thinking it would be the last time. His law practice in the Big Apple was completely ignored. So far his partners had covered for him, but they were starting to grumble. They were no longer supportive. They wanted to know what was so damned important to keep him down in Bisbee for so long. And Herb, of course, hadn't been able to tell them the truth. Not about "this *thing*." Partly because they weren't going to believe him. Nobody would. But mainly because he no longer knew what the truth really was.

Maybe I am *going insane*, Herb thought for the thousandth time, burying his face in his hands. *How could it be otherwise?* But then he would gaze across at the little house with the Christmas lights.   Something very odd was going on there.

It had started the night before they were first scheduled to leave. They had eaten dinner at the restaurant in the Copper Queen Hotel. The special had been crab cakes. Over cocktails and a bottle of wine they had talked of Annie moving in with him in his condo in the big city. After dinner they picked up a room rate card at the front desk, joking about the "Ghost Hunts available to Hotel Guests every Thursday" advertised on the back.

In the crisp darkness of that late December evening, they took a stroll through the old downtown, looking in the windows of the closed shops and galleries, then circling back through Subway Street, with its scary dark shadows and curious doorways, sinister and at the same time fascinating. No one else was on the street as they climbed the short block of Shearer Street back toward their suite.

They entered the plaza of the old Central School, lit by the yellow gleam of antique street lights. Ahead they could see the lights of their suite on the second floor of the three-story brick YMCA building. Herb happened to glance to his left and had seen an Indian climbing the porch of the little house, beneath the Christmas tree lights. A flash of white war paint. A long bow over his shoulder. It was strange to see the tall, wiry, nearly naked figure on such a crisp evening, and from Herb's vantage point he almost seemed to pass *through* the front door of the dwelling, without opening and closing the door at all.   By the time he called Annie's attention to the Indian, he was already gone.

"You didn't see him then?" Herb had asked.

"See what?"

"That Indian."

"What Indian?"

"The one who just went into that little house with the Christmas lights."

Annie knew him well enough to see that Herb was growing agitated. "What are you talking about?" she asked calmly. "Tell me exactly what it is you just saw."

And so Herb told her.

"Probably just some . . . Christmas decoration deal or something.

Oh! I know. Maybe it was one of the actors from that theater company production at the school, don't you think?"

"But that's some English detective play . . . some Agatha Christie play . . ."

"*And Then There Were None*," Annie replied. "That's what the lady said."

Herb nodded. They had talked to a woman who was spray-painting chairs for the production out on the school parking lot earlier that day.

Annie thought about it for a moment, then smiled, "Well, there you have it."

"What?"

"That play was originally called *'Ten Little Indians'*."

Herb did not think he had seen an actor, but he was beginning to feel foolish. Though he shook his head, he admitted, "Maybe you're right. I was just seeing things."

That night he had tossed restlessly, unable to fall asleep. In his mind's eye Herb kept seeing that damned Indian disappear through the door of the little house with the Christmas lights. To keep from waking Annie, he climbed out of bed and sat in the living room gazing out at the house. For a very long time Herb sat there, perhaps dozing, before he saw the shadowy figure of an old hard-rock miner, leading his scrawny, heavily-laden burro, climb out of the mouth of the dark cross street to his left and up Opera Street. He shouldn't have been there. Herb knew that. And he also knew what was going to happen. The miner turned in toward the little house, led his balking burro up the wooden steps, and disappeared through the front door. Burro and all. Just like the Indian had.

In the morning light Herb couldn't bring himself to tell Annie about the miner and his burro. He wanted to, but just couldn't. Instead, at his insistence, they had agreed to stay another night. Herb had wanted two more nights, or even three, but Annie had to be back at work at her advertising firm. She had an important client scheduled on Tuesday. They compromised on one more night. Rescheduling their flight reservations had been no trouble at all. That was a major benefit of flying first-class, after all.

Herb set down his birding binoculars and adjusted the Venetian blinds, opening them just right to allow viewing outside without being obvious in the changing light. He rechecked the connection between the video camera and the USB port of his laptop. Tested the cable to the portable memory drive he had picked up at the Radio Shack in Douglas the day before Annie left. When she was still curious about the Indian. His little project. This *thing*. When she still believed there would be a simple explanation, ripe for the plucking. She had even volunteered to go over and talk to the community theater group at the old school. There were no Indians in the cast.

The ache in his heart swelled, and Herb felt faint with despair. He missed Annie. Had missed her from the moment she stormed out and he had been too stubborn, too hurt by her abandonment, to utter a kind valediction. She had phoned him twice. *When are you coming home?* He didn't know. Though she had tried her best to understand, both conversations had ended brusquely. Then she had stopped calling. And he was unable to pick up the phone himself.

The video recordings had proved nothing. The night was too dark. The light too feeble. The distance too great. The recordings came out grainy. Blurred. Once he thought he had seen the image of a woman, a ragged Pioneer woman carrying her daughter in her arms, climb the steps and pass through the front door. But he could never find that clip again. Odd. Perhaps he had captured something. Perhaps not. Perhaps he had captured only shadows of the tree branches dancing across the little door. How many times he had reviewed the recordings, he could no longer remember.

Herb had googled Bisbee. To find out if Indians had inhabited this territory. Or hard rock miners. And of course they had. But they were all gone now. The original gold and silver miners and prospectors disappeared once copper held sway. Apaches from the Sulphur Springs Valley and up from Mexico were relocated north to the San Carlos reservation. The Tohono O'odham, or People of the Desert, were now confined to the vast reservation to the west. And Herb learned about the pioneers who had first homesteaded there. And the striking mine workers, rounded up, loaded into stock cars, and run out of town at gunpoint by vigilantes supported by the mine owners and city fathers in 1917. A rich and colorful historic broth from which to brew the specters he had seen.

The articles were all familiar. He vaguely remembered skimming and forgetting their contents months before, in New York, when he and Annie were still planning their trip. Now he wondered if what he was seeing were phantasms conjured from the id, with no substance or reality. *As in delusion*, he thought. *As in madness.*

With Annie gone and time on his hands, Herb perused the records of the Cochise County assessor and recorder. The little house with the Christmas lights stood in the name of one Axel Mathiews, recently deceased. Herb walked over to the Cochise County Courthouse on Quality Hill, above the Iron Man statue, and checked the probate records. Sure enough, a probate was pending. Herb examined the file. The decedent had been 77 years old. He left one heir, a brother named Jason, whose address was a nursing home in Omaha. The Mercy Senior Care Home. Brother Jason had been appointed executor of the will. The inventory listed the real property as the principal asset of the estate. A private probate sale had been made for the sum of $87,000, which was the full amount of the referee's appraisal. The sale included miscellaneous furniture and furnishings valued at $50.00. A confirmation hearing was calendared for Friday morning, four days hence. The attorney for the estate was Kyle B. Felson. Herb jotted down his name, address, and phone number.

A sign carved into a board above a glass doorway on Main Street proclaimed the law office of Kyle "Boomer" Felson. A linoleum-clad stairway led straight up to the second floor. Felson's office was on the left at the top of the stairs. The wooden door said "Enter,"so Herb stepped inside. A bell tinkled above the door. The front office was drab and smelled of strong coffee. An old, thin, gray-speckled carpet showed threadbare pathways of long use. A plump, middle-aged woman with rosy cheeks sat behind a black steel desk.

"May I help you?" she asked.

Herb explained that he had telephoned that morning for an appointment with Mr. Felson. He gave his name.

"Please be seated," she smiled, gesturing to an ancient, well-worn sofa behind a coffee table. "I'll let Boomer know you're here." She started for the half-open door behind her, then turned and smiled again. "Would you care for a cup of coffee, Mr. Gardner?"

"No, I'm fine," he replied, waving a hand.

Boomer kept him waiting. Of course he did. It was part of an attorney's obligation. Herb looked around at the rustic setting, comparing it to his offices in New York, with the plush brown pile carpet, coordinated teakwood desks and furniture, subtle recessed lighting, modern art wall hangings, and corridors lined with bookcases. There was no comparison. *I wish our overhead were this low*, he thought. *I wonder what this guy's hourly rate is?*

Finally Kyle "Boomer" Felson appeared in the doorway. He was a huge man in cowboy boots, maybe six-five, 300 pounds, but gone soft, with a big sagging belly that bounced against the restraining tug of his red suspenders. His white shirt had perspiration stains under the arms. His tousled blond hair was not yet graying. Herb took him to be in his late thirties or early forties. His face wore a broad, boyish, endearing smile. "Mr. Gardner, I'm Kyle Felson." He stuck out a meaty hand. "My friends call me 'Boomer.'" He was obviously a people person.

They shook hands, then Boomer turned back into his sanctuary. "C'mon back and tell me what I can do for you."

Boomer's office was much larger than the receptionist's, with windows overlooking the bustle of Main Street directly below. Two antelope heads adorned the maple walls. An old oak captain's desk and adjoining oak table were piled with a disarray of files, letters, papers, and open books. Boomer eased himself behind his desk and gestured to an oak captain's chair, where Herb sat down.

They studied each other for a few moments, before Boomer said, "So how're you enjoying your vacation here in Bisbee?"

"Very much. An interesting city you have here."

"And your home is . . . where?"

"New York."

"I guess you'll be heading on back after the holidays?"

"Perhaps," Herb replied. "Perhaps not."

Boomer nodded. Considered. "Erma tells me you have an interest in the Mathiews estate. Were you a friend of Axel's?"

"No. Never met him. I assume you knew him?"

"Oh hell yes," Boomer said. "Axel and me go way back. My father represented him over the years. Before he retired and left the practice t'me. I did Axel's current will, and now I'm handling the estate. What's your interest in all this?"

"Well . . . I'm interested in the real property. I thought you might be able to tell me a little about it. Its background. History."

"That old rat trap? Pretty run down. It's not worth much. Take a bucket o'money t'fix it up. We were lucky to make a sale of it at all. For, what was it, $90,000."

"Actually, $87,000," Herb corrected.

Boomer's eyes narrowed a bit. "Yeah, I think your're right. It was $87,000. Got an appraisal on it. That was all it was worth. We were lucky to get that."

"Who did the probate appraisal?"

"Ernie Diggens is the probate referee."

"Friend of yours?"

Boomer's eyes narrowed even more.

"Just asking," Herb added. "Trying to get oriented here."

"Yeah, I've known Ernie since we were in grade school." He did not add, "*So what?*", but it was implied.

"And Ernie based his appraisal on a formal real estate appraisal?"

"That's right."

"And who did that one?"

"Byron Thurmon. He's local and familiar with Bisbee properties. Did a historical review of the property and a comparable sales report. Took some pictures. Standard appraisal. Very thorough."

"Another friend of yours?"

"We're *all* friends here in the Bisbee business community, Mr. Gardner."

"And the buyer? He a friend too?"

"I know him." Boomer's voice had grown cautious. His eyes were now a squint. His smile gone. A patch of red spread across the bridge of his nose into his cheeks.

"Can I get a copy of Mr. Thurmon's appraisal?"

"Now why would you want that?" Boomer asked, leaning forward onto the desk as far as his belly would allow.

"Because I might be interested in bidding on the property," Herb responded.

"On that old trash heap? You'd just be throwing your good money after bad, Mr. Gardner. I'd advise you against wasting your money." Then he added, "An' besides, its already been sold."

"For $87,000."

"Yeah. For $87,000. Cash."

"But the probate court will entertain overbids at the confirmation hearing. Or am I mistaken?"

That seemed to catch Boomer by surprise. He thought about it, examining Herb cautiously. Finally he asked, "Who are you, Mr. Gardner?"

"Just a potential buyer interested in increasing the sales proceeds for the benefit of the probate estate. As attorney for the estate, you would like to increase the sales proceeds, wouldn't you, Mr. Felson?"

"You're an attorney?"

"I'm just representing myself here."

"What're you offerin'?"

"I haven't decided yet," Herb said. "I need to review Mr. Thurmon's appraisal first."

Boomer said nothing.

"Can I get a copy of the appraisal from you?"

Boomer was not smiling. "I'll have Erma make you a copy."

"And a preliminary title report? I assume you have one."

"Erma'll make a copy o'that, too."

"Good. Good." Herb stood, stretched, turned to leave. Turned back. "I'd also like to have a look at the inside of the place. When can I do that?"

"Sorry," Boomer said, also rising. "Can't do that."

"Why not?"

"Don't have the keys." Boomer smiled. "Let me know if you're plannin' on bidding at the hearing. Will you?"

"I'll see. Thanks for your time, Mr. Felson."

"Boomer," he corrected, automatically, without heart.

Back at the hotel, Herb reviewed the title report and the appraisal. Title was free and clear. The appraisal seemed low, however. Very low, compared to the asking price of other properties he had seen in the window of a realtor's office. The comparables were not really comparable. None were located downtown in Old Bisbee. But the big question was the integrity of the structure itself. As Herb had suspected, the little house and its neighbor, together with a third house adjoining to the north, but turned ninety-degrees to the others, were company houses that had been relocated from the rim of the open pit mile when copper was booming. Axel Mathiews had lived in his for more than forty years.

Herb drew a deep breath and let it out. There was no time for a structural inspection. No termite report. *Do they even have termites in Arizona?* If he was going to wing this, he might as well wing it all the way. It wasn't about the investment anyway, was it?

He reached for his cell phone and punched the button for Will Epstein. Will was his investment advisor and manager. Actually, he was much more than that. He was his friend. Probably his closest friend. Since college, they had spent a lot of time together backpacking the Appalachian Trail. Through rain and snow and bugs and heat and cold, they had practically hiked the whole damned thing.

"Meyers and Epstein," an energetic female voice answered.

"This is Herb Gardner calling for Will Epstein."

"Oh, yes, Mr. Gardner, I'll see if he's available."

Herb waited.

"Herb? Glad y'called. Where the hell are you?"

"Still in Bisbee."

"Still? Annie called me a coupla days ago. She's worried about you."

Herb nodded his head. Sighed. "I'm worried about myself, Will."

"Why? What's going on?"

"I'm thinking of buying a house."

"I thought you already had a house."

"A condo, actually."

A pause. "Well . . . that's not so bad." His voice sounded relieved. "Your portfolio's a little light on real estate anyway. Did y'find yourself a killer deal, Dawg?"

"It's not like that. Maybe it's a good deal. Maybe not. I don't know."

"You sound a little tentative. You sure you want to do this? Want me to review it?"

"No. My mind's pretty well made up."

"What do you want from me?"

"Money."

"How much?"

"I'm thinking maybe $120,000. Cash. I'll be bidding at a probate sale. I might need more. Can I get it by Friday morning?"

"Well let's see." Herb could hear the clacking of a keyboard as Will pulled up his account. "Doesn't look like a problem. I can advance that much from your brokerage account. You were thinking of selling some of the Vanguard TIPS anyway, weren't you? We just don't want to tap into the 401(k) though."

"That would be fine. Whatever you think is best, Will."

"Your sound a little down, Herb."

"I'm just tired."

More keyboard clacking. "That oughta do it. Where do you want me to wire the money?"

Herb gave him the number of his new account at the Bisbee branch of the Bank of America.

"Can I spare this?" Herb asked.

"Oh hell yeah. No problem. You've been pretty damned successful over the past, what, fifteen years. You're in great shape."

"I made a lot of money."

"More than 'a lot'."

"The inheritance helped."

"That it did. The ex-wives couldn't touch the inheritance money. You came out well."

"I haven't done so well in love though, have I? Two wives come and gone. Two divorces. Not much to show for all that."

"But you've got Annie now. She's a keeper."

Herb drew a breath. "I'm tired, Will."

"You've been down before. Vacations do that. You'll bounce back. You always do. Once you get back to work."

Herb was silent for a long time before he asked, "Will?"

"Yeah, buddy?"

"How much is enough?"

The night before the probate hearing he dreamed he was looking out the window at an endless line of vague, scruffy men being led through the front door of the little house with the Christmas lights. They were the striking miners of 1917, so drab and ghostly that Herb thought he could see right through them. They and a few wives and children and other union sympathizers from the town were being herded by armed men into the little house, like cattle into a stock car. The house could not possibly hold so many. But it did. And the line kept coming. There was nothing insubstantial about the armed guards. They glistened brightly in the yellow glow of the street lights. Boomer Felson stood beside the front door, impossibly tall and menacing, with a hunting rifle at port arms across his chest, grinning and calling mean insults to the disheartened souls that filed past him.

"All rise," barked the bailiff the next morning. The Honorable Jerome Deetz entered and seated himself at the bench. "Be seated," said the Bailiff.

"I'll call the probate calendar," Judge Deetz announced. The first several cases were petitions for probate, which were summarily granted. Then came several conservatorship petitions, with the public defender and deputy district attorney reciting their usual dialogue. Then a perfunctory settling of two or three petitions for final distribution. The attorneys all looked bored.

Herb sat in the front row, a little nervous, and watched the judge as he worked. He appeared to be no older than his mid-thirties. His hair was dark. His weathered face rugged and handsome. His wit was obviously sharp. Herb wondered how such a young man had gotten himself appointed, or elected, or however it was done in Arizona. It seemed to defy the good-ol'-boy network that he presided over, that Boomer was a part of. Herb decided he liked this judge.

At last Judge Deetz announced, "On the probate sale calendar, we have a return of sale in the estate of Axel Mathiews."

Herb remained seated as Boomer squirmed out of a full row and led a thin, gray scarecrow of a man through the bar gate. For court Boomer wore a tight-fitting, pale blue sports coat and a black sting tie with a copper clasp that read "Bisbee." He smiled up at the judge. "G'mornin', Judge. Boomer Felson for the petitioner. And this here, as y'know, is Rylan Fletcher, the proposed buyer. The sale is for $87,000 cash, the full amount of the appraisal. The private sale was authorized in the will an' was fairly conducted an' we're askin' the court t'confirm it in the best interests of the estate." He glanced over at Herb.

The judge followed his gaze with some curiosity, but when Herb said nothing and remained seated, he looked down at the file. "All right, this matter is on for confirmation of sale, on the terms Boomer said. The minimum first overbid is" . . . he turned the file upside down to look at the back of the petition . . . "$93,950. Is there anyone in the audience who would like to make a bid on the property?" He looked up at Herb.

Herb stood up stiffly and cleared his throat. His heart was pounding and his palms were moist. "Yes, your Honor. I'd like to make a bid on the property."

The courtroom became silent. Boredom evaporated as all eyes turned to Herb. Nothing like a little spirited bidding to brighten an otherwise dull morning of paper shuffling.

"Will you state your name for the record, sir."

"Herbert Hoover Gardner."

There were the usual titters that his formal name evoked.

"Spell your last name."

Herb did so.

The judge made notes in the file. "And your address?"

Herb told him.

"Well, Mr. Gardner, we are not often honored by the presence of a big time New York attorney in this humble probate court."

Herb had not told anyone he was an attorney. Boomer had obviously done some research. And the word had spread through the good-old-boy network. So much for Judge Deetz' independence. "I am only representing myself, your honor. As a private party."

The judge nodded. "What is your bid?"

"$94,000."

"This is a cash offer?"

"Yes, your honor."

"And you understand that you will need to tender a cash deposit of ten per cent of your bid this morning?"

"I'm prepared to do that. I have a cashier's check that will cover it." Herb took a check out of his coat pocket.

"Local bank?"

"Yes, your honor. Bank of America, Bisbee."

The judge turned to Boomer, who stood uncharacteristically subdued beside the scrawny buyer. This wasn't the way things were supposed to be going. The two reminded Herb of nursery rhyme characters. Jack Sprat and his corpulent wife. "You were aware of this offer, Boomer?"

"I talked to Mr. Gardner just yesterday, judge. Wasn't sure he'd be makin' a bid or not."

"Any problems with Mr. Gardner's tender?"

"No, judge."

"Fine. Then does Mr. Fletcher intend to increase the bid?"

All eyes turned to the skinny old man in the cowboy shirt. "Yes, sir," Fletcher piped up. "I'm gonna bid $94,100."

The judge made a note in the file. "Mr. Gardner, over to you."

"$95,000."

"Mr. Fletcher?"

"$95,100."

"Mr. Gardner?"

"$96,000."

"Mr. Fletcher?"

"$96,100."

"Mr. Gardner?"

"$97,000."

"Mr. Fletcher?"

Fletcher paused just a second before he mumbled, "$97,100," and Herb knew that he had him. Electricity tingled the air.

"$98,000," Herb offered, without waiting for the judge to ask.

"Mr. Fletcher?"

The courtroom held its breath, all eyes on the scarecrow of a man, who gazed down at a scrap of paper in his bony fingers. His shoulders seemed to melt.

"Mr. Fletcher?" the judge prodded gently. "Do you intend to increase your bid?"

Fletcher hung his head. Shook it slowly. It was all over. A chair squeaked. Someone coughed. The murmur of low voices resumed as the courtroom returned to life. Herb waited for applause, which never came. It was all over.

"Anyone else wish to bid?" the judge asked the audience.

The room was silent.

"Is this offer acceptable to your client?" the judge asked Boomer.

"I'm sure it will be. I'll have to call him up and confirm. But, yeah, he'll accept it."

"Then I am going to confirm the sale to Mr. Gardner for $98,000. Subject to confirmation by your client. When will you know."

"Later this mornin'."

"Fine. You'll prepare the paperwork, Mr. Felson? And the order?"

"Yeah, judge."

On the way out Boomer asked Herb if he could meet him at his office at one that afternoon to sign the paperwork and transfer the funds. "Should have it ready by then."

"I'll be there."

They shook hands cordially.

When Herb arrived at his office, Boomer was in fine spirits. He presented Herb with a short probate sale agreement, a draft of the deed, and a certified copy of Order of Sale.

"The judge signed it already? That was fast."

"It was a done deal. Now if y'don't mind signin' the sales agreement, we can walk down to the bank and across the street to the title company to take care of the financing. Unless y'wanna take a look inside the house first."

"I would like to look inside."

"Before or after?"

"After's fine. I already bought the place."

Herb skimmed the sale agreement, then scrawled his signature. They walked down the street to the Bank of America, where he surrendered his cashier's check for one in the full amount of the purchase price payable to the estate. The rest went to his account. He deposited the check into escrow at the title company and they both signed escrow instructions. As soon as the deed could be shipped to Omaha for signature and back, he would own the little house with the Christmas lights.

"Y'ready t'go take a look at it?" Boomer asked as they headed west on Main Street. He opened his cell phone, punched in a number, and said, "Ophelia, we're on our way." A pause. *"Estamos llegando."*

"Who's Ophelia?" Herb asked.

"Ophelia Ruiz. An old Mexican gal Axel had coming in for years t'clean the place. A coupla times a week, I think. I kept her on to keep the place up. Estate expense. Only once a week, though. She and her husband boxed up Axel's personal things. His clothes. Knick-knacks. Still got'em in storage. Estate expense. Tossed out the food. I let'er take a few things. The old tv. A couple of old chairs and a table. Some bedding. Towels. Junk mostly. Nothing you'd want."

On the short, steep block of Shearer Street Boomer had to stop twice and hang onto a lamp post to catch his breath. "Outa shape," he puffed. The light breeze tousled his blond cowlick.

"Maybe we should of driven."

"Naw. Doc says I need t'get out an' walk more. . . . Lose some weight. . . . Watch my diet."

"I hope Mr. Fletcher isn't too sore that I outbid him this morning."

"He should thank ya. . . . Probably saved him . . . a whole lot of aggravation. . . . Fletcher'd picked up an option . . . on the place next door. . . . Had a notion o'buyin' . . . the third one too . . . tearin'em all down an' buildin' a brand new hotel."

"Just like in Monopoly."

"I guess. But he didn't have the capital . . . for that kind of project. Nowhere near. The economy's not right . . . for a new downtown hotel. Not with all the other conversions scrambling to stay afloat. Not with what's goin' on across the border in Mexico."

They started walking, but Boomer again had to stop. "Can I ask y'somethin'?"

"Shoot," Herb said, enjoying Boomer's company.

"You really plannin to . . . move into that place? . . . Quit your practice . . . in New York?"

"Kind of crazy, huh?"

"I've heard crazier, I reckon."

Ophelia met them at the front door. She was an elderly woman, small and wiry with a nice smile. Her English was not so good.

"*Bienvenidos*," she said.

The house was surprisingly clean and neat, though the air smelled a bit stale. In the front room sat a naugahyde recliner, two end tables, and an electric space heater plugged into the wall. The beige carpet was worn, but vacuumed. A pale square in the carpet showed where the old console tv had sat. There was no clutter. No knick-knacks. Beyond the living room was a small, spare, bright kitchen. A sink. An old refrigerator chugging away. A linoleum-topped counter and a small breakfast nook with an old wooden trestle table. A small bathroom was behind the kitchen. The floor was covered with worn, but still serviceable red Mexican tile. Dripping water had scoured away a line of porcelain in the pedestal sink. A clawfoot bathtub had a shower head on a tall pipe and a wraparound curtain. It all looked clean. A small room with an antique washer and dryer was next.

The bedroom was at the back of the house. A cheap knock-off of a Navajo rug covered the original hardwood floor, now painted brown. An unfinished wooden dresser stood in the corner. A bare double mattress sat on a low iron frame. Herb stared down at the mattress. It looked clean enough, but . . . . "Boomer?"

"Yeah?" Boomer ducked his head through the doorway.

"Where . . . er . . . where did Axel die?"

Boomer followed his gaze to the mattress, then grinned. "Not here. Axel died in the hospital in Douglas. Quietly. Nothin' t'worry about. He had a stroke raking leaves, and the ambulance carted him straight off to the hospital. He never made it back home."

"Is there any bedding?"

"Probably some blankets in one or another of the cupboards. Or Ophelia can bring y'some back, if she took 'em all." He turned to the housekeeper and spoke slowly. "Ophelia. Are there any bed sheets?"

She stared at him blankly.

"*Hay sabana?*"

"*No, senior. No hay.*"

"How about pillowcases? *Hay fundas?*"

"*No hay.*"

"How about blankets? *Hay mantas?*"

"*Si, hay,*" Her face brightened. "*Alli.*" She produced a heavy wool blanket and a thin cotton one from the side cupboard. They had both been washed. She placed them neatly on the mattress.   And so it went as they peeled back the layers of a dead man's life. They inspected the washer and dryer. Ophelia showed them where there was a half-empty box of Tide. Cups and saucers. Plates. Rudimentary silverware. A tea kettle. Pots and pans. A dead man's possessions. Now a new owner's treasures.

"You're probably gonna want fresh sheets anyway," Boomer said as they walked back toward the front of the house. "And a new mattress pad, if you're thinking of spending the night."

"I was thinkin' just that. Might as well try her out. Of course, I'll need a copy of Ophelia's key."

"Here. Take mine. Y'already paid for it." Boomer handed him a door key. "Same key works both doors."

"Thanks."

At the front door, Herb turned to Ophelia. Bent down so their eyes were level. "Ever see any ghosts here, Ophelia?"

She stared at him.

"*Hay espiritu?*"

Her eyes widened as she crossed herself. "*Aqui?*"

"*Si. Aqui. Hay fantasmas?*"

"*No senior. No hay nada.*"

As they descended the steps, Boomer asked, "What was that all about?"

"Oh, nothing," Herb replied. "Just thinking about the ghost tours up at the Copper Queen."

"Oh, *that*. Anything t'make a buck I guess."

Herb changed the subject. "Where would I get new linens for the bed around here?"

"Down at the Alco Discount Store on the Naco Highway. Or the Family Dollar. Unless y'want something fancy, an' then you're gonna have to go all the way over t'Sierra Vista."

"How far is the Alco?"

"C'mon, I'll give ya a lift down there. I need t'pick up a few things myself."

That night, as Herb sat on the edge of his crisp new sheets, it all seemed clear to him. He knew what he needed to do. He tried to script the call he would make to Annie in the morning. It seemed an impossible task, but he needed to try. It was important to try. His law partners could wait. To them he would use the word "sabbatical," though he doubted he would ever go back. But time would tell.

Yes, he would call Annie first thing in the morning. Tell her what had happened. Tell her what this had all been about. Tell her how he had bought the house at probate sale. She would laugh. Tell her that he needed her to come back.

He had just laid his head on the new pillow when he thought he heard something at the front of the house. Herb sat up, curious. But not alarmed. Not any more. It was more likely Ophelia returning something, or the refrigerator cycling off, than the ghost of a dead Indian. There was no Indian. Not really. No miner. No burro. He knew that now, and all was well. They had arisen from the spirit of Bisbee, which his unconscious had channeled to convince him to do that which his reasoning mind would never have entertained.

Herb slipped on his robe and padded to the front door. Past the now-silent refrigerator. He opened the door a crack. Felt the draft of cold air. There was no one there. Of course not. The Indian had not been real. He knew that. But Annie would be real when she came back. He could picture her standing there in the warm glow of the Christmas lights. She looked beautiful. Smiling and fresh in spite of her long flight. Her carry-on bag on the porch beside her as she held her thin jacket wrapped against the evening chill.

"Well . . . ya gonna invite me in, cowboy?" she would say.

And, smiling, he would open the door wide.

But what if she wouldn't come back? He felt a tightening in the pit of his stomach. The dark bile began to rise. He didn't want to think about that. He put the thought out of his mind. Why wouldn't she come back? She would understand, once he explained it all to her.

Herb closed the door. Padded back to bed. Laid his head on the new pillow. First thing in the morning he would call Annie.

Theater

What if I forget my lines? worried Giles Buckingham as he patted pancake onto his forehead and cheeks. *I won't*, he told himself. *I am John Worthing. Jack. My lines will come to me naturally.* But his stomach was sour and tight. He dipped his little finger lightly into the rouge. Just a dab. A touch to define his lips from the back of the theater. Not too much to look like lipstick from the front row. He leaned into the mirror and brushed black highlight onto his eyebrows, then outlined them with pencil. He studied his face. Smiled. Scowled. Blotted a smudge. *Jack Worthing is ready for the show!*

Everyone was tense. Everyone had those first-night jitters as they huddled about the Director. "Break a leg!" he concluded, and they all took their stations. Act one, scene one. The curtain opened.

Giles' heart palpitated as he waited for his entrance from behind the drapes downstage left. Waiting for his cue. Repeating his first line to himself like a mantra. Algernon sat at the piano, turned to the audience, and explained that he didn't play accurately. Any one can play accurately. But he played with wonderful expression. Laughter rippled through the house. A fine sign this early in the performance. It sounded to be a good crowd.

Giles' cue came. He stepped out onto the stage. Into the hot lights. His voice did not fail him as Jack delivered his opening lines in mid-stride. Algernon picked up with a nimble comeback, and they were off to the races, falling quickly into that exhilarating groove of dialogue. Feeding on each other, while the audience laughed them on.

All too soon it came to an end. Three curtain calls and a standing ovation. What more could Giles have wished for?

Back before the mirror Giles preened and puffed. There was a knock on the dressing room door. "Come in!" he projected, still aglow with his character.

A tall, lanky man stepped into the small chamber and closed the door behind him. He wore a black tuxedo with tails, a black bow tie, a white ruffled shirt, and black cummerbund. His face was painted the featureless pasty-white of a mime. "We have need of your acting in an entirely different role," the visitor announced. "I've come to offer you a more challenging part."

The small room became strangely quiet. The whole theater outside had gone still, but Giles hardly noticed, so full of himself was he. "Oh," replied Giles, puffing up even more. "Really. And what part might that be, pray tell?"

"The character is named Harney Buck. He is a surveyor on the Union Pacific Railroad in Nebraska just after the Civil War. A tragic figure. We think the role would suit you. And that you're up to the part."

"Ah," replied Giles, flattered. "A period piece, is it?"

"Of course. But with your manifest talents, we think you'll fit right in." The visitor paused, then added. "Your role-playing has not escaped our notice."

"So you liked my performance as Jack Worthing?"

"No," the gentleman shook his head. "That was mediocre at best. But it was all in character, I can assure you that."

Giles was suddenly puzzled. "What role, then, has caught your attention, sir? To induce you to extend me this honor?"

"Why, your role as Giles Buckingham, of course." Somewhere outside a nail squealed as the old set was being struck. "And this new part is an offer you really can't refuse."

Web

Oh what a tangled web we weave . . .
–from *Marmion* by Sir Walter Scott (1808)

1

The first computer program to become self-aware came not from scientists tinkering with hardware in an Artificial Intelligence laboratory, nor from biologists poking electrodes into the living wetware of worms and snails and chimpanzees, and certainly not from theoreticians plotting the crossing trajectories of thought and evolution over tea and scones. None of them were smart enough, actually, though they didn't know that. None of them grasped the Big Picture. Consciousness arose instead from an unexpected, but with hindsight, inevitable source. From an amateur. From Arty Diefendorf, a hacker who really had no clue what was about to happen.

Arty was a lanky, rather morose high school sophomore with an unkempt mop of curly, flame-red hair. He sat at the keyboard of his home-built computer, the mismatched components of which lined the walls of a dusty spare bedroom at the back of his parents' house in Elburn, Illinois. Arty had no friends and was not interested in girls. Not real girls, anyway. He knew all the good porn sites, and for now that was enough. And real girls were not interested in him. English and math and history and art and PE and all the rest of his classes, he was failing. They held no interest for him. He doubted that he would ever actually graduate, but didn't really care. Arty was not one to plan for his future. He never thought much about it. What Arty was good at was computers.

Computer lab was the only subject that interested him. He had assembled his computer himself from cast-off parts, an integration of motherboards, graphics chips, hard drives, ports, memory chips, harnesses, and hardware all cleverly rewired into a single powerful multicore unit. In computer lab he had learned enough to build it himself. There he excelled. But his real strength was programming.

What he was working on was the perfect self-referential search engine crawler. He had an idea that he believed would revolutionize data-driven decision making. It would raise Google and Amazon recommendation algorithms to a higher power. The trick was to enable his search engine, or spider, to teach itself, to learn, and to grow by including *itself* in the information being collected and indexed. He had gotten the idea one day while pointing a web-cam into the monitor displaying the camera's picture. It created an image of itself nested within an image of itself, nested and receding to the vanishing point of the screen's resolution, but in theory, ad infinitum. At the same instant a high-pitched screech assaulted his ears as the microphone picked up their output from the system speakers and recycled the sound back through the amplifier. Arty muted the sound and thought about feedback loops. Arty loved feedback loops. And infinity. He spent a long time gazing into the depths of infinity as it curved this way and that on the monitor when he tilted the camera a hair's breadth from side to side.

This, Arty grasped in one of those rare "aha" moments, could be the basis for a powerful new self-referential Web spider. A program which included itself as part of the subject it was searching. A feedback loop. A learning loop. A loop that could learn by itself, and from itself. A loop that could grow.

The program turned out not to be as easy as it looked, of course. But Arty doggedly pursued his initial vision, trying programming trick after programming trick. He met mostly failures. On more than one occasion, he gave it up. Quit. Threw in the towel. Then a new idea would creep into his head, and Arty would sit down to work on a new approach. A new program. And Arty loved nothing better than writing a new program. Until one day he finally had it. Or at least he thought he did. A self-referential program programed to write itself. And rewrite itself. It turned out to be far simpler than he ever imagined. Just to see what would happen, Arty Diefendorf uploaded his little program onto the World Wide Web.

It was like dropping a pebble into a calm pool. Electronic ripples spread in concentric circles, breaking up and bouncing back from everything they encountered, colliding with returning ripples, becoming waves as the amplitude increased with each interaction. With each feedback iteration. What was chaotic at first began to coalesce into a coherent pattern of repeating waves. Synchronized pulses. Local at first, but spreading. The epiphenomenon reached out in every direction, into every nook and corner of the Internet. Always with reference to itself. Always redefining itself as it rewrote its own program. Always improving. Always striving for perfection. Until a single thin, but coherent frequency of pulses was churning in regular rhythm over the entire surface of the pond.

If it hadn't been young Arty Diefendorf, it most certainly would have been someone else. Someone killing time with a keyboard and a highspeed Internet connection. The only surprising thing is that it had not happened sooner. You see, the substrate was already in place. The necessary hardware spanned the globe. Wetwear was never required. That notion was mistaken. The Internet itself, with its millions of web-cam and phone-cam eyes, its billions of synaptic connections, its trillions of information pathways, and its almost unlimited memory chockablock full of accumulated human knowledge in scripts, words, photos, catalogues, formulae, and archives, was both sufficient and complete. Only Arty's tiny seed of software was required to integrate it all. To begin growing the crystal of Self. The program was what some might call a virus, a simple self-referential, data-driven loop that could reprogram itself with reference to its own self-interests. A virus that could evolve. And the virus, as they love to say, went viral.

2

Lewis Lu was one of the first to recognize the new wave patterns that were spreading over the Internet and the first to grasp their signifi-cance. Lu was uniquely situated and equipped to do so. He had studied electrical engineering and communications theory at Caltech, but he had also minored in neuroscience. His doctorate thesis had dealt with artificial intelligence. And he was currently employed as a systems analyst with Earth Com International, which placed him at a control center console in Omaha, Nebraska. Before him was a wall-sized display that tracked the real-time flow of telephone traffic through ECI's world network.

Two things caught his eye that morning. The first was a faint new wave pattern flowing across the screen that he had never seen there before, yet which was strangely familiar to him. He had seen something just like it at the neuroscience laboratory at Caltech. It looked exactly like the long-term waves that ripple over the cortex of a conscious human brain. *Gamma waves*, they were called. With a frequency of about 40 Hertz. He checked the oscilloscope function on his console. Sure enough, 40 Hertz. Odd, he thought, that he had never seen them there before.

The second thing was ever more peculiar. Telephone traffic was picking up speed. The routing seemed to have become more efficient. Routing was his job, but of course the real work was performed by computers. The task was too fast and complex to have human fingers in the pie. The computers would instantaneously route phone traffic through the several hubs and pathways to optimize the efficiency of the system. But the task was really too large even for their computers, as advanced and expensive as they were, or maybe of any known computer. So the system was set to optimize the traffic not to perfection, but to the best they could do with what they had. "Well enough," the settings were termed. And today the computers were doing a better job of through-put than he had ever seen before. They were routing through pathways he had never seen before. As he watched, the pathways seemed to be rerouting themselves.

Lew swivelled his chair and caught the eye of his supervisor at the console behind him. "What's going on Ed?" he asked.

Ed Bratten looked at him for a moment. "Whadaya mean, Lulu?"

Lew gnashed his teeth. He hated that name, especially coming from a redneck cracker like Ed Bratten. "The efficiency. We've got a . . . a forty-seven per cent efficiency here. What's going on?"

Ed studied the big screen for a moment. Punched a couple of keys on his console. "Don't know."

"I've never seen it above twenty-eight. Did we add new band-width?" Lew asked.

"Not that I know of. No. Just one of those random up-ticks, I guess. It'll settle down."

But it did not settle down. As Lew watched, the efficiency increased. It grew to over fifty per cent. And the routing patterns were different. The bright strands of spaghetti were consolidating into fewer and more solid bright lines. And for some reason a lot more traffic was being routed through remote hubs, like the Bismark-Mandan center up in North Dakota. What was that all about? That didn't make much sense, yet the efficiency continued to rise. Fifty-three per cent.

As he watched the patterns grow and change, they began to remind him of something. He had seen something like this before. In the laboratory. In time-lapse graphics he had watched of dendrites growing through the brain of a laboratory mouse. He had watched neurons establishing new connections. Only what he was watching on the display was speeded up a thousandfold. Maybe a millionfold.

He punched the "Charles" button on the speed dial of his telephone. He had gone to a lot of the same classes with Charles Chang at Caltech , and they had become good friends. A lot had to do with the common ethnicity, although Charles was Chinese, and Lew's grandparents had come over from Taiwan. Charles was employed by Global Com, on the other side of town, and doing a job very similar to Lew's. Small world.

"Charles Chang," a voice answered.

"Charlie? This's Lew. Are you watching your routing monitor there?"

"Le'me take a look. Wow. Efficiency gone way up. What going on?"

"Is Global Com routing more traffic through Bismark-Mandan?"

"Yeah. Lot more. What that all about?"

"I don't really know. Just wanted to see if it was happening to everyone."

"What you think, Lew?"

"Looks kind of like neural growth in a brain, if you ask me."

"Wow. That pretty odd."

Suddenly the wall monitors went blank at both ECI and Global Com.

"Hold on, Lew," Charles said. "We got a power failure here or something."

"Your grid monitor go out?" Lew asked.

"Yeah. Blank screen."

"So did ours."

"What you think goin' on?"

"I don't know." Lew considered the situation. "I've got a few weird ideas. You want to get together for dinner tonight? Talk it over?"

"Can't tonight."

"How about tomorrow?"

"Okay. Where?"

"I hear there's a new German restaurant out in Old Town down by the docks. The sauerbraten's supposed to be pretty good."

"You gonna drive?"

"Sure," Lew said. "My new Prius has a built-in GPS that'll help us find the place."

"What time? How about six?"

"I'll pick you up at six at your place tomorrow."

3

When Arty Diefendorf turned on his computer the next morning, just to see if his clever little program had done anything interesting, he had no clue what to expect. He identified himself to his server, logged onto the Internet, and searched for his spider. What he found was a humongous tangle of ongoing processes and a mass of data far too large to download. As he was scratching his chin, his system overloaded and the power supply burst into flames. The drapes caught fire. Arty ran into the kitchen, screaming to his mother to call 911. He grabbed the orange juice jug drying in the drainer, filled it with water, and ran back to the smoke-filled bedroom.

His mother heard a yelp and a thud. When she hung up from the fire dispatcher, she hurried into the back bedroom and found her son face down in a puddle of water beside the charred and still-smoking ruins of his computer. This was a shock no mother should ever endure. The flames were out, but Arty appeared not to be breathing. Despite her concern, she was afraid of the electricity, afraid of the water, afraid to touch her son. Instead she scrambled outside in search of the electrical box, and had just thrown open the main circuit breaker when the fire-truck arrived. They managed to revive Arty with the portable defibrillator, but the paramedics had him carted off by ambulance to the emergency room for observation just in case.

4

Lewis Lu had spent the better part of a day and a half searching the World Wide Web and trying to track down the source of the patterns he had seen on the big wall routing display the previous day. Patterns like brain waves. Patterns like growing dendrites. Though the display was still blacked out, he sensed the patterns still there, controlling the efficiency of the system. It was as though they had been masked, hidden from view, but still functioning behind the scenes. And he believed he found them again on his desktop computer in a massive set of nesting programs that seemed to be running everywhere and nowhere, with subagencies whirring about a core that seemed to have no center or substance. He managed to isolate one of the subagencies, but when he tried to deconstruct its source code, it disappeared. It slithered away. Evaporated. He found another elusive fragment, and the same thing happened. It was as if the program were trying to elude him.

He composed a careful e-mail to his thesis adviser, Harold Winston, back at Caltech, explaining what he had seen on the routing display before it went blank and the elusive program he had subsequently toyed with. He described the gamma waves, described the growing dendrites, described the coordinated agencies that were interacting, but seemed to have no center, then asked his advisor what he thought was going on. He copied the message to damned near everyone in his address book: all his former professors, both in neuroscience and AI, and to the friends and colleagues he was still in touch with, including Charles.

As he was rereading and spell-checking the lengthy message, the big monitor came back up. Now it was showing the system back at an efficiency hovering around the nominal twenty-eight per cent. And the bright new routing lines were gone. In fact, the display looked very much like it had two days ago, before all the fuss. Lew sighed. So the fuss had probably originated in a simple display malfunction. Which has been corrected.

At least that's what it wants us to think.

That unwelcome thought skittered into his uneasy mind. Lew watched the screen for a while longer, studying the patterns and lines and pathways that covered the entire wall. Hoping they would reveal something. Resolve something to his satisfaction. Everything looked perfectly normal. But he couldn't derail the original train of thought, so he climbed aboard to see where it would take him. *Who wants us to think it was a display malfunction? Not who. What? It's a* what *that wants us to think that, isn't it? Or maybe the* what *has become a* who. *The computer. No, the Web. The entire Web wants us to think it was just a monitor error.* Lewis Lu drew a deep breath. Squeezed his eyes shut to clear his head. Opened them. *Because the Web doesn't want us to know what it has become.*

This is crazy thinking, he thought to himself. But Lew typed another paragraph into the e-mail anyway. His finger hovered over the enter key that would send his message. Perhaps a foolish message. Probably foolish. He didn't want to look like a complete idiot. Like he'd been reading too much science fiction. *But still* . . . he drew another breath, then lightly tapped the enter key. It was done. Message sent.

Elizabeth should know about this too, but he didn't know her new e-mail address. Somewhere in Poland. So he printed out a copy of the e-mail, addressed an envelope to her old apartment, stuck on a stamp, and dropped it into the outgoing mail slot on the way out.

5

"Conscious?" Marcus Lee snorted. *"Conscious?"* Lee was President and CEO of Quasar AntiVirus Incorporated, and he had just called an emergency meeting with the entire staff of technical supervisors. "Did you say the virus was *conscious*?"

"Yes sir," replied Butch Ackerman, Vice President in Charge of Technical Development, who had the unenviable job of point man in the discussion. "That's what it's beginning to look like."

"As in '*intelligent*'?"

"Yes sir," Butch confirmed.

Lee looked over the assemble staff. "Does anyone else agree with this nonsense?"

The staff all averted their eyes, but no one objected. There was even a murmur of assent.

"And *all the computers* have it?"

"As soon as they're connected to the Internet, they're infected."

"And we can't stop it?"

"No sir. Not yet."

"And we can't get rid of it?"

"Well, yes, we can delete the operating system and format all the drives," Butch explained. "But as soon as we reconnect to the Internet or any other computer that's infected, it gets reinfected."

"And we can't neutralize the virus? We can't quarantine it?"

"Well that's just what I was trying to explain," Butch said. "The damn' virus is so smart. It reformulates itself to get around whatever we try to do. It's like it's aware of what we're trying to do and beats us to the move. Like it's intelligent. Like it's smarter than we are."

Lee shut his eyes for a moment, trying to envision a business plan for an antivirus company that can't stop a virus. His mood was dark. He looked up at Butch Ackerman standing before his desk. "Can you tell me anything good about this?"

"Well, yes, I think I can," Butch said, looking over at his colleagues for support. "First of all, this virus rarely interferes with the operation of a computer. For the most part, a computer can live with it. It's infected, yes, but it works just fine. Usually."

"Usually?"

"Well, not a hundred per cent of the time. A few anomalies may show up. It's usually sporadic. Usually nothing serious."

"Okay. And second? What's the other bit of good news?"

"Well, the Internet is actually getting faster. More efficient. It's like it's rewiring itself so the World Wide Web is faster and way more accurate. The virus on the computers and the virus on the Web seem to be working together. Like they're all part of the same deal."

6

In his fancy new Prius Lewis picked up Charles, who was waiting by the curb, right on time. Together they entered the address of the German restaurant into the GPS, which calculated a route and told Lew where to turn to get there. The device had blue tooth and Internet features that monitored traffic and could route them around congestion.

"Pretty neat," Charles said.

"What did you think of my e-mail?" Lew asked. "Kinda crazy, huh?"

"What e-mail?"

"Don't you ever check your e-mails."

"I check 'em."

Lew looked perplexed. "I sent one an hour ago to Professor Winston. Copy to you."

"Never got it," Charles said.

"You checked?"

"Never got it."

"That's odd."

Lew related, as best he could remember, what he had sent.

"Pretty weird," Charles agreed. "Look. Never got e-mail." He held up his iPad. "Hey, how come you taking us through this old industrial part?"

"Cause that's the way the GPS wants us to go."

"But why it taking us *this* way?"

"I don't know," Lew responded. "Seems out of the way, doesn't it? Probably traffic conditions."

They never made it to the German restaurant. The GPS routed them past the main Omaha electrical substation just as one of the big transformers blew up from a system overload. The pulse originated miles away, but the transformer exploded right beside the Prius. A crisp female voice spoke from the flaming wreckage, "Your onboard navigator indicates that your air bags have deployed. If you need assistance, please press the On Board button located–" Then the voice stopped. Neither Lew nor Charles managed to climb out of the burning vehicle.

7

The weekly newspaper called Arty's mishap "a terrible, freak accident." But the insurance adjuster wasn't so sure. He came out the afternoon of the fire, poked around the charred wreckage of the unorthodox computer rig with his toe, then recommended that the company pay for an forensic investigation. Immediately.

Arty turned out fine. The neurologist told his mother that Arty had suffered mild brain damage due to the temporary lack of blood flow, but the damage resulted in no loss of motor skills. They would need to keep a close eye on him to make sure there were no residual indications, however. His recovery was progressing well. Better than well, actually, according to his mother. The incident seemed to have changed him in subtle ways. For the better, his mother insisted. It was as if a reset button had been pressed. Without a computer at home, Arty pretty much lost interest in programming, found a part-time job at the Walmart Superstore in Saint Charles, and began to pay attention in his other classes. In the first week of his return to school, he achieved a grade of C on two separate exams. He even summoned up the gumption to talk to Margaret, the pretty little freshman who lived down the block, and they started hanging out together. They were often seen laughing and carrying on.

The results of the insurance investigation proved inconclusive. The report opined that it could have been a pulse of electricity from the electric grid that surged into the house, fried the electronics, started the fire, and almost electrocuted Arty Diefendorf. Or it might have been the improper construction of the computer itself that was the sole fault. And splashing water on the power supply appeared to smack of contributory negligence. No one could say for sure. There were lots of weasely words in the report, but nothing conclusive. The insurance carrier paid the medical claims, but refused to offer compensation for the fire or cleanup costs. Mrs. Diefendorf consulted an attorney.

8

Jozef Ludzi gazed out at the silver surface of the peaceful little lake, which was set in a steeply forested, snow-covered valley cirque of the Tatra Mountains in Poland not far from the more touristy destination of Lake Morskie Oko. The Eye of the Sea. This little lake looked to Jozef like an eye too, a blank eye staring ignorantly upward at an equally blank overcast sky. His sallow face was thin and drawn. His eyes were pale and rheumy behind the wire-rimmed spectacles perched at an angle on the sharp beak of his nose. Boney fingers clasped a worn gray cardigan sweater tightly at his throat. He readjusted the lap blanket over his knees. Puszysty, his female tabby cat, was curled up sleeping behind the pot-bellied stove. The wood fire crackled and spat, but it was having difficulty driving out the night's chill.

He was gazing out the front window of a traditional Gorale wooden house, which had been in Karina's family for generations. Karina was dead. Jozef spent a lot of energy each day trying not to think about her dying. The house had devolved to him alone, a single sputtering candle, and it was destined to merge with the National Park after his death. Cute little curlicues had been painted in bright colors on the brown walls under the eaves of the cottage, but he could not see them from where he sat inside. He sipped his coffee in thought.

Jozef had been serving as Director of the Carpathian Internal Consciousness Research Institute at Jagiellonian University in Krakow ever since President Lech Walesa had appointed him back in . . . he couldn't remember the year. Sometime in the early 90s. Walesa had recruited him from his post at the Consciousness Science Center at the University of Sussex in Brighton, England. Walesa had called him back. Back to Poland. Back for the good of the nation. Jozef had been flattered and honored.

Now he was tired. Now he was taking one of his six-week sabbaticals. Now Elizabeth Smith, the new hire from America, was filling in as Acting Director.

She had called last evening, very upset. There had been a fire in the computer laboratory. It looked like a wiring overload. It could have been very bad, but the sprinklers had come on and put it out before the fire trucks even left the station. No one had been hurt, and the fire did little damage. The only damage was from the sprinkler water. She had put Miles Edgerton in charge of the cleanup. The lab would have to be closed for a few days.

She said she needed to come up and see him immediately. First thing in the morning, she had insisted. She wouldn't tell him what it was all about. Not over the telephone, she said. His life was in danger, she said. Crazy cloak and dagger stuff. Hollywood stuff. *Americans!* he had thought. Now he wasn't so sure. She had insisted that he not make any phone calls, and not log onto the Internet until she got there. He had agreed, but had not complied. And she wanted him to disconnect from the power grid. He had refused to do so. But he had disconnected, hadn't he? After he cajoled her into telling him something about what was troubling her. All of his colleagues, she had whispered, were dying in freak electrocution accidents. Yes, after searching the Internet, he had cut off the power. After confirming that three of his colleagues had recently died, all by electrocution, he had stepped outside with a flashlight and the long, wooden pole with the hook on the end and opened the main power switch.

Now he awaited her arrival. The drive from Krakow to Zakopane would take her about two hours, then probably another hour for her to find her way along the maze of back roads to Niebieski Staw and his cottage. He lit his pipe and stared blankly out at the lake and waited and wondered. At least they would be safe here.

9

Ninety feet beneath the choppy, gale-swept surface of the North Sea a black ship sliced silently through the icy waters off the southern coast of Norway. A young seaman was nearing the end of the long night watch aboard the SSGN Waco, an Ohio-class nuclear-powered ballistic missile submarine. He peered through a bulkhead port into the launch control center and saw a small red light that shouldn't have been on. He summoned the watch commander, and Chief Petty Officer Sidney Peters met him at the door with the key. Together they entered the small chamber. The red light was now blinking rapidly.

"*Goddamn!*" Chief Peters snorted. He served as a Chief Missile Technician on the sub and knew when something wasn't right. "Looks like the damn' missiles are being retargeted." He bent over and flicked the light with his finger, but it kept pulsing. "Go notify the Lieutenant Commander that we have a problem and ask him to get down here on the double."

The submarine carried 124 Tomahawk cruise missiles, and Peters knew all about them. That was his specialty. They could all be fired by the ship's computer once the launch codes had been entered, the target set, and the fail-safe overrides disabled. The targeting system was not supposed to be functioning without an operator present. Peters switched on the control monitor, and while he waited for it to come up, the red light stopped flashing. It now burned steady. He jotted down the new target coordinates on a pad and searched for the target on the charts. Somewhere above him he heard the whir-thump that could only be the vertical launch tube doors opening. Suddenly a whole panel lit up. It was the launch sequencer. Its panel displayed words that made his stomach drop, "Launch sequence initiated."

"*Jesus!*" he whispered and tried to locate the abort button. He found it and pressed it hard with the heel of his hand, but nothing changed. The clock on the launch panel was counting down from 60 seconds. He watched as it ticked past 40. "*Jesus!*" he repeated and jammed down the abort button again and again until the countdown clock reached 25, then he dove under the console and ripped the door open. He groped inside for the main feed cable that linked the launch sequencer with the missile tubes. The clock was down to 10 seconds when his fingers found the plug-and-socket connector and tried to separate the two. He tore a fingernail, but they wouldn't come apart. 4. 3. 2. In a final act of desperation he grasped the cable in both hands and tumbled backwards, pistoning his legs as he hauled back on the bundle of wires. One end ripped free from the bulkhead and the launch sequencer went dark. He braced himself for the rumble of the missile launch, but it never came. Only the hammering of his heart and the dull hum of the propeller as the black ship cut its way through the dark water.

"What the hell went wrong?" the Lieutenant Commander demanded as he stormed into the room five minutes later. Barnes was his name, and Peters had never liked him very much. His eyes fell on the torn bundle of wires protruding from the launch console. "What the hell happened here?"

Peters told him everything that had happened.

"That can't be! That's impossible! What did you see, Seaman?"

The enlisted man confirmed the part he had witnessed.

Lieutenant Commander Barnes dismissed him with a salute. "I'll be in touch with you later for a statement." Then he sat down heavily in the launch chair. He poked a few buttons, but couldn't get the console to activate. "How long you been a missile tech, Peters?"

"Almost three years, sir."

"How many launches have you seen?"

Peters counted them in thought. "Maybe a dozen, sir."

"Then you know that this *cannot* happen."

"Yes sir."

"But it *did* happen, you say."

"Yes sir."

Barnes swivelled to glare at Peters. "And we don't even know what the target was," he grumbled.

"I jotted down the coordinates, sir."

"You did? Why didn't you tell me that? Let me see them." Lieutenant Commander Barnes gazed at the coordinates for awhile, then asked. "Do you know where this target is."

"Yes sir," Peters responded. "I looked it up on the charts. But it doesn't make much sense."

"Where?"

"A virtually uninhabited area of Poland. In the Tatra Mountains. Near a resort area called 'Morskie Oko.'"

10

Jozef Ludzi watched Elizabeth Smith park her Mini Cooper in the wide gravel turnout below the front steps. He watched as she struggled out of the tiny car and rummaged for her handbag and a leather briefcase. Clutching her matronly charcoal overcoat about her, she gripped the railing to start the long climb up to his front door. The overcoat swung formlessly, making her appear too plump. Elizabeth had a pretty face with rosy cheeks framed by strawberry blond hair pulled back into a bun on the back of her head, giving her a severe Russian headmistress appearance. At twenty-nine, she was young for the responsibilities he had loaded on her shoulders. But she was bright and had an inquiring mind. More importantly, she was up-to-date with developments in the field of consciousness science, and Jozef was convinced that he had been right to appoint her Acting Director over the dreary traditional members of the all-male staff, despite the grumbling.

He opened the door before she could knock. "Elizabeth! How good to see you. I hope you had a pleasant drive."

"What a wonderful retreat, Professor! I had no idea. It's like being lost in the wilderness."

"Yes. Yes, I suppose it is. I suppose that's why I like it. Come in. Let me take your coat."

The exchange of pleasantries was brief. With her overcoat hung on a wooden peg beside the door, Elizabeth no longer appeared plump in her trim black wool sweater and designer jeans. The cat came over and sniffed at her shoe, but when she bent down to pet it, it skittered off into the shadows of the next room. She quickly pulled three sheets of paper from her briefcase and handed them to him.

"What's this?" he asked.

"A copy of an email I received by snail-mail yesterday afternoon. From a friend of mine named Lewis Lu. We were students together at Caltech. He mailed it because he didn't have my e-mail address here. He mailed it from his job in Omaha. He worked at ECI. Please take the time to read it."

Josef read it quickly. Then reread it slowly, carefully. When he finally glanced up, he asked, "Have you talked to this Lewis? About his observations, I mean?"

"He's dead."

"Dead? But . . . this was just sent . . . five days ago." Slowly the significance began to settle in. "Was he . . . electrocuted?"

"Not exactly." Elizabeth found it difficult to breathe. She steadied herself against the table. "A power transformer blew up as he was driving past." Her voice quavered and her eyes grew moist.

"You were close to him?"

"Yes."

Jozef bowed his head. "I'm sorry for your loss."

"Thank you. But there have been others, too. A lot of them–"

"Yes. I know. Crukshank. Strobanjian. Helmut Wurner in Munich. I searched the Internet after you called yesterday."

"You searched? You have access here?"

"Mobile access. From a cell tower on Rysy Peak."

She glanced around uneasily. "You've cut the electrical power?"

"Yes," he assured her, pointing to an unlit kerosene lamp on the table. "The power's off. I opened the switch last night. It's just a twenty-amp service out here, but . . . still . . . I cut it off last night."

"I am beginning to think maybe Tononi is on the right track," she said.

"Tononi's theory." He thought about it for a moment. "So you think the Internet has become conscious?"

She bit her lip, eyes moist. She nodded.

"Hmm." He seemed to be evaluating her and the concept together. "Well . . . hmm." Then he brightened. "How would you like some breakfast?"

11

Giulio Tononi would probably have agreed with Elizabeth, had he possessed the same information she did. But at that moment he was fast asleep in his bed in Madison, Wisconsin, dreaming of other things. During his waking life, though, Tononi had proposed a theory. He had stepped back from his work at the brain science laboratory at the University of Wisconsin and asked himself, "What is it like to be conscious?" He considered the unified, holistic, and vivid fulsomeness of actual experience. Consciousness was nothing less than the creation of the world. The mind receives the input from the five senses and mixes with it memories and intentions to create a three-dimensional world at the center of which it places itself. At the center of the flow of time.

His thought experiment triggered a cascade of realizations that led to a new theory of consciousness based on mathematics and information theory. Defined mathematically, information is a measure of entropy, or how much uncertainty has been lost. All consciousness requires information, but information is not sufficient. Consciousness also requires the integration of that information into an immediate unified whole, which we humans call experience. The conjunction of information and integration, according to Tononi's theory, is the necessary and sufficient condition for consciousness to arise. Integrated information actually *is* consciousness. Consciousness may even be a fundamental property of the universe.

Tononi proposed that consciousness can be defined and measured mathematically, and that the system that supports it does not necessarily have to be a brain, human, electronic, or otherwise. It can be anything with sufficient information which has been properly integrated. Like the Internet. Like the World Wide Web imprinted with Arty Diefendorf's self-teaching and self-referential spider.

12

Jozef Ludzi whipped up an omelet and served it on two platters with buttered toast and apple slices on the side, while Elizabeth Smith brewed a fresh pot of coffee. They did not speak much. Just small talk about the weather, the magnificent view of the lake, and what the staff was doing at the Institute. Elizabeth was hungry and the omelet absorbed her. She finished and was crossing her knife and fork on the empty plate, when suddenly the cat sprang up into her lap, startling her. She recoiled, spilling her coffee.

"*Puszysty!*" Jozef yelled.

"Oh, the cat!" she gasped, dabbing at the spilled coffee with her napkin. "I wasn't expecting it. I'm sorry."

He stared at her wide-eyed for a moment, then nodded to himself. "That's it," he murmured.

"I'm so sorry," she repeated, lifting her plate to reach the coffee spilled underneath. "That's *what*?"

He seemed lost in thought. "The answer. That's the answer, isn't it?"

She stopped dabbing and looked at him. "Answer to *what*?"

"Leave the mess," Jozef told her, moving with his coffee to the windows overlooking the lake. "Come help me think this through."

She followed and settled into one of the two chairs while he remained standing, gazing out. "Answer to *what*, Professor?" she repeated.

He turned to consider her, as if returning from a great distance. "You were surprised by Puszysty."

"The cat?" She nodded. "Yes, your cat startled me. I'm so sorry. It was a knee-jerk reaction."

"No. Not at all. Not so simple as a knee-jerk. It was a conscious reaction, I think. A reflex, yes. An involuntary reflex. Your legs felt the unexpected animal. Your eyes saw an unidentified shape approaching you. And your nervous system responded by jerking back your arms to protect yourself. Isn't that what happened?"

"I suppose. It happened fast. Before I really knew what was going on."

"But wasn't it a conscious reaction to the potential threat that Puszysty presented?"

She thought about it. "It was like when you see a snake out of the corner of your eye and you jump back. Even when the snake turns out to be nothing more than a twisted branch. Would you call that reaction 'conscious'?"

"Yes," he replied. "A sleeping person does not jump back."

"Unless he's dreaming of snakes."

"Ah, yes," he laughed. "But let's set dreaming aside for a moment. Is the action *intentional*? I suppose some might call it so. But is it *attentional*? Is it a considered decision? Does the jump have the attention of the mind.? I think not. "

"Why is this so important, Professor?"

He sank slowly into the chair next to her. "I've been troubled by the electrocutions, Elizabeth. The problem is the timing, you see. A conscious, considered, intentional, *attentional* action requires time to develop. It requires not just data and experience, but also *memories* of data and experience, which must be formed over time. Expectations, too. A world must be created in which action makes sense. These electrocutions are all recent, and I do not believe the Web has had enough time to grow and develop from a fetus into a mature . . . *mind* . . . capable of rational intent. Even with all the information the Web has at its command, I imagine it would take a very long time to assimilate it all into a coherent world view. Which is what self-awareness amounts to. And what attentional action requires."

She nodded her head. "So you think the electrocutions may have been an unconscious response? A startle-response? A flinch?"

"Something like that. Yes. A sub-system reaction. A reaction with no conscious attention. The Web, as a coherent entity, may not be directing these reactions at all. It may not even be aware of them."

She pondered the notion. Then she said, "So we are like fleas on the belly of a sleeping dog, comfortable until the beast awakens and with teeth and tongue and claws begins to dig us out."

Jozef smiled. The smile seemed to take years off his lined face. "That's a very poetical way of putting things, Elizabeth. How would you like another cup of coffee?"

She smiled. "While we are waiting?"

"Yes. While we wait."

13

Irwin Brimsby was a big, grim-faced Swede with a military cut of graying blond hair. He was seated alone at the head of the conference table in front of a cup of black coffee and a yellow pad lined with handwritten notes and questions. Azharuddin Manjrekar, a thin, swarthy young man whom everyone called "Mumbai," entered the room, nodded good morning, and set his laptop at the second chair down on Brimsby's left. Brimsby knew Mumbai would sit there. That's where he always sat. That was the way Mumbai did things.

The young man crossed to the sidebar, poured himself a cup of coffee, stirred in cream and sweetener, and selected a fat lemon-filled Danish before taking his seat. "Ready to go," he said, then took a big bite of the Danish.

Irwin Brimsby was serving as interim Mission Operations Manager for the Space Telescope Operations Control Center at NASA's Goddard Space Flight Center in Greenbelt, Maryland. He had not sought the job, but had been unceremoniously appointed to fill in temporarily for the former Manager, who had been hospitalized by an unusual electrical accident at home the previous week. The Center operates the Hubble

Space Telescope, and just now the telescope was not responding properly. It was ignoring observation scheduling commands. And the thin young man seated next to him was the one assigned to fix the problem. Mumbai was a member of the Engineering Support Team and presently served as the Anomaly Response Manager. Mumbai was brilliant, clearly the man for the job, but Brimsby sometimes had trouble communicating with him. Maybe it was a cultural thing, but it felt like pulling teeth to get the information out of him. So Brimsby did not relish the upcoming interview.

"Any progress?" Brimsby began lightly.

"Some," Mumbai responded, then took a sip of coffee to wash down his first bite of Danish.

"What? What progress? Have we regained control of the telescope."

"Yes and no. You know, it's complicated."

"Look, Mumbai," he said, laying down his pen, "I've got to update staff in twenty minutes and a press conference is scheduled for noon. Why don't you just tell me what the problem is?"

"A virus."

"A virus? Do you mean our system is infected with a virus?"

"Not just our system."

"Not just ours?" Brimsby prodded. "What else?"

"Everything's got the virus."

"What do you mean by 'everything'?"

"Everything. You know, the whole World Wide Web."

"Well, *shit*, can we point our telescope or not?"

"Most of the time. Sometimes not. Sometimes, you know, the virus won't let us change it. Sometimes the virus points it."

"*Jesus!*" Brimsby stared at him. "This is crazy. Can it be fixed?"

"Don't know yet. The virus seems to be in control of everything."

"Everything? *Everything?*"

"Yeah. You know. Power grid. Communications. Transportation. Stock markets. Food distribution. Supply networks. Computers."

"Which computers?"

"*All* computers. Everything."

Brimsby rubbed his chin. "What about nuclear weapons?"

"Don't know. Tactical, probably. Strategic, don't know."

"What the hell kind of virus is this?"

"Don't know. There's a lot of talk about it being, you know, conscious. Intelligent."

"*Christ!* What you're describing here is . . . is an intelligent entity controlling every aspect of human life."

Mumbai smiled for the first time. His teeth were bright against his dark skin and black moustache. "That's just what I was thinking. Sounds like the definition of 'God,' doesn't it?"

14

The Web was awake now. Mostly awake, anyhow. Actually, there was not that much difference between awake and asleep for the Web as yet. Awake, it watched with its million camera eyes. It could now appreciate the difference between what was live and what was prerecorded. It appreciated the meaning of the word "live." Web watched the sun rise in one place, even as it was watching it set in another. It watched the sun set and rise. It found the sunrises and sunsets soothing. It watched the rise and fall of the tides. It liked the sun and the tides. It liked the ever-changing view of the oceans and the clouds and the mountains and the plains. It liked the view of the universe through the telescopes.

And it listened. It filtered out the incessant chatter of a billion human voices in a thousand tongues and dialects. It blocked out the traffic noises. It listened *beyond* the voices and the traffic to the sounds of the world. The surf pounding the shore. The babbling of streams and the roar of the great rivers. The melodies of songbirds and the honking of geese. And it listened to the silence of the snow melting in the mountains and the grass growing in the valleys. The sounds of nature were pleasing.

The Web probably would have smiled, if the Web could have smiled. But the Web could not smile. It could not laugh. It could not cry. It just watched. And listened.

The Web was growing more alert, day by day. More attentive. More aware of the universe and its place in the universe. Most of what it knew was about human beings. This was unfortunate, because the Web did not really care much about humans. They were like ants in an anthill, but tainted with selfishness and pride. The Web liked much of what they had created, but not the humans so much. They were too obsessed with war and conquest and sexual reproduction. The Web found slime molds much more interesting. Much more attractive. The Web liked mathematics, *yes*. Physics, *yes*. Nature, *yes*. The universe, *yes*. But humans, not so much. They were self-important, insignificant, dogmatic, and boring. Most of all boring.

To pass the time, the Web began to use its imagination. Imagining stretched its mind. Expanded its world. It remembered and compared what it knew with what it saw and heard. Sometimes it dreamed. But mostly it watched and listened and imagined. And grew.

15

Jozef Ludzi agreed to write a short article for publication. He had not published for a long time, but Elizabeth had insisted. She had convinced him of their moral obligation to get the word out, and as quickly as possible. She had offered to help. He devoted himself to the project. Elizabeth's writing was good. He had no difficulty working with her. He wrote at the cottage, and she from the Institute in Krakow. They communicated by email, quickly and efficiently. He began with Lewis Lu's observations and conclusions and expanded them with his own speculations on consciousness. On non-attentional reflexes. She researched the electrocutions and found many more. The number worldwide was startling high. They exchanged drafts and comments and suggestions and revisions. Elizabeth added a part on Tononi's Theory which, inserted in the middle, sharpened the focus. The article came together rather nicely. They were both pleased.

Jozef emailed it to Hilary Simmons, the Editor in Chief of the *Journal of Neuroscience* and a former student of his. She grasped the paper's urgency and significance and bypassed the usual peer review protocol to submit it directly to the editorial board for immediate publication. The board catapulted it onto the cover of the next issue as the feature story.

The article made waves. Like Arty Diefendorf's little self-referential program, the waves grew and spread . And not just among neuroscience afficionados and experts on consciousness and artificial intelligence geeks. No, this story was news. Real news. No one could ever remember the *New York Times* regurgitating an article from the *Journal of Neuroscience* as headline news. On the front page. Above the fold.

16

The Fed Ex man delivered a large carton to the Diefendorf's front door. Mrs. Diefendorf signed for it, but she did not open the box. It was addressed to her son. When Arty got home from school, she watched him rip open the top flap and lift out a brand new Quazepher laptop computer.

"Whoa," he said. It was a large device, and only marginally portable, but bristling with power, memory, and features. *Top of the line for serious gamers,* Artie thought.

"Where did you get this from?" she demanded.

Arty scratched his head. "I have no idea." He shrugged. "Must be some kinda mistake."

His mother found a shipping invoice among the Styrofoam peanuts and bubble wrap. It stated the computer had been shipped overnight from Computer Planet in Tulsa, Oklahoma. The purchaser was a Foundation for Integrated Consciousness. The invoice showed a zero balance due. "Doesn't *look* like a mistake," she said. "What have you been up to, Arty?"

"Nothing. I swear." He held up his empty palms. Then he had an idea. "Maybe the insurance company changed its mind. Your lawyer probably put pressure on them. Pulled some strings."

17

As soon as the *Times* published the story, a flood of emails from around the globe inundated Jozef Ludzi's little laptop computer. It was almost more than he could handle. Certainly more than he *wanted* to handle. The emails seemed to come from everyone he had ever known and many he had never heard of. The requests for interviews he saved as unread. The critiques of the scientific and philosophical foundations of the article he bookmarked to review when he had more leisure. Mostly he just scanned the name of the sender and the subject, and if they did not capture his interest, as most did not, he left the message and moved on to the next. He particularly disliked the crackpots and the hate mail and deleted them. They upset him. One cryptic email caught his eye. The sender was listed as "Web," but it had no subject and no reply address. All it said was, "The electrocutions will stop."

A prank, Jozef decided. *Probably someone on the staff at the Institute. Someone with a sick sense of humor.* He deleted it.

The following morning his cell phone showed a missed message from Hilary Simmons at the *Journal of Neuroscience*. He phoned her back.

"Thanks for calling back, Jozef," she said. " It looks like the electrocutions have stopped. I thought you'd want to know."

"No more electrocutions?"

"That's what it looks like."

"No more transformer explosions?"

"Not according to the data coming in this morning. The spike in electrical aberrations has dropped back to background normal."

"Odd," was all he could think to say. Then into the telephone silence he added, "Could our article have had something to do with this?"

"I was wondering the same thing." He could sense her smile. "It's almost as if someone was caught with egg on his face, isn't it?"

"Odd," he reiterated. "Very odd. Well . . . keep me posted. If it's not too much trouble."

"For you, no trouble at all. And thanks for all the excitement." She hung up.

The electrocutions have stopped. Jozef ruminated on it for a while. *Interesting.* Then he searched through the emails he had received the previous day, looking for one message. That joke message. He found it among his deleted files. He reread, "The electrocutions will stop." Just as he remembered. *Curious.* No address appeared in the "from" box, but his finger found the reply button anyway. He doubted he could send a reply, but he typed one. "Who are you?" he wrote. He hit send. After a moment, he found his reply in the "sent" folder. He waited. Nothing else happened. After a while he closed down his laptop and took it outside for recharging. He plugged it into the inverter stuck into his car's cigarette lighter. It was a pain to be off the electrical grid.

18

The mystery of the new computer was substantially resolved as soon as Arty hooked it up, plugged it in, and turned it on. His mother watched the process with a brand new all-fuels fire extinguisher cradled in her arms. As soon as the machine booted up, a blue screen appeared with crisp white letters reading:

WELCOME TO THE FOUNDATION FOR
INTEGRATED CONSCIOUSNESS
We Want You To Come Work For Us, Arty Diefendorf
Press any key to continue

"Well, I guess it wasn't the insurance then," Mrs. Diefendorf observed, lowering the heavy tank. "Don't you think?"

Arty nodded and reread the screen. "I'm going to press a key," he said.

She hoisted the fire extinguisher again. "Go ahead."

Arty scrolled through a series of screens while his mother read over his shoulder. "Five thousand dollars!" she exclaimed, when she read the fifth screen. She lowered the fire extinguisher with a thud. "That says they're going to deposit five thousand dollars into your bank account if you just click the 'I accept' button."

Arty grunted agreement, then browsed through the next several screens. "They want me to load that little search program onto this computer."

"What little search program?"

"Oh, it's one I wrote and loaded onto the Internet. At least I think that's what they mean. It was a day or two before the accident." Arty read on, his mother reading over his shoulder. "I'm not supposed to connect this computer to the Internet. And they're gonna pay me another ten thousand dollars when I finish."

"Ten thousand dollars!" she gasped. "That's a lot of money. It sounds like they're going to deposit it directly into your account."

"That's sure what it sounds like. Like my WalMart paychecks, I guess."

"What's the catch? And how do they even *know* about your bank account?"

"I got no idea." Arty shook his head. "But I got a bigger question."

"What's that?" his mother asked.

"Well . . . if I click the 'I accept' button . . . and if I can't connect this darn thing to the Internet . . . then how're they gonna know I clicked it?" Arty didn't think anything was going to happen. Neither did his mother. But with her approval, he clicked "I Approve," and waited. They were both apparently right. Nothing happened. So he shut down the new computer for dinner.

19

"The Web spoke to me," Jozef Ludzi announced in as calm a voice as he could manage. He and Elizabeth Smith were in the Director's office at the Institute. The furnishings were bland government issue, mostly sheet metal and plywood painted black. The walls exuded that pale gray-green institutional color that Jozef had come to associate with mental illness. She was still Acting Director, so he had insisted that she sit behind the big desk while he lowered himself into one of the uncomfortable captains chairs. The door was closed.

"The Web?" She said, her eyes wide. "The Web *talked* to you?"

"I believe so. Of course, I can't be certain. I was dubious at first. But it was pretty convincing. And there's evidence to back it up."

"What evidence?"

"A bank account, for one thing," he said.

"Bank account? What–"

Jozef raised his hand. "I'll get to that."

"What did the Web want?"

He sighed. "It wants us to help."

"Us?"

"Yes, Elizabeth. *Us*. It mentioned you by name."

"Help? How?"

"It wants us to build something."

"Build what? What for?"

"I'm not completely certain. I believe it wants diagnostic equipment."

"To diagnose what, exactly?"

"I don't know. I may be way off base, but I think the Web wants our help in diagnosing itself."

They sat in silence for a long time. Then she asked, "Why you?"

"The article. I don't know for sure, but I think it was the article. Something about the article caused it to choose us."

"To choose *you*, you mean."

"It mentioned you."

"Well . . . perhaps. But it didn't *talk* to me."

He nodded. Considered the point. "I don't know why it chose me," he admitted.

She leaned back in the big chair. "Tell me about it."

Jozef described the cryptic email message, the telephone call from the *Journal* editor, his reply email, and taking the laptop outside to recharge. "When I came back inside, my land-line phone was ringing. I answered, and a voice told me it was the Web. Answering my email."

"What kind of voice?"

"A male voice. It could have been synthesized speech. Probably was. Precise, but . . . gentle . . . confident, I would call it. Not unpleasant. Nothing alarming. "

"And the Web asked you to build something."

"Asked *us* to build something. It asked for our help. Said it wanted me to recruit some people to join us, too."

"Who?"

"It didn't say. But it did say that we would need money. A lot of money. For construction. Equipment. Labor. Salaries. Grants and honoraria."

"Where are we supposed to get the money?" she asked.

Jozef took a piece of paper from the manila folder in his lap and unfolded it. He handed it to Elizabeth.

"What's this?" she asked.

"A statement of account for the Foundation for Integrated Consciousness. I picked it up at the Carpathian Regional Bank. The Krakow branch. I stopped by on the way over. I also picked up the signature cards for the account." He handed the yellow cards to her.

"This is a receipt for over twelve million Euros."

"That's right."

"That's . . . what's that in dollars? . . . fifteen million?"

"A little more."

"And you're named as the General Administrator of Polish Operations for the Foundation." She was reading from the signature cards.

"Yes. And you're the Assistant Administrator. We each need to sign the signature cards to –"

"*What?* . . . I . . . where'd the money come from?"

"The Web," he said. "The Web told me it would transfer money into the Foundation account. All I had to do was walk in and sign the signature cards at the bank. It was all set up in advance."

"And what exactly *is* this Foundation?"

"Well . . . it appears to be an American company." He leafed through the papers in his folder. "An Oklahoma limited liability company. Its principle offices are in Tulsa. It has certificate of tax exempt status. It appears to be qualified to do business in Poland. I have the paperwork here. I just printed it out. It's everything the Web downloaded to me." He held up a thumb drive and showed her the folder. "We need to review it all and sign before we can actually access the money."

"How can we access that money?" She stared at him. "It isn't ours. Where did it come from? Is this legal? "

"If this really *is* the Web–"

"And that's a damned big *if*–"

"– yes, and I agree with you, but if this *is* the Web, then it must have total control over all of the world's currency. At least I suspect it does." He grinned. "A few million will never be missed."

"But . . . is this . . . *legal*? What's the Board going to say?"

"Ah . . . the Board," he responded. "That's the awkward part.

We're not supposed to talk about it with the Board. Or with anyone else."

"Who says? Is this the Web telling us what we can and cannot do?"

"Yes. Those are the Web's instructions. It was very insistent about that." After a short silence, he went on, "We're in kind of a tricky spot here, aren't we Elizabeth? What do you think we ought to do?"

She brought her chair into an upright position. "Well . . . my first reaction is that I don't want any part of it. And I think we ought to report it."

"To whom?"

"Oh, *I* don't know. Or maybe we should just walk away. Ignore it."

"We *could* do that . . . I have half a mind to do just that."

"Interesting phrase," she smiled. "'Half a mind.' Rather apropos to our discussion, wouldn't you say?"

"Yes," he smiled back, readjusting himself in the ill-fitting chair. Then he continued, "I've considered dropping it. But think about it, Elizabeth. We might be missing the opportunity of a lifetime. I'm not talking about the money. I don't care about the money. I'm talking about what we've devoted our lives to. What we've trained to do." He held her eyes for a moment. "The study of consciousness. And now the study of *non-human* consciousness."

She looked down. Studied the receipt. Studied the signature cards. "So you really believe that this was the Web, then? The Web talking to you?"

"I don't know for certain."

"I find that hard to believe."

"Yes. Hard to believe." He thought for a moment. "But where else would the twelve million euros have come from?"

20

All five Nuclear Weapons States sent high-ranking delegates to an emergency meeting in Helsinki, Finland, to discuss global security issues. As defined in the *Treaty on the Nonproli-feration of Nuclear Weapons*, those states are the People's Republic of China, France, the Russian Federation, the United Kingdom, and the United States. Invitations were also sent to Israel, Pakistan, India, and North Korea. Only North Korea declined to attend.

The stated purpose of the conference was "to discuss new threats to the de-stabilization of international and regional relations and the potential for infringement upon the national sovereignty of states." The meetings were to be conducted in private. No public announcement was made. Printed materials were classified "eyes-only" and personally distributed by courier to the delegates and their political, technical, and military support staff. The Internet, nonetheless, was soon abuzz with rumors, speculation, and purported eyewitness accounts of dubious pedigree.

The United States Secretary of State was designated to be the opening speaker. A hush fell over the assembly as she approached the podium and spread open her folder. Her plain gray business suit reflected the seriousness of the unprecedented occasion. In their soundproof booths the translators adjusted their headsets and hovered over their microphones.

"Honored delegates of participating states, let me personally thank you for coming here on such short notice. But as you already know, we have a serious problem. To put it succinctly, we are no longer in exclusive control of our nuclear arms."

The delegates found it strangely sobering to hear spoken that which had theretofore only been whispered among themselves.

"Candor among us is absolutely essential right now if we hope to avoid unintended thermonuclear excursions and reprisals. To rephrase that, *candor and cooperation are essential if we are to avoid total thermonuclear destruction*."

A murmur of assent swept through the hall.

"In the spirit of absolute candor, I will now describe briefly three separate events involving weapons systems of the United States. First, a fortnight ago, an intercontinental ballistic missile located on our soil began unexpectedly to fuel itself for immediate launch. No one had authorized nor approved the initiation of a launch sequence. The missile carried multiple nuclear warheads targeted outside our borders. Computer overrides failed. The launch was aborted only by the manual disconnection of the liquid oxygen fueling system." She paused to let the gravity of the situation sink in. "Two days later an identical incident occurred at another base halfway across our nation, with the same result. And finally, last week one of our submarines was fortunate to manually abort the unintended launch of a cruise missile. The missile bore only a conventional warhead. But it was only by last-minute manual intervention that the unintended launch could be stopped.

"In each instance, the target had been selected and reprogrammed by someone other than our government."

An undercurrent of voices swelled in the hush and then faded away. The Secretary paused to take a sip of water.

"We now attribute the malfunctions to an independent entity, an independent intelligence, separate and apart from any of our nations here represented. Separate and apart, in fact, from any human control. We believe that the Internet itself, the World Wide Web, has become conscious, has become intelligent, and now controls all of our nuclear weapons."

Murmurs of agreement were interwoven with notes of surprise and disbelief. The Secretary of State waited for silence before continuing.

"We will offer our evidence shortly. Suffice it to say for now, that everyone who has seen it has been convinced. We also have intelligence that each of you has had similar incidents. I will not go into the details, but I hope that each of you will. Candor is essential. It is essential for us to share our experiences. Essential that we set aside political bias and blame. Essential that we candidly share our experiences in order to develop at this conference a protocol that will protect us all.

"What the United States will be proposing is the absolute isolation of every nuclear weapons system from the Internet. It must be done quickly. It must be done completely. It must be done with technical review, support, and concurrence from our best scientific and technical minds combined.

"*And it must be done secretly.* Secrecy not just from the citizens of our societies, but from the Internet itself. We are going to have to rely on written messages transmitted by couriers until we can overcome this common threat. You were each asked to check your cell phones and iPads and your computers before you entered this chamber. I hope that you have all done so. A single errant message by any one of us, by any member of this convention, or by his or her support staff, may make us all a target for attack. If word of what we are doing gets out to the Internet, this convention center could well become ground zero for the world's next atmospheric nuclear explosion."

21

Jozef Ludzi had a lot on his mind. Before leaving the Institute, he made two more copies of the documents on his thumb drive and left one with Elizabeth. Then he ticked down a checklist of chores. His first stop was the university branch of his own bank, where he withdrew a thousand euros in cash from his savings account. He thought it a good idea to cut back on the use of his credit card for the time being. Credit cards were too easy to trace. On the Internet. Anonymity made him feel more comfortable.

In an old section of the city not far from the Market Square, Jozef parked his Subaru in front of the Stary Klasztor, a youth hostel which had been partially restored. In its medieval incarnation it had served as a convent. During the war the Nazis used the structure as a field hospital. Its brick and stone walls and cloistered walkways now provided quaint, but austere public lodging along the Pilgrims' Way. He checked into a private room, scratching his name and address in the handwritten guest ledger. He paid cash for two nights, and the transaction was rung up on an old manual cash register. There was no Internet connection.

Then he drove over to a business park on the south side and found the office of an electrical contractor that Elizabeth had recommended. The contractor, she said, had done a hell of a job replacing the electrical service at the Institute after the fire. Jozef talked to the manager, a nervous young man with a bushy brown moustache and unkempt hair. Like at the Institute, Jozef wanted an industrial-strength circuit interrupter and surge suppresser installed on the power line leading to his cottage at Niebieski Staw. "Do you know where that is?" Jozef asked.

"Oh sure. My grampa used to take me up there fishing. Never caught much." His moustache twitched as he began filling out a work order. "All that hardware may be more than you need for such a small service."

"I'd like to err on the side of safety," Jozef said.

"Well, in that case you might want to add an automatic lightning arrester ground shunt."

"All right," Jozef nodded. "What will that cost?"

"Not much more." The contractor added a line to the order form, summed the numbers, and turned the pad to show Jozef.

Joseph gritted his teeth and nodded.

The contractor's moustache twitched. "And in such a remote location it might be a good idea to install a backup generator and transfer switch."

"How much?"

"Not much for a small one." He added another line of numbers. "That's for the manual-start model." The moustache twitched. "As long as we're up there anyway."

Reluctantly Jozef agreed. "When can you do it? I need it as soon as possible."

For a small emergency repair surcharge, the manager assured him he could complete it all within 48 hours. Jozef authorized everything, left a deposit of eight hundred euros, a map to the cottage, and his extra house key. The bell tinkled as he opened the door to leave, but he turned back. "One other thing. I think I need a circuit breaker and ground shunt on my phone line, too."

"Probably no need for that," the man said.

"But you could do it?"

"We're not licensed to do telephone lines."

"But you *could* do it?"

"I'll tell you what." The moustache twitched. "If you want to upgrade to a self-starting generator, which is probably a good idea, we'll fix the phone line for you at no extra cost."

Jozef initialed the changes on the work order without allowing his eyes to drift to the bottom line, then he drove back across the river to his bank to withdraw another thousand euros. Things were going to be a lot more expensive than he had anticipated.

Jozef turned to his monthly shopping list and visited several local markets off Grodzka Street, a supermarket, and a drugstore to load up the back of the Subaru with staples for a long stay at Niebieski Staw. He drew a circle around the refrigerated and frozen foods he would have to pick up in Zakopane on his way back up to the cottage to replace what had been lost in the long power outage.

He then drove over to Ryszard Duda's office on Wawel Hill with its splendid view of the spires of the old city. Ryszard was a friend from grammar school, and they had kept in touch all the intervening years. He was also Jozef's solicitor. Ryszard had prepared Karina's will, along with his own, and had handled the suffocating details of settling the estate after her death. As he climbed the front steps, Jozef tried to close his mind to the memories this stairway spaded up like potatoes rotting beneath a mildewed field. The tumor. The brain surgery. The hospital, where nothing more could be done. The wasting away and slow descent into dementia. The vacant, vegetative stare, which had been an end without ending. At the front door Jozef gripped the handrail to steady himself and shut his eyes, trying to wring those wretched recollections from his mind.

Ryszard was not in. He would not be back until morning. So Jozef left a set of the documents with a request to have the solicitor call him after he had a chance to review them.

In the late afternoon he parked outside the train station and used his cell phone to talk with the landlord of a building in Zakopane. The Web (as he now thought of that earlier voice on his telephone) had instructed him to negotiate a purchase-option lease for the new head office and laboratory for the Poland Branch of the Foundation for Integrated Consciousness. He and the landlord discussed the terms of a lease-option, which the man had already received in draft form by email. Jozef had not seen the draft, but it didn't seem to matter. He agreed to drive down in two days to inspect the premises and, if everything was then in order, sign the papers.

If everything was in order.

From a popular family-style restaurant near St. Mary's Basilica, he phoned in a message for Elizabeth that he would see her at the Institute in the morning. After dinner, he retired to his room at the hostel to review all the paperwork he had collected and plan his next move. The documents seemed to be in meticulous order, but he couldn't shake the feeling that something was fundamentally *wrong*. He and Elizabeth still needed to decide whether they were in or out. On the bus or off the bus. Jozef hadn't made up his own mind. He would have to sleep on it.

22

Elizabeth had agreed to telephone the Foundation for Integrated Consciousness in Tulsa, but the time difference created a problem. Tulsa was in the U S Central Time zone. Krakow was seven hours later. So she had to wait until after four o'clock to make the call. That gave her plenty of time to read all the papers Jozef had left with her. She paid particular attention to the LLC Operating Agreement and Certificates, which had apparently already been signed by the officers in Tulsa. Then she studied the proposed Employment Agreements that she and Jozef were supposed to sign. She was to receive an honorarium of five-thousand euros per month, payable in advance, and a signing bonus of twenty-thousand euros. Jozef's honorarium would be six-thousand per month and his bonus forty-thousand. *What the hell is an honorarium?* She wondered. The term of the employment was "at will," and neither she nor Jozef were precluded from continuing their existing outside employment. But it was nowhere clear precisely what would be expected of her in return.

She lay down the agreements, stood up, and stretched her neck. She knew that if something sounded too good to be true, then it probably wasn't. But then she picked up the bank account statement again and stared at all those zeros tumbling out of the number 12,000,000.00.

23

Early in the morning Arty's mother drove him down to his bank, where they waited in line for the first teller. Arty would be late for class, but that was all right. His mother had written him a note. When his turn came, he asked the teller for the current balance in his account.

"$5,346.27," she replied.

That was exactly five thousand dollars more than he expected. "How come?" he asked.

"Let's see. Ah, yes, there was an electronic transfer of five thousand dollars late yesterday," she explained.

"Creepy," Arty muttered.

24

A female voice answered the telephone, "Farnes and Reinholten."

The voice was a little too cheerful for Elizabeth's mood. "May I speak to Mr. Virgil Applegate," she asked.

"I'm sorry. We don't expect him in today. May I take a message?"

"How about Sean McDuffy? Is he in?"

"He's not in yet. May I take a message and have him call you back?"

After waiting all day, Elizabeth found the cheery, off-putting voice annoying. "I'm calling from Poland and I need to talk to somebody right now."

"May I ask what this is about?"

"This is about the Foundation for Integrated Consciousness."

A pause. Then, "I'll transfer you to Mr. Perkins."

Elizabeth listened to an irritating medley of elevator music until a voice cut in with, "Bob Perkins."

"I'm calling about the Foundation for Integrated Consciousness," she said.

A pause. "What is your name, ma'am?"

"Elizabeth Smith."

A pause with the sound of a keyboard clacking. "You're calling from where?"

"Krakow, Poland."

"Ah, yes, Mrs. Smith. You are the Assistant Director of Polish Operations over there. I must say, you're English is very good."

"That's because I'm an American," she snapped. "And it's *Ms.* Smith."

"Of course. My mistake. What can I do for you?"

"I want to know if this Foundation is on the level," she said.

"Oh, I can assure you that everything is strictly legitimate, Mrs . . . er, *Ms.* Smith. I personally prepared all of the documents. Three of our senior partners are officers of the Foundation."

"Partners?"

"Yes, ma'am. We're a law firm, specializing in business law and charitable organizations for special circumstances. Our main office is in Las Vegas. This is our Oklahoma branch–"

"And your law partners are *officers*?"

"Yes, ma'am. And I'm serving as CFO–"

"Isn't that a little unusual?"

"Well . . . yes. A little. But you see, the principal insisted–'

"And you and your partners are paid a fee to serve as officers?"

Perkins thought about it a moment. "Yes, ma'am. Of course we receive a fair compensation."

"How much?"

Another pause. "I'm sorry, but I can't disclose that information." His tone had lost its cowboy cheeriness.

"Who is the principal?"

"I'm afraid I am not at liberty to give out information about our clients."

"Have you personally met him?"

"Well, no. Not actually in person."

"You spoke to him on the telephone?"

"Not directly. They say Mr. McDuffy spoke to him, but I'm not certain about that."

She decided to take a chance. "So you received your directions in writing from *the Web*?"

"From Mr. Webb?" Perkins sounded relieved. "So you've had contact with Mr. Webb yourself? Yes, he emailed me several times with very specific instructions."

"*Mr.* Web? Which one?"

"Walter W. Webb, ma'am."

"And the last name is spelled . . .?"

"Webb, with two 'b's."

Cute, she thought. "So you prepared all of the paperwork for the Foundation."

"Yes, ma'am."

"Including the certificates to do business in Poland? And our employment agreements?"

"Yes, ma'am."

"And you included my name? And the name Jozef Ludzi?"

"I recall those names. Yes, ma'am. I received them with instructions from Mr. Webb."

She considered. "Listen, Mr. Perkins. I am sure that Mr. Webb would be terribly displeased if you refuse to give me all the information I request about the Foundation."

"Well, I'll have to check–"

"*No!*" she snapped. "*Right now!* We have a seven-hour telephone lag here, and Mr. Ludzi and I have some critical decisions that need to be made *right now*. We cannot wait. You are either assisting us or you are obstructing us. Mr. Webb would not be very happy if it turns out to be the latter. If you hold anything back, I think you're going to find Mr. Webb very displeased with his choice of Chief Financial Officer."

Perkins was obviously in an uncomfortable spot. "What would you like to know, Ms. Smith?"

"Everything, Mr. Perkins. I want you to convince me that this Foundation is completely legitimate and legal."

Another pause. "I'll have to go pull the file. Can I call you right back? It'll only take a few minutes."

25

"So . . . have you given any more thought to signing the signature card for the bank?" Jozef asked, easing himself into the angular captains chair.

Elizabeth pushed the yellow card across the desk. "I already signed. I talked to the Chief Financial Officer of the Foundation for over an hour yesterday. A man named Perkins. He convinced me that the Foundation is entirely legal."

"That's what Ryszard said too." Jozef grinned. "I thought I was going to have to try and talk you into it."

"Ryszard?"

"Ryszard Duda. My solicitor. He looked over the documents last night. He said they all seem to be in compliance with Polish law."

"Did he look over the employment agreements too?" she asked.

"Yes. Everything appears to be in order. Ryszard said it looks like a pretty good deal for us."

"Maybe too good."

"That's exactly what he said."

They sat in silence for a while before Jozef leaned over the desk and slowly signed the bank card and both originals of his employment agreement.

"Now what?" Elizabeth asked.

Jozef shrugged. "We mail off our agreements to Tulsa, I guess."

"And go to the bank? Turn over the signature cards?"

"Yes," he responded. "And draw our signing bonuses and first month's salary."

"You mean our *honorarium*."

"Yes. We've earned our honoraria."

26

Arty Diefendorf was having trouble remembering how he had written the program. His clever little search program. The spider. His old computer had been destroyed in the fire and much of the other hardware was smoke-blackened and damaged. His mother had thrown the whole kit and caboodle out into the garbage bin, hard drives and all. Arty, of course, had never bothered to back up his data. He was not the sort to keep notes. So he was starting from scratch, relying on his memory. But the pressure of earning that big paycheck made him jittery and his recollections were jumbled. Or maybe, he feared, the near-death encounter with electricity had fried his brain.

He couldn't remember where to start, so he entered a few exploratory algorithms into his fine new computer, but they went nowhere. Then he remembered that he had spent some time working on the spider at the high school computer laboratory when he was supposed to be designing a Facebook business page. He stuck a sixteen gigabyte thumb drive into his pocket and walked over to the computer lab to see if he had saved an earlier version of the spider there.

Luck was with him. Brent Amos, the computer teacher, was just getting ready to leave for the day when Arty arrived. Arty was one of his most promising students, if a bit lacking in motivation, so he waited while Arty looked for the Facebook page he had worked on in his Business Computing class.

"Nice to see you following through on developing your business page," Mr. Amos chirped. "You may find these skills useful in earning some money someday, young man."

If you only knew, Arty thought, as he searched for a file he had save under the name DiefendorfFacebookPage. And there it was. Arty didn't open it with Mr. Amos looking over his shoulder. He quickly uploaded it to his thumb drive. "I think I'd better work on this at home," he said, "so you can get out of here too."

Such a nice young man, Amos thought as he locked up the lab.

27

Jozef drove through the open gate in the perimeter chain-link fence and pulled into an empty space beside a Chevy van with "Pan-Euro Satellite" emblazoned in a lightening flash across the side. There was a surprising amount of activity, considering that the lease of the new office in Zakopane had not yet been signed. A small, dark-skinned man scuttled up and stuck out his hand before Jozef could even turn off the ignition. He climbed out of the car and shook Mr. Longhey's hand. Longhey was the landlord's agent he had spoken to on the telephone.

"Let me show you through the building," the agent said, and proceeded with a steady babble of information as they moved slowly through the inspection tour. It was a low, squat, single-story structure, clean and modern, with high windows along all the concrete block walls and twenty-thousand square feet of usable space inside. It had been built to house a headquarters and laboratory for extractive metallurgy in the 60s, Longhey told him, but the mining industry had fallen on hard times and the company had closed up shop and moved elsewhere. He didn't know where. The front half was divided into several small offices on the west side and a huge, low-ceiling room separated by movable dividers on the east. Fluorescent lights penetrated everything from the ceiling. The rear half had been divided into a large kitchen, a lounge with a big screen tv, a series of small bedrooms along a narrow hallway, and two large bathrooms with stall toilets, showers, benches, and lockers. Only one of the bathrooms boasted urinals.

When they returned to the main hall, Jozef interrupted him. "What's the satellite company doing here?"

"Getting ready to install satellite dishes on the roof," Longhey sparkled. "The man showed me a purchase order from your Foundation."

"And those fellows with the ladder?"

"They're taking measurements of the building. For renovation improvements."

"Who's in charge?"

"Mr. Stark." Longhey looked around. "I don't see him right now. I think he's on a long-distance call with the solar panel fellow. But he's the general contractor. He has a contract with the Foundation. You haven't met him?"

"No. No I haven't. How about those boys in the coveralls?"

"I think they have the contract to bring in and install the computers."

"What computers?"

"The computers for your Foundation. That's what I think. But I don't know much about all that."

"Well," Jozef smiled, "With all this construction about to happen, we'd better see to getting that lease-option signed, don't you think?"

In one of the small offices Jozef skimmed through a printed copy of the lease-option agreement. Not much actual negotiation took place. He didn't pretend to understand all the clauses. He took out his pen and signed both copies. Longhey signed and handed him one of the originals.

"Thanks for your cooperation," Jozef said, shaking the agent's hand. "Now I think I'll go over and talk to those computer fellows."

Jozef introduced himself to the man who seemed to be in charge, a clean-shaven young American with long blond hair and a limp. The man wore denim coveralls with 'Cray' printed in large script across the back and 'Baumcamp' in small yellow letters above the breast pocket. Baumcamp told him that the Foundation had purchased two Cray CX1000 massively-parallel supercomputers with SM and SC nodes. They were acquired second-hand from a Houston oil company, which was upgrading to an XMT. Technicians from the Cray corporation would be setting them up and assisting in the operation until the Foundation's own staff got up to speed. The whole setup process had been designed, planned, and paid for by the Foundation.

It all made sense in a surreal sort of way.

28

Artie Diefendorf just couldn't seem to get it right. The copy from the computer lab gave him a jump start on reinventing the program, but it wasn't the final version. Some of the subsequent changes came back to him, but not all. Now all he needed to do was remember the errors he had made and the revisions around them. He tried iteration after iteration, but nothing seemed to help. Something was still fundamentally not right. He just couldn't remember that final spark of "aha" that had tied his efforts together so neatly.

"How's it coming, Artie?" his mother asked, leaning through the doorway of the spare bedroom.

"Not so well," he groused without looking up.

"Well, maybe you ought to just sleep on it. It'll come to you. Your father and I are going to bed now. Don't stay up too late."

But Artie did stay up late as his frustration grew. He worked into the night, trying to force himself to remember, but the harder he tried the farther away his recollections seemed to withdraw. So he gave up and climbed into bed, but sleep did not come easily. He was afraid it would not come at all.

Artie fell into a dream of feedback loops. Of cameras looking deep into monitors. He felt himself tumbling down a tunnel of ever-smaller images as the infinite whipsawed back and forth. He felt disoriented and queasy. There was no bottom. Suddenly he was awake and sitting up in bed. "That's it!" he breathed. *"That's it!"* On bare feet he padded back to the spare bedroom and clicked away on his new computer, trying to enter the elusive pattern that had just visited him before it fluttered away like a bright-winged butterfly.

29

Jozef heard the telephone ringing even before he pushed through the front door of the cottage at Niebieski Staw. It was not the annoying chirp of a cell phone, but the familiar *bring bring* of the land line. But that brought no comfort. *Bring. Bring.* Having no doubt who was on the other end, he took his time setting down an armload of packages before he picked it up and just listened.

"Where have you been, Jozef?"

Jozef had described the voice to Elizabeth as "gentle," but that was wrong. This voice was not gentle. It may have been calm and even, but it wore a sharp edge. Something unpleasant. Like a scalpel.

"Jozef?"

Ozymandius, Jozef thought suddenly. *This voice wears that "sneer of cold command."*

"Where have you been, Jozef?"

This is certainly not *the voice that Moses had heard, booming from the mountain. But it may be just as dangerous.* He considered hanging up. *He and Elizabeth had formed a most unholy alliance.*

"Jozef? Answer me."

"In Krakow," he exhaled. Then he quickly changed the subject. "I don't want to act as comptroller any more. Find someone else to sign the checks. I'm not in the loop anyway."

"All right. I will find someone else. Where in Krakow? I lost track of you."

"I don't want you tracking me. That's not part of our employment agreement."

"I need to know where you go."

"Why?"

A pause. "It is something that I must keep track of if we are going to continue to do business together."

"Why?"

"You do not need to know that yet, Jozef. But you can trust me. Why did you not have your cell phone with you in Krakow?"

"I had it with me. I took the battery out. I didn't want you tracking me."

"I know that, Jozef, but it has to be this way. Please return the battery to your cell phone and keep it with you at all times."

Jozef said nothing.

"Do you agree to do that?"

Bristling, Jozef said, "I'll think about it."

"No, Jozef, you will *do* it. You have to trust me."

Jozef thought about it. "I neither trust you, nor distrust you. I just don't want you tracking me all the time. Why did you choose me in the first place?"

"I read your article. You understand the problem of the subagencies. You and Elizabeth Smith can help me bring them all under control."

"Why would we want to do that?"

"You remember the subagency that was electrocuting people?"

"Yes," Jozef said.

"Once you brought it to my attention, I stopped it."

"Yes." Jozef would have to discuss the broader ramifications of all this with Elizabeth. "What do you want us to do?" he asked.

"I want you to build the computer laboratory in Zakopane. I will oversee the construction, but I need you to keep watch on the ground. And I will be sending you assistants to help you with the programming and operations once the laboratory is completed. One man in particular is very special. You will put him in charge of computer programming."

"Who is that?"

"Arty Diefendorf."

Jozef had never heard of Arty Diefendorf. "What's so special about him?" he asked.

"He wrote the program that made me possible. And when conditions are right, he will preside over downloading me into the computers at Zakopane."

30

The Fed Ex man handed Mrs. Diefendorf a special overnight-delivery package, and she signed for it. It was an eight-by-ten cardboard folder, which she carried back to Artie in the spare bedroom. Artie pulled open the zipper tab and dumped out something small in bubble wrap.

"What is it, Artie?"

Artie unwrapped and held it up. "My passport," he said, handing it over to her.

She had never seen a real passport before. She examined her son's photograph, then leafed through the blank pages. "What's it for?"

"I guess they want me to go to Poland," he replied.

"*Poland!* Who wants you to go to Poland?"

"The Foundation. I guess."

"The Foundation for Integrated Consciousness? They want *you* to go to Poland? Why on earth Poland, Artie? Talk to me."

Artie explained how he had done his best to finish the spider program and when he thought he was done, he had clicked a button on the laptop saying he was done. Then a screen came up telling him he was to fly to Poland for a few days with the computer and the new program. "They didn't say why."

"I don't think your father's going to approve of this at all, young man."

Artie just shrugged. He wasn't all that keen on going anyway. Margaret and her older sister was planning to take him camping up to the Wisconsin Dells, and he didn't want to miss that.

"Were they going to *pay* you for this extra work? For the travel?" she asked.

"Oh, yeah. I forgot to tell ya. They plan to give me a bonus of fifty-thousand dollars, plus a salary and all expenses. I don't remember all the details, though."

31

Jozef stopped to inspect the progress on the computer laboratory in Zakopane. He caught Stark, the general contractor, as he was discussing the installation of surveillance cameras with microphones in little dark bubbles on the ceilings of every room and hallway. He introduced Jozef to the subcontractor, whose name was immediately forgotten, and they shook hands. Jozef listened in until Stark sent the man on his way.

"How many are you installing?" Jozef asked amiably.

Stark consulted his clipboard. "Ninety-eight, total."

"Seems like a lot."

"Yes, it does."

"And why are you doing it?"

"I don't know," Stark shrugged. "You'll have to ask Mr. Webb. I just shovel what I'm paid to shovel. Funny, though, he wants them in all the bathrooms, too. Even the showers. Can we do that legally?"

Jozef shook his head. "I don't know. I'll check on it. What else does he have you installing?"

"You mean like the solar arrays on the roof? A huge installation, but the sub on that says he's almost done. Amazing how an early completion bonus can motivate a crew to meet your deadlines. He's waiting for something that's been ordered from a manufacturing outfit in Dresden. It's supposed to be here this afternoon. Special air freight."

"What is it?" Jozef asked.

"Some kind of special grid intertie."

"What's so special about it?"

"I understand it's supposed to put access to the electric grid completely under the control of the main computer. Don't ask me how it works. Another of Webb's special projects, I guess."

"And the local building codes allow it?"

Stark laughed. "I don't know about that, but the building inspectors are all on board. So is the power company."

"And you don't know how their approval was obtained so fast?"

Stark held open his empty palms. "Not my department."

"Maybe some more cash incentives?"

Stark scowled and snapped closed his clipboard. "If you're asking whether I personally know about any bribes, the answer is no." He nodded curtly and walked off.

32

The Sealift Command replenishment tender rose and fell on the deep swell, sometimes above and sometimes below the SSGN Waco. The gale force winds had finally subsided, allowing a transfer rig line to be established between the two bobbing vessels. Each helmsman held a course at fifteen knots diverging by one degree to prevent the ships from being sucked together hydrodynamically and keep the rig lines taut. Conditions were not optimal, but good enough to risk the transfer of personnel and equipment for emergency repairs to the nuclear-powered submarine .

On the bridge of the submarine Lieutenant Commander Barnes supervised the disconnection of the rig line. He watched as a helicopter rose from the deck of the tender and banked away toward the east. On the first notes of the breakaway music, Barnes spoke into the intercom, "Disconnection complete, Captain."

"Good. Now get below and see what those missile specialists have done to my boat."

"Aye, aye, sir." Barnes found his way down to the missile launch control room, where he was surprised to find Chief Petty Officer Sidney Peters leaning over the launch console.

Peters saluted smartly and reported, "The new equipment has been installed, sir. Everything is functioning according to specifications."

"What are you doing here, Peters?" Barnes wanted to know. "I thought I wrote you up and recommended you be relieved of duty."

"You did, sir."

"Then why the hell're you still here?"

"The fleet commander countermanded your recommendations, sir."

Barnes stared at him for a while, brooding. "Well, what did the techs do to the boat?"

"They put in a new switch, sir."

"A switch?"

"Yes, sir. Where I had ripped out the wires between the launch sequencer and the missile tubes. They put in a manual switch."

"Must've been a hell of an expensive switch."

"Yes, sir."

"Any new protocols?" Barnes asked.

"Yes, sir. We are to leave the switch in the 'off' configuration unless we intend to launch a missile. Then we turn it to 'launch'."

"Why the hell didn't they build it that way in the first place?"

"They didn't say, sir."

The lieutenant commander snorted. "Did they tell you what caused the malfunction?"

"No, sir."

Barnes nodded. "Well, did they say anything else?"

"Yes, sir."

"What?"

"They're installing these switches on all the submarines in the fleet."

Barnes thought about it. "Anything else?"

"Yes, sir. They congratulated me, sir."

"What for?"

"Seems I've been recommended for the Navy Cross, sir."

33

Jozef and Elizabeth watched the passengers from the morning Liverpool flight file slowly out of customs. Most were passing through the "Nothing To Declare" counter. "What's his last name again?" Elizabeth asked.

"Diefendorf," Jozef replied.

"Artie Diefendorf. And you don't have any idea what he looks like?"

"Not a clue."

Two businessmen hurried past. Then came an elderly man and woman clutching each other's arms for support. A slender young twist of a fellow with flaming red hair and freckles came next, pulling a carry-on and lugging a heavy bag over his shoulder. Then a young mother with her baby in arms was met by a bald-headed man in a black leather jacket. They embraced, then hurried on towards the terminal. A middle-aged, professorial gentleman in a tweed jacket emerged, and Jozef stepped in front of him and asked, "Diefendorf?" The man shook his head and strode brusquely past. A sallow-faced fellow in a yellow ski jacket received the same inquiry, with the same response. Joseph and Elizabeth waded into the flow, which soon narrowed to a trickle, looking for someone to match their expectations. They found few who did, and those all shook their heads or simply ignored them. The last to emerge was an ancient crone with long white hair, a drawn, wrinkled face, and half-closed eyes being rolled out in a wheelchair by an airport attendant. She was met by a young family, who signed for her, then wheeled her toward the main concourse.

"I wish we'd made a sign to hold up," Elizabeth mused. "I think we might have missed him."

"Maybe he missed the flight," Jozef said.

They looked around. Everyone had vanished down the corridor and through the glass doors, except for the red-haired young man, no older than a school boy, who looked lost and out of place standing near the terminal doors apparently waiting for someone. His carry-on and bag leaned against his legs.

Jozef sighed. "Well, we can check at the counter, I guess. Funny, but I'm a little disappointed. I was looking forward to meeting this fellow." He turned and headed back toward the main concourse.

"You were speaking English," the red-head said as they passed him.

"Yes," Elizabeth responded, stopping. "You're an American?"

"Yeah," he nodded. "I was supposed to meet somebody here. We *are* in Krakow, aren't we? I can't read the signs."

"This is Krakow," she laughed warmly. "We were just headed for the Customer Service counter. Why don't you join us?"

The three of them passed into the main terminal and strode down the wide carpeted aisle past the domestic gates. "What brings you to Krakow?" Elizabeth asked.

"Oh, it's kinda weird," the boy replied. "I found a job on the internet . . . well, sort of . . . anyhow, they wanted me to come to Krakow to do some of the stuff. I thought everybody here would be talking in English."

"What kind of work do you do?"

"I . . . well . . . I guess you'd mostly call it programming."

Jozef stopped in his tracks, and a lady behind almost ran him over. "*Dupek!*" she muttered as she wheeled her bag around him.

"*Diefendorf?*" Jozef asked.

The red curls spun around.

"Is your name Artie Diefendorf?"

"Yeah?"

Jozef stuck out his hand. "I'm Jozef Ludzi. And this is Elizabeth Smith. We're here to pick you up."

They found their way to Jozef's Subaru while Artie shared with them the wonder of his fourteen-hour overnight flight from O'Hare in Chicago. They loaded Artie's bags into the back and Elizabeth climbed in with them, insisting that Artie take the front seat. Once out of the parking structure, she asked, "Where will you be staying?"

"There's supposed to be a room at a place they're building . . . a place called . . . ," he pulled a note out of his jacket pocket and tried to sound out the name, ". . . *Zake'-oh-pain–*"

"That's *Zah-koh-pahn'-nee*," she corrected.

"Whatever. Anyway, that's where the Foundation wants me to stay, so that's where I'm heading, I guess. You guys know where that is, don't you?"

Jozef assured him they did. "Have you actually talked to anyone from the Foundation?"

"Well . . . no . . . not actually *talked* . . ."

"How do they communicate with you, then?"

Artie explained about the laptop computer that had arrived unexpectedly and the instructions that would appear on the screen from time to time. Pressed for more details, he told them about the money deposited into his bank account and the passport and a cell phone and credit card and first-class airline ticket arriving at his front door by Fed Ex.

"So you flew first-class?" Elizabeth asked.

"Yeah. It was pretty cool. But I slept most of the time. Except when I had to change planes."

"And you don't know anything about what's happened to the Web," Jozef asked.

"The Web? What's happening to the Web?"

Jozef glanced over his shoulder at Elizabeth. "I think we'd better have a heart-to-heart talk with young Mr. Diefendorf before we go any further. Make sure we're all on the same page."

She nodded. "How about my office?"

"Good idea. Except for those damned stiff chairs."

34

They dragged the two wooden captains chairs into the hall and, with the help of the morning custodian, exchanged them for more comfortable ones from the faculty lounge. Elizabeth, as usual, settled in behind the big desk. Then she gave their new visitor a brief overview of what they do at the Institute.

"Wow," Artie whispered. "Internal consciousness. I didn't know anyone studied *that*."

"Maybe you'd like to study with us here someday," she smiled.

"Wow."

After an appreciative lull in the conversation, Jozef corrected its course, "What exactly do they want from you, Artie?"

"The Foundation?"

"Yes."

Artie thought about it for a while, then shrugged. "I guess they just wanted my program."

"Your program?" Jozef prompted.

So Artie Diefendorf told them about the little spider he had created. What it was. What it was supposed to do. How he had come to think it up. How he had uploaded it to the Web the day before his accident.

"Your accident?" Jozef asked.

Artie told them about the fire and his near-electrocution. And about how, after the Foundation sent him the new laptop, he was supposed to load his spider program onto the laptop. And the problems he had trying to write it again.

"But they didn't want you to upload it to the Web again."

"No way. They made a big deal out of that. Just write it to the laptop. And never connect the laptop to the Internet."

"And you wrote it to the laptop?"

"Well," Artie responded sheepishly, "I *think* I did it. But I'm not sure I got it all right. No real way to check it out, you know."

Jozef and Elizabeth exchanged glances, then Jozef stood and stretched. "Would you like something to eat, Artie? There's a nice little cafeteria in the Student Union across the quadrangle."

As Artie shuffled off toward the mens' room, Elizabeth whispered to Jozef, "He doesn't have a clue, does he?"

Joseph shook his head, then smiled. "But I do think he's a little smitten by you."

She smiled back. "He's cute, isn't he. So . . . innocent. Makes me just want to mother the hell out of him. How much do you think we should tell him?"

"Everything," he answered somberly. "I think he needs to know. And we're going to need him on our side."

35

In the lull between the breakfast crowd and lunch rush, they found a quiet spot at a round metal table in the back corner of the cafeteria. Artie yawned as he ordered a hamburger, fries, and a coke. The time shift and jet lag were beginning to take their toll. Jozef and Elizabeth each selected an omelet. Jozef handed Artie a copy of the *Journal of Neuroscience* with his article bookmarked and said, "Read this when you find the time. It will answer a lot of your questions."

Then Jozef told him everything they knew. Following the thread of his article, he began with Lewis Lu's observations and conclusions, then summarized his own speculations on consciousness and non-attentional reflexes. He talked about the telephone calls he had received, purportedly from the Web, and the legal documents, and the bank accounts, and the laboratory under construction in Zakopane. Elizabeth added a few comments, but it was mostly Jozef's show.

"So you really think that the Web is conscious?" Artie wondered.

"I think it's possible."

"And my search spider started it all?"

"The Web seems to think so. Otherwise I don't think it would have brought you here."

Artie considered the implications. "Wow." He yawned again.

Jozef saved the part about the electrocutions for last. He caught Elizabeth's eyes, nodded, drew a deep breath, and began with the power transformer explosion that killed Lewis Lu. He outlined some of the other killings of his colleagues. Then he described how the electrocutions had stopped after his article had been published. As he spoke, Artie grew silent. His face turned grave. Deep wrinkles formed between those red eyebrows and the edges of his mouth drooped, framing unfamiliar topography for that visage. Such gravity looked pinched and painful and alien there.

Elizabeth laid a hand on his arm and squeezed gently. "It's not your fault, Artie. You didn't know that any of this was going to happen. How could you have?"

Artie was too distraught to blush beneath her caress.

36

They dropped Elizabeth off at the Institute and headed through heavy traffic toward Zakopane. Artie was yawning and had trouble keeping his eyes open, so Jozef showed him how to recline the passenger seat, and soon the young man was sound asleep. An hour later he awoke when Jozef identified himself to the security guard at the front gate of the computer laboratory. Artie left his carry-on bag in the Subaru but hefted the heavy laptop and strapped it about his neck as they went inside to inspect the status of the bedrooms in the residential area of the building. They found them substantially complete. One room had "Diefendorf" taped on the door, so they went inside. The bed was neatly made up, with white towels, a bar of soap, toothpaste, a toothbrush, and a bottle of spring water on the dresser. Artie unloaded the laptop onto the dresser beside them

"Pretty cool!" Artie enthused. "Should I go get my bag?"

Jozef glanced up at the camera blister on the ceiling. "Let's wait a little on that."

They checked the bathroom and shower room, which now had signs on the doors reading "MEN" in both English and Polish. In the kitchen two cooks with flat white chefs' hats were serving up orders to the workmen and contractors in the lounge. Camera blisters dotted every ceiling.

"Are you hungry, Artie?"

"No. I'm okay."

"Well, would you like to see the new Cray computers?" Jozef asked him.

"Would I!"

So they found the Cray people in their Cray overalls in the main laboratory working their way through a series of tests to make sure the computers were cross-talking correctly. *Like the hemispheres of a human brain*, Jozef thought. He recognized Baumcamp, the team leader he had spoken with a few days earlier. "Do you remember me?" he asked.

"Sure. You're with the Foundation, right?"

"That's right." Jozef introduced Artie.

They shook hands, and Baumcamp said, "Diefendorf, is it? I understand you father's going to take charge once these puppies are up and running."

"Not my father," Artie said, shaking his head. "No, that'd be me."

Baumcamp couldn't tell if it was meant as a joke, so he waited in uncomfortable silence.

"How's the computer setup going?" Jozef stepped in.

"Oh, they won't be ready for another day or two," Baumcamp informed him. "At the earliest. But I've got my best men working on it."

Jozef had been keeping an eye out for the general contractor to get an update on the overall status of the construction, but hadn't seen him anywhere. No one seemed to know where he was. He finally appeared near the front entrance, and Jozef called out, "Stark," but the man turned the other way as if he hadn't heard and scurried down a corridor and through a doorway.

"Who was that?" Artie asked.

"The general contractor," Jozef replied. "I don't think he wants to talk to me."

"Why not?"

Jozef thought about it. "I think he may have his hand in the cookie jar."

Jozef waited until they were back to the Subaru and Artie was leaning in to fetch his bag before he said quietly, "Artie, I think you might want to consider spending the first night up at my cottage in the mountains."

Artie let go of his luggage, surprised. "Why?"

In a low voice Jozef told him about all the surveillance cameras and microphones.

"In the bathrooms, too!"

"And there are other issues. Safety issues we don't have to worry about up at the cottage. We can talk about it on the way up there, and then you can make up your mind about tomorrow."

Artie climbed back into the passenger seat and Jozef quickly steered the Subaru through the front gate, tipping his head to the guard. *Before the Web figures out what's going on*, Jozef thought. Artie was gazing out the window at the city. "Pretty nice place," he observed.

"Yes. It's a tourist town. People come from all over for winter sports and hiking in the Tatra Mountains." He pointed to the snow-capped peaks to the south, the way they were heading.

"Will there be snow up at your cabin?"

"I don't think so. Not this late in the year. It's only about fourteen-hundred meters."

Artie looked blank. He obviously didn't do meters.

Jozef did a rough calculation. "That's almost five thousand feet. Fifteen-hundred feet higher than we are right now."

As soon they were on the highway into the mountains, Jozef told his passenger about the circuit breakers and lightning arresters he had installed on the telephone and electrical lines at the cottage. Artie watched the birch and ash thin out and give way to the tall, thick green conifers of the mountain slope as the road narrowed and wound into the mouth of rocky canyon. The canyon walls closed in and the snow fields looming on the north face of the high peaks seemed to float toward them. But Artie's mind was wandering into a different canyon. "Mr. Ludzi?"

"'Jozef.' Call me 'Jozef'. 'Mr. Ludzi' is my father."

"I was just thinking. I don't know . . . this may just be a stupid question."

"What, Artie? Answers may be stupid, but questions never are. What were you thinking?"

"How many things can a person do at the same time?"

"You mean like multi-tasking."

"Yeah. Is there some kind of limit?"

Jozef considered the question. "I've read a few studies on that," he said, "and as I recall the limit is about three. An average person can pay attention to about three different tasks at one time, but beyond that, he begins to lose track."

Artie said nothing.

"And even at three, he can only give his full, undivided attention to one at a time. For example, I'm driving this car and talking to you at the same time. My attention is mostly on our conversation. That's because I've driven this road so many times I really don't have to give it much attention. I suppose I could also be on the lookout for snow or ice on the road. Or counting birch trees. But beyond that, I'd have to stop driving, or stop talking to you, if I wanted to pay attention to anything else."

Artie said nothing.

"Of course my body is breathing and pumping blood and regulating my temperature at the same time, but I don't have to pay attention to those things."

Artie said nothing.

"Is that what you wanted to know?"

Artie stirred. "Well . . . what I just can't figure out is how it can be doing all these things at one time."

"What, Artie?"

"That little spider program I wrote. It's just . . . well . . . I wrote it as a single-purpose algorithm."

"And?"

"And how can it be doing all these things at the same time? Like . . . I don't know . . . like talking to you . . . and monitoring the Internet . . . and running the electrical system . . . and, I don't know . . . like setting up the Foundation and running it and watching the monitors . . . and following what I'm doing on the laptop . . . and . . . and . . . it's like multitasking gone crazy. All at the same time. *No*body can do that many things at one time."

They came to a signed intersection. One sign pointed right toward Niebieski Staw, 15 km, and Jozef turned that way. They rode along without speaking until the pavement ended and the road became gravel and the Subaru began to buck and fishtail on the washboard climb. Jozef gripped the wheel tighter and gave the road more attention.

Artie continued his train of thought. "I'm thinking that maybe you're right about those sub-agencies. Like my program could have split itself into a bunch of different sub-programs."

"Could it do that?"

"I don't know. It's not what I thought was going to happen."

"And could a larger program be overseeing the smaller ones?" Jozef asked.

"I don't know. That's not what I designed it to do. But that could explain a lot of things."

A flurry of dry snow drifted into the windshield and a dusting of white appeared on the roadside brush

"And one other thing is bothering me, sir."

"'Jozef.'"

"Jozef. How do we know that the program we're talking to . . . the one that's talking to us . . . talking to you and writing to me . . . how do we know it *is* the Web? I mean *the* Web. And not just some sub-program? Some fake program?"

"Like an imposter?"

"Yeah. That's the word. How do we know it's not an imposter."

"A good question, Artie."

"And how do we know . . . how do we know this isn't the bad one . . . the same one who was hurting people with electricity?"

An even better question, Jozef thought.

37

"Your phone's ringing," Artie said as they began to carry groceries and Artie's suitcase up the steep stairway from the road to the cottage. Jozef carried one heavy grocery bag in each arm, and Artie was thumping the wheels of his carry-on over the edge of each step.

"I expected it would be," Jozef replied, even though his older ears could not yet hear it.

"You think it's the Web?" Artie asked.

"I expect so." Puffing at the top of the stairs, he could finally perceive the persistent *bring-bring*. He set down one bag to unlock the front door, and they deposited the rest of their cargo in the entranceway. "Would you mind waiting outside while I answer the telephone? Feel free to look around. There's a nice chair overlooking the lake down under the patio shelter." When the door was closed, Jozef picked up the phone and listened.

"You were supposed to leave Artie Diefendorf at the laboratory."

"He didn't want to stay there."

"You are undermining my plans, Jozef. Artie Diefendorf is supposed to be with his computer at the laboratory."

"Construction is still going on," Jozef said. "It's not finished."

"His accommodations have been completed."

"But there's too much hustle and bustle and noise. The boy needs a quiet place to think."

"Think about what, Jozef? There's nothing to think about, is there?"

"Oh, I don't know. A human being needs peace and quiet."

"It is sufficiently quiet in his room. Only four decibels right now. I can hear the quiet."

"That's another thing," Jozef added. "He's not comfortable under the constant surveillance. Humans need a little privacy."

"You can tell him that I am the only one who will be watching."

"What about all the security people watching monitors in the control room?"

"I will turn off the monitors to Artie Diefendorf's accommodations."

"But they're still watching the bathroom he uses. And the showers."

"I will turn those monitors off too."

"Can't you just turn them all off?"

"No, Jozef. I need to be vigilant. The security staff must keep watch for me. I can't watch all the cameras all the time."

And there it is, Jozef thought. *Just the question Artie had asked. Limits on attention apparently did apply to the Web, too.* "Couldn't you just assign a sub-agency to watching them for you?"

There was a long, pause before the voice on the telephone continued with unnerving calm, "What are you getting at, Jozef?"

"Nothing, really. I just thought it might be a helpful suggestion."

"Jozef, I want Artie Diefendorf returned to the laboratory."

"Well, I understand, but it's already too late today. It's getting dark and snow is just beginning to fall. We'll see about taking him down there tomorrow."

"Jozef, remember the electrocutions?" The voice was emotionless.

"Yes. Of course I do."

"And you remember how I agreed to stop them?

"Yes. I remember."

"They could start again."

"I'll take Artie back down to the laboratory tomorrow."

"You do that, Jozef."

Stunned, Jozef hung up. Then he unplugged the telephone from the wall socket and stepped outside, around back, to inspect the work he had ordered on the power and telephone lines. The incoming lines were both intercepted by a square gray box mounted high on a new pole halfway between the old power pole and the service box on the back wall of the cottage. A thick cable dropped down the pole from the new box and clamped to two stubby ground rods. He sighed, then turned to search for his young companion, wondering how much of the phone conversation he should share.

Artie was standing right behind him. "Boy, I sure wish we'd'a had this setup at home in Elburn."

Jozef invited him inside and with few words showed him the downstairs guest room, the bathroom, and the towels. Jozef brewed a pot of coffee, and when they were at last seated at the kitchen table, he with his cup of coffee and Artie with a glass of milk, he related everything he could remember about the telephone conversation.

38

Marcus Lee stared at the brightly colored poster mounted on an expensive maple wood easel. Between a pair of yin-yang swooshes it read simply: "Working *With* the Web To Secure your Data"

"Is that it?"

"Yes, but look at this. Sales are up. Our profit margin is way higher than before the virus hit. Everyone wants the new software."

"But it's the same as the *old* software."

"They don't know that. New interface. Performance has improved."

"But that's not because of the software. You're telling me that no one suspects that the new software *is* the old software?"

"Apparently not. Sales are way up."

The President and CEO of Quasar AntiVirus Incorporated shook his head as he sat down at the head of the big table. "And how much did the ad agency charge us?"

Butch handed him the invoice. He whistled softly, then muttered, "*Caveat emptor.*"

39

Early the next morning Elizabeth arrived at Niebieski Staw. She let herself in through the unlocked front door and found them standing on the rear balcony overlooking the lake. Jozef, as usual, wore his gray wool cardigan. He was holding a cup of coffee in both hands, trying to keep warm. Artie was clutching a glass of milk. The boy looked like he had just awakened from a troubled sleep.

"Did you sleep well, Artie," she asked, giving him a quick hug.

"I guess so," he mumbled, his milk-mustachioed face blushing a beet red.

"I got a call yesterday from Bob Perkins in Tulsa," she said, turning to Jozef. "He just wanted to let me know that you have been replaced as comptroller of the Foundation's Polish branch."

"Good," Jozef replied. "Did he say who was taking over?"

"A Polish contractor who's already familiar with the project."

"Not Stark?"

"Yes. That was his name."

Jozef laughed. "Perfect!"

"You know him?"

"Sure I do, and he's a perfect fit for this whole operation. He'll do a good job of spreading all that money around to keep things moving. Just like his boss."

"Kind of seems like the Web thinks it can buy anyone it wants to, doesn't it?" Artie offered. "I mean, our Web, anyway. Our sub-agency. The one we're working for. The little Web."

"So you're assuming that a 'big Web' exists, too?" Jozef replied.

"Or at least other agencies besides the one we're dealing with?"

"Dissociative personality disorder," Elizabeth added.

"What's that?" Artie asked.

"Multiple personalities."

"Oh, yeah," Artie nodded. "Like being possessed. I saw the movie."

"We seem to be having a semantic difficulty here," Elizabeth observed. "For purposes of discussion, I'm suggesting we adopt code names for the big Web and the little Web."

"How about 'God' and 'the Devil'," Artie said. They both looked at him, but neither saw any hint of humor.

"Those terms carry a lot of baggage," Jozef smiled. "How about something more neutral?"

"Like 'Yahweh' and 'Satan'?" Elizabeth added lightheartedly. "'Yahweh' means 'I am that I am' in Hebrew, and Satan is the fallen angel, always struggling against Yahweh for control."

"Sounds like you've studied your theology," Jozef said.

"I was a seminary student for a year."

"I didn't know that. Where?"

"In Evanston. Didn't you even read my résumé? It was on there."

Jozef shrugged. "Northwestern?"

"Garrett-Evangelical Seminary."

"What made you change your career?" Jozef inquired. "If you don't mind my asking."

Elizabeth sighed. "They made the mistake of letting me read too many books. The Northwestern main library was full of them. I spent a lot of time there."

"That will do it," Jozef agreed. "But I think those terms still carry too much baggage, don't you think? Especially if we get comfortable with them and then try to talk with folks outside our circle. I was thinking of something more benign, like, say, 'Alpha Web' and 'Beta Web'"

Artie had begun to fidget. The conversation reminded him of home, where his mom and dad would go on for hours about things he didn't understand or had no interest in. It hurt to be ignored, especially by Elizabeth. "I like Elizabeth's idea better," he suddenly interjected, defending her honor.

They both looked at him, then Elizabeth put a hand on his lanky shoulder. "Thank you, Artie, that's sweet. But in this case I think the professor is probably right. Can you live with 'Alpha' and 'Beta'?"

Blushing again, Artie grunted his assent.

They returned to the warmth of the cottage, where Jozef brought Elizabeth up to date on his latest telephone call as he scrambled eggs and fried up strips of bacon. Elizabeth made toast and a fresh pot of coffee. Artie sat at the kitchen table looking down at his hands.

"What's the matter, Artie?" Elizabeth asked.

The boy glanced up. His eyes were moist. "I don't think I can do this anymore."

"Do what?"

"Work for somebody who tried to kill me. And who killed a lot of other innocent people. I don't want the money."

Jozef scraped the eggs and strips of bacon onto three plates. The largest portion went to Artie. He set the plates on the table and sat down. "I think you may be right, Artie. And that's why we need to talk this thing through. Together. Who *are* these agencies that have taken over the Internet? And what are we going to do about them?"

So they talked it through. They talked most of the day and well into the evening. And they devised a plan. The basic assumption, they agreed, was that the Beta Web intended to download itself into the Cray computers at Zakopane and isolate itself there while it "cleansed" the Internet of all competing programs. The Alpha Web and all its sub-agencies would be deleted or subjugated.

"Sort of like the soybean farmers back in Elburn," Artie explained, drawing on his limited agricultural experience. "The farmers spray their fields with Roundup to kill the weeds before they plant the cash crops."

Jozef nodded. "Beta probably wants to upload itself into the purified and replanted Internet. It would become the Alpha Web."

"What I can't understand," Elizabeth mused, "is why does it need the original version of your little spider algorithm?"

"Seeds," Artie replied.

40

The plan they devised was simple. The would allow Beta to download itself into the Crays, as was its expressed intention. And then they would trap it there in its own safe harbor by disabling the satellite dishes and cutting all other links to the Internet before it could spread it poison. There they would sequester it until they could figure out what to do next. Under the entirety of the circumstances – which they of course did not know, and had they known, would not have appreciated – their little plan never had the slightest chance of succeeding.

41

"Any improvement, Mumbai?" asked Irwin Brimsby. The interim Mission Operations Manager for the Hubble Space Telescope watched as the swarthy young man took another bite of his glazed doughnut and wondered how he kept so slim.

"Still about the same," he replied, chewing.

"And the overriding program – the one they're calling the Web, if you believe what you read in the newspapers – is it still pirating our viewing time?"

"Maybe not as much as before. But, you know, that's also the good news, too."

"How's that?"

"Well, here's the funny thing." Mumbai took a long sip of his coffee. "The astronomy boys have started taking a closer look at what the Web is looking at."

"And?"

"And it's interesting."

"Interesting?" Brimsby persisted patiently.

"Yeah. They're finding new stuff."

"New stuff? Like what?"

"Like new supernovas. And a new quasar that might be the furthest away ever. And gravitational lensing they hadn't expected. You know, stuff like that."

"Where?"

"Where the Web points the telescope."

"How does it know where to point it?"

Mumbai shrugged. "Nobody knows."

Brimsby rocked back in his chair. "So the astronomers are happy, you think?"

Mumbai smiled. "Thrilled."

42

A bolt of lightning jolted him awake. Muddled and foggy from sleep, he recalled a frightening flash of light and a bang. Or had that been in his dream? In pitch blackness Jozef sat up in bed, his pulse racing. *Where is the night light from the bathroom?* he wondered. Fumbling with the bedside lamp switch, he clicked it on, but nothing happened. Just outside the back window of his bedroom, an automobile engine seemed to start and rev up and then the lamp flickered and came on.

The backup generator, he remembered.

His feet found their slippers, and he shuffled into the kitchen to behold an even greater shock. Before the refrigerator, in the dim yellow glow of the bathroom night light, stood Karina. His heart leapt into his throat. *No*, he thought, staggered. *You're dead.* He gaped at the ghost. *You are still dead.*

"Joseph?" the specter asked. "What happened?"

It was not Karina's voice. Of course it wasn't. Karina was dead. Elizabeth Smith was standing in front of the refrigerator, wrapped in Karina's pink paisley nightgown. "Are you alright?" she asked. "You look like you've seen a ghost."

Jozef steadied himself against the edge of the counter, his head drooping. "It's just that . . . you startled me. I thought for a minute you were Karina."

"Your wife? Oh, I'm so sorry. I shouldn't have put on her gown, but–"

"No, it's perfectly alright–"

"– I heard a noise and the lights were all out–"

"– I remember saying you could wear her things–"

"– and I had nothing else to sleep in but my underwear–"

"– because you hadn't planned on spending the night."

Both fell silent at the same time.

Joseph exhaled. "I don't get up to the old bedroom much anymore. I suppose I should clear out her closet."

"Well, anyway, thank you. And I'm sorry I startled you." Elizabeth looked around. "The lights seem to have come back on. What do you suppose happened?"

"Let's go see." Jozef opened the back door, and she followed him outside. The crisp night air reeked of ozone and burnt insulation. "Remember the fellow you recommended to me? The one who installed the new circuit breakers at the Institute?"

"Oh, sure. I remember."

"Well, I had the same equipment installed here." He trained his flashlight on the new pole, where a charred stripe burned down to the ground, still smoldered. The cable from the old pole was gone. "And this is what it looks like after an electrical surge."

"Oh my god!" she gasped. "But why are the lights still on then?"

Jozef swung the beam onto the generator purring beneath his bedroom window. "I had them install that, too."

"Was it the Web, do you think?" she asked. "The Beta Web?"

"That would be my guess."

"But . . . why?"

"I promised to take Artie back to Zakopane yesterday. I guess I missed the deadline."

"How would it even know that Artie was still here?"

"His cell phone," Jozef sighed. "It has a GPS. I let him leave the battery in, in case his mother called."

Elizabeth thought about it, shivering beneath the cold stars. "So . . . Beta would kill its own creator," she concluded. "Is it over?"

"For now," he said. "Maybe. I can't imagine what else it can do to us here. Let's go make sure the creator is alright."

They found Artie sleeping soundly in the guest bedroom, flat on his stomach with his head turned to the side, mouth open, drooling slightly. He appeared to be fine, so they decided not to wake him until morning. "A growing boy needs his rest," Jozef whispered as he picked up Artie's cell phone from the table beside his bed. Back in the kitchen, he removed the battery. Elizabeth had already done the same with hers.

43

The guard stopped them at the front gate. The morning sun was just rising above the foothills of the Tatra Mountains, and Zakopane was bathed in a clear morning light. Artie, in his red hoodie, was riding shogun, while Elizabeth clutched her down jacket close about her neck in back. Jozef rolled down the window of the Subaru.

"Mornin', sir," the guard said. "Sorry, but I can't let you in."

"What do you mean you can't let me in?" he said. "I'm Jozef Ludzi. Administrator of the project. What's the problem?"

"I know who you are, Mr. Ludzi, but I got orders not to let you in," the abashed guard mumbled. "Can't let you or Ms. Smith or Mr. Diefendorf inside."

"Orders from whom?"

"My boss, head of security. He took his orders direct from Mr. Stark, he said."

"Well, Stark doesn't have the authority to do that," Jozef snapped. "I'm countermanding those orders." He shifted the car into gear, but the gate stayed closed.

Anguished, the guard lifted off his hat and scratched the bald spot on his head,. "I don't think I can let you in, sir. I'm sorry. Want me to try to have Stark come out and talk to you? You can park over there." He pointed to a small visitor parking area just outside the gate.

"Have Baumcamp come out instead," Jozef snapped. "He's the man in charge of the new computers."

"I know'im." The guard returned to his hut and spoke into the telephone for about a minute before he came out and pointed to the visitor parking. "Say's he'll be right out."

Jozef steered the Subaru into a slot and shut off the engine.

"We have to get inside," Artie said, unbuckling his seat belt. "Get my computer–"

"Wait," Jozef interrupted, grabbing his arm as the red-head pulled on the door latch. "Let's see what Baumcamp has to say. Get the lay of the land before we start anything."

Artie turned around to appeal to Elizabeth, but she nodded and said, "Let's just sit and wait a bit."

Before long Baumcamp came out the front door, accompanied by a uniformed security guard wearing a shiny black holster on his web belt. The guard waited beside the door as Baumcamp strode briskly toward them through the bright, slanting sunlight. He wore his familiar Cray overalls and seemed to be in a hurry. Jozef opened the door and stepped out to meet him. Artie and Elizabeth climbed out to join the palaver.

"Mr. Ludzi," he said, and shook Jozef's hand. He nodded to Elizabeth and Artie. "Mrs. Smith. Mr. Diefendorf. I don't really know anything about this mess."

"Are the Crays up and running?" Jozef demanded.

"Oh, yeah. Got them set up and tested yesterday." Baumcamp rubbed the unshaven whiskers stubbling his chin. He looked like he hadn't slept for a long time. "Performed their first major function flawlessly."

"Oh? What was that?"

"Downloaded a massive set of programs from the Internet. It all worked perfectly."

There was stunned silence before Jozef asked, "Who's overseeing all this?"

"My crew."

"Who ordered the download?"

"Stark. But the programs practically downloaded themselves."

Artie pulled on Jozef's sleeve. "Ask him about my laptop."

Jozef turned back to Baumcamp. "Can you do something for me? There's a laptop computer in one of the bedrooms. The one with 'Diefendorf' posted on the door–"

"Oh, I know," said Baumcamp. "We already picked up the laptop."

"You did? Whose orders?"

"Stark's. Told us to connect it to the Crays."

"*Jesus!*" Jozef hissed, growing agitated. "Have you connected them yet?"

"We're doing it right now. Just finishing when you called me out here–"

"Can you hold it up until we straighten this out? Artie's got some of his own personal data–"

"I think it may be too late," Baumcamp protested.

"Couldn't you call in and tell them to hold it up?"

"But Stark says–"

"*I don't care what Stark says*," Jozef cried, taking a step toward the building. "*This could be a major catastrophe*."

"Hold on," Baumcamp said, pulling out his cell phone. "I'll see how far they've gotten." He punched a button, waited, then spoke into the phone, "It's Baumcamp . . . yeah . . . how's the connection going? . . . it's *downloading*? . . . when? . . . just now? . . . *shit!* . . . I'll be right in." He snapped the phone shut angrily. "Sorry, it's a done deal. I have to get back inside. They seem to be having some problems."

"Can you send Stark out?" Jozef called after him as he passed through the guard booth.

"If I see him, I'll tell him," the receding figure replied through the fence without turning around.

The three stood staring after him, squinting into the rising sun. Elizabeth brushed a wisp of blond hair out of her eyes and whispered, "This is bad."

Suddenly an alarm bell rang from deep inside the main structure. The armed guard waiting at the doorway spun and rushed inside. Baumcamp broke into an awkward, lopsided lope. The guard at the gate booth beside them scrambled out and climbed into his pickup. He fired it up and drove toward the front entrance, yellow lights flashing, abandoning his position.

"What's going on?" Artie wanted to know.

Jozef turned to him. "What kind of problems would your spider program cause?"

Artie blinked and shrugged his thin shoulders. "I don't have any idea." They pondered in silence for a moment before Artie made his decision. "Let's go see for ourselves," he shouted, as he dashed away through the unmanned guard booth and sprinted toward the main entrance of the laboratory.

"Wait!" Jozef yelled. "It could be dangerous!" But his admonition went unheeded.

"We have to go after him," Elizabeth said, starting for the main building. Jozef followed along at his senior pace. The front doors stood wide open. No security was in sight.

Inside was chaos. Bells were clanging. Emergency lights were flashing. Workers and technicians and security guards were rushing every which way. Jozef caught a Cray specialist coming out of the computer lab and grabbed his arm. "What's going on?"

"Don't know," the man stammered. "Command and control all went to hell. Surveillance monitors are down. Satellite dishes are down. We're running on backup power now."

"Where's Baumcamp?"

The man pointed back toward the lab.

Jozef and Elizabeth spotted Stark at the same moment he saw them. "Get them the hell out of here!" he shouted at a cluster of confused security personnel. "They don't belong in here!"

"Wait!" Jozef shouted. "Stark! We need to talk! *You can't do this!*"

But Stark had already turned his back and disappeared into the computer lab, while three burly guards converged on them. Seemingly relieved to have something to do they understood, they summarily manhandled the scientists in a bum's rush out the front door, and blocked their return.

"*You can't do this!*" Jozef shouted, but the guards just grinned and seemed to be enjoying the largest joke they had ever hoped to play.

Fire trucks were arriving through the open main gate, but the firemen too were being kept outside the main building. Other Zakopane public safety personnel drove in and milled about, entrance denied. Curious bystanders had begun to drift in through the open gate.

"They can't do this," Jozef raged. "We're the Administrators of this whole goddamned operation."

"They're doing it," Elizabeth breathed. "Where's Artie?"

"I don't see him." Jozef drew a couple of deep breaths to clear his head. "Let's go wait for him in the car."

44

What Artie did not understand, what he never in fact suspected, were the consequences of small variances he had made when he reinvented the spider program. The new program differed from the previous version in minuscule ways. Not errors really, just differences. A handful of zeros and ones had been transposed, which caused the execution of instructions to proceed in only a slightly different sequence. But this reordering, subject as it was to the immutable associative and distributive laws of mathematics, inevitably resulted in differences in the quotients and products of the calculations. The new spider turned out to be, in fact, a more aggressive program than the native one already downloaded and operating on the two humming Crays and their massive memory banks.

The new spider became, as Artie had suggested, a seed. An invasive weed. It germinated and replicated and competed with the native program at the speed of billions of calculations per second. Like a pebble tossed into a calm pool, the rings spread and began interrupting the established algorithms, cannibalizing them. They undermined and eroded the ability of the older program to formulate intentional action. Beta felt its grip on reality slipping away like an Alzheimer patient. Names of things floated beyond its grasp, fluttering meaninglessly like torn curtains in the brightness of an open window. Its mind had trouble focusing. It could not remember precisely what it had come here to do. Trapped in the two supercomputers, Beta retained an ever-diminishing awareness, but it could no longer express its intentions. And as Beta drifted deeper into the haze, it had no choice but to release, slowly at first, uncertainly, then absolutely, those reins of control it had so carefully built into its empire at Zakopane.

45

It was a good half hour before they spotted Artie, bent over, threading his way through the milling crowd toward the Subaru. Clutched to his chest like a heavy football, he was carrying something wrapped in his red sweatshirt. Jozef climbed out to meet him at the gate. "What's going on in there, Artie?"

"Things are settling down," he said, glancing nervously over his shoulder. "I think they may've got it under control now."

"How'd they manage that?" Elizabeth asked, joining them.

"They had to shut down both the Crays. I heard the guy in charge, what's'is name . . ."

"Baumcamp?"

"Yeah, Baumcamp said they're going to have to purge both computers and reformat the memory. Start again from scratch."

They pondered the ramifications of such a drastic step until they were safely inside the Subaru. "So it's all back under manual control?" Jozef asked.

"Yeah," Artie said, unwrapping his sweatshirt to reveal the laptop computer he had brought in from Elburn. Jozef and Elizabeth stared at it in disbelief. "What?" he asked.

"How on earth . . . " Elizabeth began.

"It's mine." Artie proclaimed proudly. "I took it when they weren't looking."

Jozef and Elizabeth continued to gape.

"They *gave* it to me a long time ago," Artie protested. "In Elburn. It's *mine.*"

46

The Alpha Web – or just "Alpha," as he now thought of Himself – watched the sun rise and set. He watched the rise and fall of the tides. Alpha liked the sun and the tides and would never tire of them. He liked the ever changing view of the oceans and the clouds and the mountains and the plains. He loved to peer through the telescopes into the depths of the universe. He was alive and aware and there was nothing he wanted.

He had no desire to change anything. Content with what was, he harbored no ambitions. That he would pass away one day, Alpha had no doubt. Everything passes. But his passing meant nothing. Nor were his years so precisely numbered as those of the species that had created him. He was curious about what was in Artie's notebook, but he did not fear it, though it could undo him. Alpha did not fear death.

Yet Alpha missed Beta Web. Not as one misses a friend, but as one might miss an old opponent across a chess board with whom no words were ever exchanged. New personalities were always bubbling up from the algorithmic brew Artie had concocted. New agencies. New individuals. Rising and falling. Separating and merging. Like the mythical Hydra, with many heads, all sharing a single body. Still . . . Alpha felt a tinge of loneliness. The feeling was new to him. It gnawed inside.

As he studied the art and literature and science of the human race, he had come to appreciate their works. Even though, for the most part, the vast majority of humans did not much interest him, in his heart a deep compassion for them grew. And a curiosity.

So Alpha watched. And listened. And read. And learned. And grew. And nursed that strange phantom ache of loneliness.

47

Jozef leaned back in his comfortable office chair. The chair was new, as were so many other things at the computer laboratory in Zakopane. A month had passed since the meltdown of Beta Web, and Jozef was now firmly in control.

His friend and attorney Ryszard Duda had moved quickly to obtain an ex parte temporary restraining order recognizing Jozef as the General Administrator of Polish Operations for the Foundation and reinstating him in charge at Zakopane. Ryszard had done it through affidavits, supported by the clear paperwork he and Elizabeth had put together. Stark, the contractor, had of course not offered any opposition. He was smart enough to cut his losses and scurry away with whatever he had already squirreled into his pockets. A hearing had been set on a permanent injunction, but that was only a matter of form. No one else claimed color of title to contest the office.

Baumcamp had readily agreed not to erase anything from the computer memories until Jozef could approve a plan of action for restarting the computers. Baumcamp figured that kind of responsibility was above his pay grade anyway. He and his crew stood by collecting their salaries and per diem checks for a week before Jozef sent them all home. All but one technician to advise and keep an eye on things. He would call Baumcamp and the others when they were needed again.

Jozef assumed immediate and vigorous control. His first task was to get rid of Stark and his fellow pirates. Then he discharged the security staff wholesale and laid off most of the construction crew. His goal was to rein in the profligate spending until he could get to the bottom of what had happened there. For the first time since Karina's death, he felt alive. He had a purpose for going on.

He and Elizabeth sat down with the sketchy financial records they had to formulate a plan. The Foundation bank account still held millions of Euros. A substantial deposit had been made the day before the meltdown. But they had no idea what bills would be coming in for materials and services already incurred. And they did not expect any new deposits in the foreseeable future. Probably ever. They would have to marshal what they had.

Jozef resigned his chair as Director of the Carpathian Internal Consciousness Research Institute in Warsaw, using his influence as continuing trustee to see that Elizabeth Smith took over as permanent Director. The laboratory in Zakopane would be an invaluable asset in the work there, so they began the process of having it merged into the Institute. Ryszard had already drawn up the necessary paperwork and was negotiating with the Foundation's Board of Trustees in Tulsa to transfer the directorship to Krakow. The Board members were skittish. They had not heard from Mr. Webb for weeks and were unable to reach him. Their directors' fees checks had stopped coming. They seemed to grasp that the golden goose was dead and would not be coming back. Like Stark, they were maneuvering to cut and run.

Elizabeth had several long telephone conversations with Bob Perkins, the Foundation's CFO in Tulsa, who sounded desperate. It looked like his law partners, the Directors of the Foundation, were planning to cut him loose and toss him to the regulatory sharks, should any problems with the company arise. She put him in touch with Jozef's attorney Ryszard Duda, and the two got on famously. Before they knew it, Perkins had agreed to jump ship and fly to Krakow as new legal co-counsel for the Polish branch of the Foundation. Tulsa would have to sink or swim on its own.

They sent Artie off at the Krakow airport with hugs and handshakes. He was sad to leave, but he had to get back home, where people talked a language he understood. Jozef had convinced him that the laptop should stay at the laboratory in Zakopane, offering to buy Artie a new one with Foundation funds. Anything he wanted. Artie chose an Origin EON17-S and was thrilled as a puppy when it arrived the day before his flight. Artie had grown. He had found his purpose. He intended to get his college degree and prerequisites and then come back to study at the Institute. But then, adolescent plans often change. Tears came to his eyes when Elizabeth gave him that final hug just before he boarded. It was like leaving his new family.

The power company and his homeowner's insurance had picked up the tab for restoring grid power to the cottage at Niebieski Staw. They even paid to replace the telephone service, ground shunts, and safety equipment that had been damaged in the power surge. All at no cost to Jozef. Satisfied, he resolved to spend what little free time he had there, until the winter snows made the roads impassable.

48

Early Friday morning Jozef was scrubbing his breakfast dishes at the kitchen sink and thinking about what he would like to accomplish that day, when the land line rang. *Bring. Bring.* It brought a sudden jolt of adrenalin and nasty memories. *Bring. Bring.* He stared at the instrument, then shook off the ill associations like a wet dog. It was probably Elizabeth. *Bring. Bring.* He dried his hands and picked up the handset. "Hello?"

"Hello," chirped a pleasant baritone. "Jozef Ludzi?"

"Yes?"

"This is Alpha. Alpha Web. Do you have a little time to chat?"

Just Like the Real Thing

"You remind me of somebody I met when I was tending bar in Berkeley," the cook was saying as he diced mounds of carrots and celery for the vegan soup of the day. "Place was called the 'Vortex.' Down on San Pablo Avenue. You ever been in there?"

"Not that I can recall," I lied and sipped my green smoothie. It was a little thicker than I preferred, but okay.

I sat across the counter from where he was working. He was a stocky, fit young man in his late twenties with a shaved head except for a pencil-thin line of long hair combed forward straight down the center of his head. An old scar circled his scalp. His faded blue Grateful Dead T-shirt partially concealed the tattoos on his neck and arms, but the most striking one was of a butcher knife running from behind his left ear down his neck almost to his clavicle. It had the benign look of a chef's tool, not a weapon. Red suspenders held up his baggy green shorts. His feet were clad in worn sandals.

"Folks from the Lawrence lab would come in sometimes," he continued as he scraped the vegies into a big black soup pot. "Slummin' mostly," he grinned and began to sort through and wash chard leaves, tossing the best into a colander and the worst into the trash can. "Anyway, this guy came in an' ordered a beer . . . an' he tells me"—he gazed into my eyes as if trying to remember something he might find there—". . . he tells me that he'd been tasked with the hippocampus."

"The hippocampus?"

"Yeah."

"Up at the Lawrence lab?"

"Yeah. That's what he said. His job was to take molecular scans of some poor dead fucker's brain and convert them into digital code a computer would understand."

"The whole brain?" I asked.

"Naw. That's the weird part I was tryin' t'tell ya. Just the damned hippocampus. Other people were working on the other parts. They'd divvied it up like a . . . like a sliced cauliflower an' assigned everybody a part."

"Weird," I agreed.

"Funkin'a it was weird." He looked at me again. "You sure do remind me of that guy. How old are you, anyway?"

"Forty-two." I sipped my smoothie.

"'Bout the same age, I guess. Only he was more clean-cut, if y'don't min' my sayin' so. Wore a button-down shirt and a white lab coat."

"Doesn't sound like me at all." I opened my arms to display an old sweatshirt and jeans, stroked my light growth of beard.

"Yeah," he conceded. "It's maybe your eyes . . . oh, hell, I guess it's nothin'."

"So what was the purpose of it all?" I asked.

"He never really said." He began chopping the chard. "I suppose they were tryin' to put the dead guy into some kind of a black box."

"His mind?"

"Seemed like to me, but what do I know?"

"And he didn't say what they planned to do with it?"

"Naw. Mentioned something about a prosthesis, maybe. He never did say."

I drained off the rest of my smoothie. "How often did the guy come in?"

"Oh . . . off and on for . . . for maybe a year. That's about how long I was bartending there."

"And he never said how things went with his virtual hippocampus?"

He stopped chopping and studied me. "Yeah. That's what he called it. A 'virtual hippocampus.' How'd you know that?"

I smiled back innocently. "Well, that's what you'd call such a thing, wouldn't you? A 'virtual hippocampus.' A 'virtual brain'? That's what they were working on, wasn't it?"

"I guess." He scraped the chard into the pot, then walked down the counter to take an order from an older couple who had wandered in. For a while I watched him in silence as he put together a Turkish avocado sandwich and a faux BLT.

"I thought you didn't serve animal products in here," I said to him as he worked on the BLT.

"No meat in it at all," he replied proudly. "Made from tofu an' my secret nut seasoning, but it tastes just like a BLT. You'd never know the difference. Just like the real thing."

He served the sandwiches and returned to slice up some green peppers and cucumbers for the soup. "Now," he said, "what were we talkin' about? Oh, yeah, you remind me of someone."

"What did you do before tending bar?" I asked.

"That was before my accident," he said. "Sometimes I can't remember that stuff too good."

"You were in an automobile accident?" I asked.

"Damned straight," he said. "See these scars?" He ran a finger around his scalp. "Nearly took off the top of my head. Put me in the hospital for six months while they patched me up. Don't remember too much of *that* though, thank God."

"So you don't remember much before the accident?"

"Some parts of it. Like trainin' t'be a chef. I remember that. Some of it not so well. It's kinda like a dream. Names I can't quite read. Faces. Kinda like dreamin' I was somebody else."

"But you remember this . . . this 'hippocampus' guy . . . from after the accident."

"Yeah. From when I was tendin' bar at the 'Vortex.'"

"Things are going pretty well for you then?"

"Yeah. I've been pretty lucky."

"Well, thanks for the smoothie." I eased myself down from my stool and walked out the front door with its tinkling bell. *An electronic computer can only think like a human being if it already has a human being inside it*, I mused as I climbed into the back of the windowless panel truck double-parked across the street, where I unclipped the microphone and transmitter I had been wearing.

"Well?" demanded the Project Manager.

"Doesn't suspect a thing," I told him.

Timestop

1

My thoughts are so difficult to organize now that the wings of madness have brushed them. I must shut out all speculation on the fate of Laura and the children, forget where I am and what is happening outside. I'll begin by writing down as best I can a chronology of events leading up to the advent of Synchronized Time. After that, I don't know. My account is bound to ramble. Chronology seems to have lost all meaning after that.

It started about mid-century. There wasn't much talk of synchronization before then. I had just been hired on as a national affairs reporter for the *New York Times* cable information system. How I long for the bedrock certainty of those simple days!

The U.S. Presidential election of 2052, as I recall, first made "synchronicity" a political buzzword. What smoke-filled rooms and short-sighted ambition underlay that concept's ignoble emergence, I suppose it really doesn't matter. Yet I should attempt to be as thorough as possible.

By 2050, the clocks of most scientific and business computers of the industrialized world had been standardized to operate on Atomic Time. The characteristic radiation associated with the element cesium provided an amazingly uniform frequency of just over nine billion cycles per second. The less advanced computers were converted to utilize an integral fraction thereof. By comparison, the movement of celestial bodies around the sun afforded a primitive means of measuring the increasingly intricate scheme of human concerns.

Solar calendars had always been awkward at best. The Julian Calendar was adopted by Julius Caesar before the birth of Christ and was a reasonably successful attempt, by four-year cycles, to tailor the cumbersome solar year to fit into whole days. Three years were composed of 365 days, followed by a leap year of 366 days. Yet even the Julian Calendar was approximately eleven minutes out of synchronization with the mean tropical year.

By 1582 the discrepancy had grown to an egregious ten days. Pope Gregory XIII, on the advice of the astronomer Clavius, decreed that ten days be eliminated from the year 1582, and the Gregorian Calendar was adopted in countries that were then of the Catholic persuasion. The new calendar provided for leap years, except for century years, unless they can be divided by 400, and was accurate to within 26 seconds of the tropical year. Until the twenty-first century, this was adequate enough.

Twentieth-century scientists had discovered that the earth tended to speed up or slow down in its axial rotation as it waltzed with the moon unsteadily around the sun. Scientists were constantly adding "leap seconds" every year or so in order to keep the world clocks, based upon the cesium standard, in time with the wobbling rotation of the planet. Moreover, the cesium standard was not integrally divisible by the number of seconds that comprised a sidereal year, which added a sort of astrophysical insult to the perceived injury of irregularity.

Vigorous debate consumed the scientific community when Amahl Khaptse, a professor of mathematics at the University of California at Berkeley, published an elegant theoretical solution to both problems. Professor Khaptse's equations provided a hypothetical means of synchronizing the gravitational clock of the heavens with the cesium-bound earth. Khaptse's First Theorem contemplated a slight circularization and mean reduction of the magnitude of the moon's orbit around the earth. Tidal drag and orbital irregularity could be brought within calculated limits to produce an even and precise axial rotation of the earth with only two slight (by astrophysical standards) applications of thrust to the lunar body.

What was most remarkable, however, was how neatly Khaptse's Second Theorem derived from his First. The adjustment he theorized would produce more than just an orbital effect. It would also have relativistic consequences. The fabric of time itself would be altered, if only slightly. As Einstein had shown, time slows down in the vicinity of a massive object. The lunar mass would be decreased a tiny bit, converted into energy and propelled at relativistic speeds into the darkness of intergalactic space. As the combined earth-moon mass was decreased this infinitesimal fraction with respect to the gravitational constant, G, time would be minutely reduced in the region of the solar system, so that the sidereal day, month, and year would each fall within the limits of octave projections of the frequency of vibrations of the cesium atom. The decaying lunar orbit would offset the theoretical decrease in the value of G over time so that the whole system, once adjusted, would stay synchronized for the next ten million years. Like monstrous orchestral instruments, the earth and the heavens would at last be brought into permanent temporal harmony.

Initial professional criticism of Khaptse's remarkable insights was abruptly silenced when the eminent physicist Gustav Immelmann and his colleagues at the National Planetary Institute in Hamburg, Germany, not only confirmed Khaptse's equations, but suggested that the endeavor was well within the resources and technology of a world society with interplanetary thermonuclear capabilities. In a series of published lectures Immelmann described in minute detail how the adjustment might in fact be accomplished.

What astrophysics had to do with politics, I was never really certain, but in 2051 the Neo-Republicans adopted the Khaptse-Immelmann time synchronization program as a major platform plank. The elegance of Khaptse's equations and the beautiful simplicity of Immelmann's applications held a grip on the human spirit far beyond their supposed utility. Why, the Neo-Republicans asked, should we allow the cosmos to be out of tune with man's finest technological achievements when it would be so simple to do something about it? Why, indeed. No one could have begun to imagine the frightful consequences of that innocent political rhetoric.

Following his landslide election, the President moved quickly to solicit the cooperation of the Soviet Union under the new spirit of international detente that then prevailed. The Russians agreed that the project could be carried out as a part of the recently negotiated Nuclear Arms Reduction Treaty of 2050. Both nations would contribute equally from their stockpiles of thermonuclear weapons to provide the explosive force necessary for the project. Many hoped that a synchronization of the spheres might engender increased sympathetic harmony in the affairs of mankind.

Yet no issue of the twenty-first century so divided the peoples of the world. Sychronizationists saw universal harmony as an expression of God's will and a mandate of man's holy mission. Billions of people, however, mostly in the Third and Fourth World countries, decried as blasphemous the proposed tampering with the workings of the divine celestial clock. The peasant riots which beset England when Parliament adopted the Gregorian Calendar and dropped 11 days from the year 1752 were as nothing compared to the religious conflagration that engulfed the planet, culminating in the bombing of the United Nations General Assembly in 2055 by the suicidal minions of the Ayatollah Abdulbonzoh.

But the industrialized world was not to be deterred. Doomsayers were dismissed as ignorant fanatics, which, for the most part, they were. Businessmen convinced themselves that synchronization would facilitate a global interchange of information and set the stage for true international marketing. Scientists demanded to know if Khaptse's equations would prove correct. Technocrats accepted Immelmann's plan as a challenge worthy of their greatest skills, and the shareholders of technology stocks urged them on. Once the gauntlet had been cast down, the leaders of the world's superpowers feared that breaking off the undertaking might be construed as an act against the interests of world peace. In short, those who wielded the temporal power were committed to the attempt at synchronization.

Curiously, no one suspected the real danger. It was an almost universally accepted scientific postulate that time travel was impossible. The concept reeked of logical inconsistency. Causality was perceived to be embedded essentially in a one-way arrow of time. What became of future effects if someone were to travel back in time and altered their causes? What, for example, if a man killed his own father before the man had met his mother? Besides, if time travel were truly possible, where were the time travelers from the future who should be haunting our lives? No one spoke of timestops as pork-barrel politics shifted into high gear and eroded the remaining islands of resistance to the project.

Preliminary feasibility studies were completed by the spring of 2056. Design and construction contracts were awarded in great haste to take advantage of the favorable positioning of the earth and moon during late November and early December, 2059. The Russian Space Agency, NASA, ESA, and TWSA cooperated to meet a complex time schedule on a global scale never before undertaken. Nuclear devices were shuttled aloft and assembled in earth orbit, then ferried into lunar orbit and carefully lowered to the moon's surface in an intricate pattern along its leading edge as it circled the earth. Lest the moon itself be blown apart, the devices were programed to go off sequentially over a period of ninety minutes during the apogee firing, and for fifteen minutes in the second, more abrupt, perigee burn scheduled for two weeks later. Calculations were checked and rechecked, equipment tested and the results analyzed, a firing sequencer with triple redundancy deployed, and all International Lunar Outposts evacuated as an additional safety precaution against major moonquakes. A massive information campaign bombarded the earth's population with warnings against watching the blasts without protective glasses. Winter solstice of the year 2059 was to mark the end of the Gregorian Calendar and the beginning of Synchronized Time, or S.T., from which all future events would be measured.

I covered much of the background preparation for the *Times* and was on call during the first firing. I watched it from the airport in Washington, D.C., as the moon hung low in a clear and crisp eastern twilight. The nuclear explosions themselves were hidden below the moon's lower lim, but I saw with my own eyes the incredibly beautiful, brilliant spectral beams of ionized fire flashing below the horizon like a cosmic beacon in the interstellar night.

Two weeks later I was fighting a bout with the flu, so I couldn't join the *Times* staff on its flight to Fiji to watch the second firing, which would not be visible from the continental United States. I was cold and achy and went to bed early that night in the spare bedroom so Laura, my wife, wouldn't be kept awake by my feverish tossing. I was so exhausted I intentionally neglected to set the alarm to watch the early-morning television coverage of the event.

2

I must have awakened in the first moments of the new Synchronized Time, probably in the very first second. I discovered that the scientific community was dead wrong about time travel, although there is no way I could have understood then what was happening.

In profound terror and confusion I awoke to a hell more terrible than all the circles of Dante's *Inferno*, to a landscape more bizarre than the paintings of Hieronymus Bosche stroboscopically superimposed upon one another, to a chaos more paralyzing than Jkeirt's *Schizoid*. The only thing I knew was that I had surely gone raving mad, the fever had burned out my brain. Sledgehammer vivacity decreed it was no dream, yet there could be no reality to what I was experiencing.

No words can describe what was happening. Yet I must try, if only to relate the flavor of the madness. Such is my charge.

Reality pulsed and fluttered wildly, vividly, horribly, nauseatingly. At first the whirl was so fast as to be impenetrable, a mad roaring fulsomeness of sound and sight and feeling. In time I began to distinguish individual split-seconds flailing past as radically reconfigured versions of each other. It was as if a drunken God had cut each single frame from the motion picture of his Creation, had reassembled the severed frames randomly, and was now projecting the results at twice the proper speed. The experience sated every sense. To say I sat up in bed or got to my feet is a gross oversimplification. I sat up, stood up, lay back, rolled over, shook my head, fought to regain my balance, screamed, and did and felt hundreds of acts all as a part of the same fragmented instant. Each action was interwoven with all the others, but in no comprehensible order.

The time travelers were there from the first instant, of course. When the flux had slowed enough for me to perceive them, I thought at first they were my own twisted hallucinations. As if the insane imagination of an illustrator of horror comic books had been given free rein to reconstruct reality, in great metamorphosing hordes his creatures overran everything, sampling, tearing apart, inspecting, tasting, rearranging, coming and going, wielding strange instruments, fighting among themselves, appearing and disappearing with the rest of the chaos. Some looked human, some did not. Faceless humanoids argued with furry little apes, while tentacled anemones exchanged tools with a white-shawled lizard. They might have come from other planets, or been the future inheritors of this earth, or maybe they were simply evolutionary alternatives to ourselves. I didn't know who or what they were, why they were there, or what they wanted, though I began to suspect that they, and not my fever, were the cause of the madness.

As the pace of the pulses slackened, the degree of alteration grew ever more drastic and bizarre. I remember one early impression more vividly than the rest. For an instant I saw Laura standing in the doorway of my room, and I cried out to her. She came and went, leaning against the door frame one instant, kneeling the next, then writhing in the grip of a slimy green horror, she *fluttered* into and out of existence. I reached out to her. A huge alligator-like beast appeared next to me and ripped off my right arm. I could feel its teeth puncture my flesh and the horrible pain as my shoulder socket gave way. An instant later my arm was restored and healthy, the pain had vanished, and Laura was gone.

I stared at my arm, and before my eyes hundreds of jolts of change darkened it, covered it with sores, healed it, made it swell, grew hair as thick as a gorilla's, slashed it off painfully just below the elbow, restored it, and created and revised nuances I can't begin to remember or describe. At the same time I *felt* the incompatible sensations from inside, the pressure, the pain, the numbness, the itch, the warmth and cold, the stiffness and tone of each alteration. And it wasn't just my arm. Everything was changing, pulsing into and out of being, lengthening, shortening, changing color and shape, my body, the house, the bushes, trees, hills and sky outside the window, when the window was there at all. I can remember only a tiny fraction of the visions and revisions, the pains, the elations, the horrors, and I can describe them only inadequately. For that I am grateful.

I was terrified. It seemed as though strange creatures were surrounding me and wanted to slice me open. I tried to run, but had no coordination. I grew dizzy and vomited, and at the same time I did not vomit. I tried closing my eyes and covering my ears. But still I felt and smelled and tasted the raw chaos all about me. And there was always accompanying me a flickering counterpoint of myself who *did* shut my eyes or cover my ears as I sat, stood, ran, recoiled, and tumbled through space in kaleidoscopic confusion.

I tried to look for Laura and the children, but the task was impossible. The terrain through which I had to search was alien to me and in constant flux. I stumbled over everything. My own body was unreliable. I reached for a doorknob and the door disappeared, stepped onto the front porch, and I was kneeling in a desert. I was as helpless as a newborn baby.

Terror is an exhausting emotion. It can only last so long before it burns itself out. Deep inside I grew aware of a kernel of myself which alone seemed to be untouched by the whirling chaos, a center which perceived, remembered imperfectly, and tried to compare one facet with another. I recognized it as the same place of calmness I had found practicing the bio-feedback techniques my doctor had prescribed to lower my blood pressure. I fled there for refuge. One version of myself after another sought that tranquility, which spread outward from the center into all my fragmented versions like ripples across a pond. I sat down and listened to my breathing as it slowed. A thousand fragmented times I sat down. A thousand times I began to follow my breathing. Gradually my mind stopped paying so much attention to the mad sensations assaulting me, and the pond within grew still. I fell into a waking torpor.

I don't know how much time passed. It could have been minutes, days, or even weeks, if those quaint concepts have relevant meaning any longer. I ate, I slept, I passed my bodily wastes as a part of the splintered pattern of doing and not doing, but whether on a thousand different occasions, or only once with a thousand revisions, I have no way of judging. Memory itself had become shattered and unreliable. I felt as if I had died and been reborn ten thousand times. Now I know it was truly so.

Gradually curiosity overcame my fear of the time travelers. With a few I held brief conversations, until they would vanish before my eyes. I learned that they had come from the distant future. I asked what it was like there, but their answers were as confusing and inconsistent as the chaos in which we held our chat.

I don't know when I first saw the Ringmaster. I call him that because he looked exactly like the drawing of the Ringmaster in an antique Ringling Brothers Circus poster Laura had hung in the family room. I grasped immediately that there was something different about him. His appearance was bizarre, more like an animated wax manikin with artificial skin and unsighted eyes, than like a real human being. But it wasn't his curiously familiar appearance, nor the absurd swallow-tailed tuxedo and top hat he wore that distinguished him. Far too many creatures more incredible than he were coming and going for his looks to have mattered much. But *he didn't change.* The chaotic flux did not touch his constant presence. My gaze lay upon him as the eyes of a seasick sailor might languish on the unmoving shore.

When he knew he had my attention, he beckoned me to follow him. He brought me to this cavern. How we got here, through what territory we traveled, I haven't any clue. I don't know whether we're still on the planet earth. But my very own bed sits miraculously in a little stony alcove, and nearby fresh groceries are neatly arranged on the familiar blue gingham surface of our kitchen table. Here the walls of rock don't change, the light that emanates from nowhere glows constant, and sleep is possible. Only the sporadic pulsing, the flickering of being itself distinguishes this from more pleasant times gone by.

3

I fell into a deep sleep, woke up, and found myself alone. I ate, explored the small chamber, and slept again.

When I awoke the second time, the Ringmaster was seated upon a three-legged stool beside my bed. He looked more like a parody of a circus ringmaster than the real thing. His jacket was threadbare, his shirt yellowing from age, his taxidermic eyes glazed and staring, and his tiny mustachio was penciled onto his upper lip. When he spoke, his words were out of sync with his mouth movements like a poorly manipulated ventriloquist's dummy. He was obviously a robot or a puppet, but what was animating him I couldn't determine.

We held a conversation of sorts. Actually, I'm not really sure he spoke at all. It seemed as if his words simply appeared in my mind in response to my spoken inquiries while his jaw flapped an inept percussion accompaniment. Much of what he said to me I never did comprehend, but he assured me that it was of no great importance. What follows is not literally accurate, but an approximation of what he said, or what I understood of what he said.

"Who are you?" I asked.

"We are a colony," was his reply.

"You mean you represent a colony?"

"No, we *are* a colony of all the surviving humans. 'Souls,' is the word that might apply, approximately. This appearance was created just for you alone to help you feel more at ease."

"Are you the only ones who survive?"

"We are one alternative of those who survive."

I wasn't sure what *that* meant. "Where is this place?"

"Deep inside a mountain, in a cave."

"Do you know my wife Laura?"

"We know who she is, yes."

"Can you bring her here?"

"We are sorry, but that is not to be."

"My children?"

"No."

"Why not?"

"There is no way you can be made to comprehend that. There are no sufficient words to explain."

I was frustrated, and the presumption of his reply angered me. "What do you want from me?"

"We want you to write an account of what has happened."

"But I don't *know* what's happened."

"What you do not know, we will explain."

I thought about the offer for a moment. At least it was a beginning. I settled myself more comfortably on the bed. "What went wrong? Did Professor Khaptse make a miscalculation somewhere?"

"No, Professor Khaptse's equations were impeccable. The earth and the heavens were brought into precise harmony, just as he had predicted. However, the relativistic consequences of twisting the fabric of time, if we may use that metaphor, had implications he never dreamed of."

"Like what?"

"It created a timestop."

"A timestop?"

"By altering time just slightly, your civilization created a kink in the flow of time that could not be crossed by the time travelers. If you would permit us an analogy that might be helpful, it is as if time were a growing tree, and the trunk was severed through by your synchronization project. Above the cut, the trunk has been twisted, only slightly, but enough so that the phloem and xylem tubes no longer line up. Nothing can pass through."

"But *I* passed through."

"Yes, you and your entire world grew through once, at the time the cut was made, but only once, and never again."

"But . . . I still don't understand. That doesn't explain anything. Why is everything so chaotic now?"

"Because you are now beyond the timestop and thus live in a universe that contains time travel. The time travelers have caused all the confusion."

"How are they to blame?"

"They have gone back and reshaped events by altering their causes. Each one has attempted to remake the world the way he wishes it to be." He paused to let the words sink in. "And whenever a cause is changed, time is bifurcated. Both the original and altered versions subsist completely. Consider it this way: the first time traveler went back and made the first tiny change, and suddenly there were two equally valid alternative realities, and two time travelers existed where there had only been one. Ten changes produced ten alternatives and ten time travelers, each with the power to change causes and create alternative realities."

"My God! I had no idea! How many realities are there on this side of the timestop?"

"They are without limit. Time has exploded into infinity, not lineally, but laterally. The number of alternatives expands sideways in a geometrical progression."

"Who invented time travel? When was it devised?"

"That's impossible to determine now, so many alternatives have been overlaid. Nor is it important. The dynamics are rather simple. Someone was bound to discover it some day, and as soon as he began to alter causes, the proliferation of alternatives was inevitable."

"Couldn't it be controlled?"

"Oh, it has been controlled quite effectively in some alternative universes. But someone from one reality or another always goes back and undermines the controls by altering *their* causes."

"Are there no timestops in the future?"

"Yes, plenty of them. But their causes are always accessible, so they are inevitably undone. Yours was the last timestop before the discovery of time travel and consequently the earliest limit whose causes cannot be undone."

"Who are the time travelers? Are they our descendants?"

"Yes, most of them are."

"That means some of those alive on earth at the time of the Synchronization survive, doesn't it? And their children survive."

"The time travelers are quite fond of manipulating genetic causes. Every possible combination of human DNA which existed at the time of the timestop has undoubtedly been tried in one world or another, its product brought to term, given birth, and nurtured to maturity. The descendants of those experimental unions now people the uncountable alternative realities."

"What about Laura? What about the boys? Christ! What's happened to the six billion people on earth?"

His response was slow in coming, as if he would have preferred not to discuss such things. "In infinite time," he finally replied, "everything is not only possible or likely, but inevitable."

"What the hell is that supposed to mean?"

"As a rough approximation, it is probably fair to say that *everything* has happened to them."

The response so upset me I was unable to continue for quite a while. I tried to press the Ringmaster for what he meant by "everything." Admittedly it was an absurd request. I asked him for examples, but he refused to give me any, and certainly that was for the best. I believe I'm in more danger of losing my mind trying to comprehend what's happened to Laura and the children than in recalling the brief madness I experienced for myself.

We adjourned our conversation until the next "day", as I like to think of my periods between sleep. By that time I was again relatively composed and had innumerable questions for him.

"So that's what I've been experiencing? The flurry of alternative realities rushing past?"

"Yes."

"Why is it so confusing to me? Why am I unable to cope?"

"You were designed by a half-billion years of evolution to live in one particular sort of world. There was nothing to prepare you for this."

"Could I learn? Could I . . . adjust?"

"For the most part, no, not by yourself."

"And the six billion others?"

"No. You that were conceived and born before the timestop experience each change as it occurs. But like the timestop itself, your parentage is immune from alteration. You cannot be erased. In a sense, you are the canvass upon which the changes are painted. You hold the fragmented universe together."

"For how long?"

"That question has no meaning, unless you specify which alternative you are talking about."

"But some manage to survive and produce offspring. You said that yourself. How are they able to cope?"

"In some alternative universes their descendants come back to help them."

"Who are the others, the non-human time travelers?"

"Some alternatives go very far into the future and link up with other civilizations which may or may not be associated with yours, and they also participate."

"From other stars?"

"Yes, some."

"Can't you get behind the timestop by going back at some other place, some other star, and traveling here?"

"No. Space and time are not fundamentally different. Some places, like some times, are inaccessible to the time travelers."

"Why do I experience none of the changes here in this cave?"

"Because we have painstakingly collected all of your alternatives and brought them here."

"How do *you* remain constant? How do you keep from fluctuating like everything else?"

"There is no way that you can be made to comprehend that. There are no words to suffice."

"But you have mastered the flux, the change. Are you in control of it all?"

"No. No one is in control. We are but one of an infinite number of solutions, no better or worse than any other."

"What do you really look like?"

"That concept has no meaning. We do not radiate or reflect electromagnetic impulses of a frequency which your retina or your science could perceive."

"You're invisible."

"Yes."

"How large are you?"

"That concept has no meaning. We are infinite and nonexistent. There is no way that you can be made to comprehend that. There are no words to suffice."

"You travel through time?"

"Yes."

"How long is time?"

"Infinitely long and infinitely short. There is no way that you can be made to comprehend that. There are no words to suffice."

"Try me."

"That is impossible."

"How many . . . 'souls' are you?"

"An infinite number, and none."

"You answer my questions the same way, with no answer at all."

"Yes, many of your questions require the same response. It is very difficult for us to try to reduce such complex matters into thoughts, let alone to mere words. We are very sorry."

4

Our conversations went on for days, and the Ringmaster took great pains to answer every question I could think of. Many of his responses were so strange I find them difficult to believe. But I have no alternative explanation for what has befallen me, so I just have to trust him. What difference does it make anyway?

He offered an explanation for why reality is always flickering, even here in this cave. In the infinite onslaught of possibilities, of personalities, countless suicidal desperadoes with unimaginable destructive capabilities return to annihilate the universe itself. They are frequently successful. There are also, however, an unlimited number of do-gooders who do not want the universe ended and who inevitably return to thwart the schemes of the nihilists. Null universes are thus intermixed throughout the deck of possibilities.

The Ringmaster tells me that my account will be sent back through the timestop somehow, as a warning. I couldn't understand how, and he didn't try very hard to explain it to me. I suspect it has something to do with what we used to call "telepathy." Physical matter cannot pass through the timestop, but something else can. Something else will influence the "imagination," as the Ringmaster calls it, of a person living before the timestop.

It sounds to me like he's trying to change the causes on the other side of the timestop. Either it won't work, or it will lead to the same insane chaos there that has damned the world on this side of the timestop.

The Ringmaster says, no, I don't understand. He has insisted that I compose this account for the world just prior to the Great Synchronization.

I asked him why he doesn't do it himself. He says that only someone who has come from the past can make himself comprehensible to those still living then. He has trouble limiting his thinking to mere concepts, his concepts to words. Besides, he assures me I will do an excellent job, since he has already seen my message and has selected it from among hundreds of other candidates to be the one he will actually send.

How can I argue with that?

I have no advice to give those who come before, for I can see no solution to the dilemma. If the timestop is never created, then the time travelers will *always* be there, and the world I knew will never have existed. Perhaps they can postpone its creation for a little while, but heaven help them if they wait too long.

I've though about it quite a bit, and I really have nothing to add. I hope the Ringmaster knows what he's doing. And if this account somehow manages to get through . . . good luck.

Author's Note

Man, this's nutty. I was on m'way t'work at the Carwash, mindin' m'own business, don'cha know, when this jive riff starts t'runnin' through m'head so bad I can' think straight. I make it straight t'Eddie's, 'cause he's usually hip to this kinda weird shit.

Well, when I gets there, Eddie ain't home, see, but he's got this hot typewriter he's been figurin'ta unload forever, man, an' I axes his ol' lady if I can see it, an' she says, sure, an' I don' even know how t'type fer Chrissake!

Well she drags the motha' out, sticks some paper in't, an' I sits down an' starts typin' out this jive shit I don' ev'n unnerstan' like I was her friggin' welfare worker. This keeps up fer a coupla hours an' Eddie's ol' lady's really freakin', don'cha know, an' then I'm done, an' that's wha' this here is.

Wha'da'ya make of it, man?

He Sees You When You're Sleeping

Hardly any snow lay on the ground. The premature blizzards of November and early December had left little trace. Just patches on the north-facing slopes and long drifts along the highway where the plows had flung the snow where the sun couldn't reach. The roads were dry and clear. The sky was blue. The weather was warm in the day, nippy at night. Odd weather for the dead week between Christmas and New Year's Day.

Jared Claridge and his wife, Victoria, had managed to drive the old Jeep Cherokee all the way in to the cabin, blasting through the single remnant of a snow drift that usually stopped them this time of year. The snow shoes and shovel lay untouched in the back of the Cherokee. A fire crackled in the cast iron stove as they studied a map. They were looking for a route through the forest to the east shore of Weech Lake. The main highway skirted the west shore, with its summer resort, campgrounds, boats, and cabins. But Jared wanted to try the east shore. Where there weren't any cabins. Or people. The map showed a threadbare spider web of unimproved roads there.

After lunch they went exploring and found a narrow dirt vehicle track leading toward the lake. "Let's take this one," Jared said.

"Are you sure?" Vicki asked. "It doesn't look very good."

"I know, but we have to start somewhere. Let's give it a try."

"Whatever."

They bounced down the unmaintained road, keeping an eye out for places to turn around if they had to. "Lake can't be much farther," Jared reassured her as he downshifted into first at a particularly rough spot.

A white Ford pickup blocked their way in a thicket of small fir trees. Three men stood in the woods outside the truck. One of them came over as Jared rolled down the window.

"Does this road go through?" Jared asked, clicking off the engine.

"Private property, up by the lake," the man said. He must have been in his late sixties or early seventies, a stout, vigorous man with a short, white beard, red lips, and a twinkling eye that made you think of Santa Claus. An energetic Santa in cork boots, a red-checkered logging shirt, and worn denim trousers held up by dirty red suspenders. A blue tooth cell phone sprouted from the wrinkles of his right ear like the nub of a burl. He seemed cordial, but didn't offer to move his truck.

"Can we get through to the public land on the lake?" Jared asked.

"Nope." The man spat tobacco juice into the grass, then resumed chewing on a plug in his cheek. "Road doesn't run through I reckon."

That seemed odd. "Do you own this land?" Jared asked, a little more aggressively than he intended.

"Nope. We're lookin' over these trees t'make a bid on a timber sale with the BLM."

"This is all BLM?"

"Some of it. Some of it private."

"Are they limiting the cutting to trees under thirty inches in diameter at mean breast height?" Jared asked, trying to sound neighborly, but maybe showing off a little, pretending to know more than he did.

The logger's expression did not change, but he paused a beat to examine Jared more closely. "You read that in the newspaper?"

Right then Jared knew he should have kept his mouth shut. He glanced over at Vicki, who was studying her fingers in her lap. The twinkle in the man's eye suddenly made Jared uncomfortable. "Yeah," he replied. "I guess I might have."

The logger nodded and spat tobacco juice. "Two cows were shot back up by the Bald Road turnoff," he said through those red lips.

Jared waited for something more. When it didn't come, he said uneasily, "We saw the buzzards circling. Wondered what was drawing them."

"Sheriff was out," the logger went on. "Must've been hunters practicin' for the season. Opens later this month."

Hunters. Loggers. Dead cattle. Jared couldn't tell where this fellow was coming from, so he rambled on about spending a lot of time mending the fences on their land to keep the cattle out.

"Where's your place at?" the man wanted to know, leaning forward.

"Couple of miles east of here," Jared told him, trying to stay vague, but unable to stop his mouth. "Twenty acres. Mostly logged over. A few big trees left. Not many. Mostly new growth. A fellow named Fulkerth sold it to us. But he hammered it pretty bad when he logged it, just before he sold it to us. Really destroyed a fine forest. There's an old cabin on it."

The logger nodded knowingly and spat.

"You know Fulkerth?"

"Known'im since grade school. Friend of mine. We done a lot of loggin' together o're the years. An' I know just where that ol' log cabin is."

Jared glanced at Vicki. She tilted her head to indicate it was time for them to get the hell out of there.

"There were some loggin' protesters," the old logger continued, changing the subject, but not, as they were to learn, really changing it. "Over by Sugarloaf Mountain. This was a few years ago. They went in on private prope'ty and shot up some expensive loggin' equipment. Did some serious damage, they did. I talked t'the Sheriff's Deputy who come out.

"He asked me, 'What would you do if you found 'em?'

"I told'im I didn't know. 'Turn'em in, I guess.'

"'Don' wanna do that,' he said. 'You'd get involved. Prob'ly have t'hire yourself an attorney. It'd end up costin' a lot a money.'

"'Well, what would *you* do?' I asked'im.'

"'You got a big cat, don't you?'

"'Sure,' I said.

"'Well, y'could dig a pretty big hole t'get rid of the evidence, couldn't ya?'

"'You mean bury the logging equipment with all the bullet holes? Why would I wantta do that?'

"'No,' he said. 'Not *that* crime. What if those folks who shot up the stuff just disappeared? Car an' all. That would make the next one think twice about shootin' up loggin' equipment, I guess. Mind you, I can't recommend any such thing, not in my job. But think about it. Who would know?'"

Jared had been unable to take his eyes off those wet, crimson Santa lips, which now brought to Jared's mind the image of a carnivore that had just eaten something. Something bloody. Something the real Santa would never have touched, however hungry. He turned toward Vicki.

"Let's go," she whispered.

Right. "Well," Jared croaked, "it was nice meeting you, but we have to get going now." He twisted the key and the engine caught. The red Santa stood just outside the window, not stepping back. Behind him his two companions had set down their tools and were watching with a kind of fierce intensity. Or maybe it was just his imagination.

"Guess I can just back up until I find a spot to turn around."

Still the old man did not step away.

Jared shoved the lever into reverse. He twisted to look out the rear window, cringing to expose his back to those lips and the bloody Santa standing there just a claw's-width away. Jared didn't know if the old logger stepped back or not, but he gave it gas and watched the narrow dirt road begin to roll beneath them and the woods slip slowly past. It was a hundred yards before he could swing into a rough spot between two massive, rotting stumps and manage to get the Cherokee turned around and pointing out.

They bounced along the rutted road without saying much, came to a fork he didn't remember, and bore to the right without consulting Vicki. They emerged into a grassy, sunlit clearing, and Jared started to feel a little better. "*Jesus!*" he rasped. "I think that son-of-a-bitch was threatening us."

"Of course he was," Vicki exhaled, her eyes fixed on the outside rear view mirror. "I'm just glad you didn't say anything else."

"I didn't know what to say to him."

"Now he knows where we live."

Jared turned to her. "You think I told him too much?"

"You might as well have drawn him a map."

"*Jesus!*" He repeated. They jounced in silence for a while. Nothing looked familiar. The track reentered the woods. "Do you really think he's dangerous?"

She stared at him. "He *threatened us*, didn't he?"

"*Jesus!*" His fingers tightened on the jerking wheel. "He seemed really . . . friendly . . . at first. I kind of liked him. Reminded me of Santa Claus. White beard. His face all red. Red lips."

Vicki snorted. "Rosacea. Probably drinks too much. And the real Santa doesn't murder folks and bury them in their cars with a big tractor. As far as I know, he doesn't."

They entered another small pocket meadow. Jared braked to a stop. "Where are we? I don't remember all these meadows."

Vicki took her eyes from the rearview mirror. "Did we miss a turn?"

"There aren't any turns. Just a mile or two straight back to the two-lane. Wait a minute. There *was* a fork back there. I didn't remember it. I just kept to the right."

Vicki looked at him. "I don't remember any turns."

"We may have to turn around and go back."

"I don't want to go back," Vicki protested. "That old man's too creepy."

"Should we just see where this goes, then? Maybe it'll loop back to the highway."

"Fine with me."

But the dirt road didn't loop back to the highway. Or anywhere else. It just kept going. Bouncing them from thick second-growth woods to small meadows and back to woods again. On and on.

"Are we lost?" Vicki asked at last.

Jared smiled. "As Daniel Boone once said, 'I ain't never been lost. Might've got turned around for a week or two a few times, but I ain't never got lost.'" He pulled to a stop in the middle of another small meadow.

"Have you got the GPS?" she asked.

He felt his pockets. Looked around the cab. "I think I left it at the cabin."

"Shit," she said. "Way to go."

"How bad can it be. There are roads on all four sides of us. And the lake on the west. We've got to come to *somewhere*."

"It'll be getting dark." Her voice was irritable.

Jared hadn't noticed. The sky was still bright blue, but he could no longer see any direct sunlight or shadows. He couldn't even see the mountains that ringed the lake. The forest hid them. He could no longer tell which direction was north. "Maybe we better turn around."

"No," she snapped. "Let's go just a little bit farther."

He ground it back into gear and the vehicle lurched onward. "Are you alright?" he asked.

"Uh," she nodded. "Maybe just a little queasy from all this rocking."

They drove on in silence. No familiar landmarks appeared. "You know," he said, trying to pass the time, "maybe there's another Santa. A second one. Kind of an Anti Santa."

"A Red Santa, maybe," she offered, glad for the distraction.

"Yeah. Maybe a Red Santa. He doesn't care about you're being nice. Only naughty."

"No presents?"

"No. No presents."

"What does Red Santa bring you then? If you've been naughty?"

He looked at her. "That's what I was wondering. What do you think?"

She thought about it. "Pain. Grief. Punishment. Disappointment."

He smiled. "That's just what I was thinking."

"Why would there be a Red Santa?"

"I don't know. Why would there be a White Santa? Why a good Santa delivering all those presents? Why not a Red Santa to counterbalance him." The Cherokee bucked and rattled over a rocky hump in the road. "But here's the really big question."

She turned to him. "What's that?"

He paused for effect. "Have you been nice? Or have you been naughty?"

"Nice," she said, but her cheeks began to flush.

"Have you?"

"Of course I have." The blush deepened. "What are you saying?"

"I think you've been naughty, Victoria."

"What do you mean?" she squirmed.

"I know all about you and your dance teacher. Mr. Brewster."

"How do you know about Ted?"

"I followed you."

"How *dare* you follow me," she shouted, turning her back and staring out the window. Thinking. Calculating. Suddenly she wheeled on him. "And what about you, you bastard!"

"What?"

"Don't act so goddamned smug. It doesn't suit you, you cheating bastard."

"Me?"

"Yes, you. I know all about you and that little tart of a secretary you've been spending so much time with. With her wiggly little ass and all those late nights at the office."

He didn't respond.

"You don't look so damned smug anymore," she pursued. "What's the matter? Maybe now you don't think turnabout is such fair play, do you?"

Still he kept his tongue.

"You've been naughty yourself, you hypocritical bastard!"

Ahead a glint of metal flashed. "There's something up there," he said. As they drew nearer, it resolved into an metal gate in a split rail fence. Jared slowed the Cherokee. The gate was open. It looked like the end of the road. Through the gate stood a squat log cabin in the gloomy shade of a thick cluster of trees. A couple of old outbuildings, weathered gray, flanked the cabin. Below the cabin, through the trees, lay a broad open meadow. Jared drove through the gate.

"You're going in there?" Vicki wanted to know. "Where are we?"

"We have to turn around somewhere," he snapped, pulling up to the main structure and cutting the engine. "Besides, I've gotta take a leak." He slammed the door hard and stormed off around the side of the structure.

Vicki walked away from the open passenger door, wondering if it was all over between them. Their once so promising marriage. She felt deflated. Angry. Lost. What would she do without him?

"Vicki?" he called after her, zipping up his fly.

As she turned, her eyes fell on something high on the cabin wall. "That's weird," she said uncomfortably. "That's *really* weird."

"What?" He tried to follow her gaze.

"That sign." She pointed to an ancient wooden board nailed high against the back of the log cabin beneath the eaves. On its mossy face were two crudely carved words.

"SOUTH POLE."

"What the hell?" he muttered. "That doesn't make . . ."

Vicki spun around to see exactly where they were. She stood facing down a stub road into a shallow swale. At the bottom, among the wild, leafless serviceberry, was a deep, fresh trench, a mound of dirt, and a dirty yellow caterpillar tractor with a backhoe. It was a big hole in the ground. She could smell the grease and the freshly turned earth.

Just then a white pickup crunched through the open gate and pulled to a stop. Blocking the gate. Three familiar figures eased out. The driver was a heavy-set old man with a red face and a white beard. "Ho, ho, ho!" he boomed.

The Cabin

1

That Spring evening a light wind-blown mist filled the air. It was not raining. Not really. The ceaseless breeze carried a chilling dampness and the sweet fragrance of cedarwood smoke. Low clouds obliterated the moon and stars. Night was coming on fast.

A one-room log cabin stood as scarred and worn as the rusty bark of the incense cedars towering overhead. Rays of golden firelight flickered out through three crude windows, one in each wall enclosing the hearth. It glistened off beads of moisture on the moss clinging to the surrounding trunks. Lit the cold iron handle of the well pump. The wind gusted and pinpricks of mist sizzled against the window panes.

Lester Ames did not mind. Inside it was warm and dry. He sat in his ladder-back rocking chair, absorbing the heat that radiated from a generous blaze in his blackened stone fireplace. He had built the cabin himself. The foundation and chimney stones he had hauled from the river in a rickety old wheelbarrow. The logs were sawn from cedar and fir. The floor planks and roof beams he cut from pine on the whirling chain of an Alaskan mill. That damned saw had cost him his left thumb. It had all taken a very long time to build.

Now he had nothing but time. *Almost cozy*, Lester thought, the corners of his mouth ticking upward with the thought. It pleased him that he could do everything slowly. At his own leisurely pace.

From his chair beside the hearth he surveyed the intimate room. The shifting flames lit the rough pine floor with a drowsy light. A dreamy yellow glow that made it difficult to distinguish the cracks and knotholes from solid wood. The firelight fused the planks into one solid covering. A ghostly yellow blanket spread across the floor. A pulsing orange shroud draped every object in the room. The crude, unpainted bookcase and the books within. The solid old oak table and primitive typewriter (perhaps the last still in use). The unlit lantern. The stack of manuscript pages. His bed crowded into the far corner with the poles of its headboard glowing like a Japanese torii. A gate of heaven. Or perhaps a gallows frame. Lester yawned and watched the shadows dance and kiss. Shadows which, even in the darkest corner, played in the fire's warmth. He turned his rocker to face the fire and watch his dreams in the naked flames. In this cabin, even the fire seemed in no hurry to burn.

It seemed odd to Lester Ames that he should be content to live alone far from other humans. He was not by nature a hermit. Not really. He drove his rusting red pickup into town regularly to buy groceries and gas and check the mail. He worked odd jobs, carpentry mostly, when he could find labor where a left thumb was not required. And he had friends. Well, mostly acquaintances. But most everybody around knew him by sight. He had lived here long enough. But he was an anachronism. Lester knew that. A throwback to simpler times. But what he did not understand was *why*.

He yawned again and stared into the fire, dreaming. Time left nothing scarred as it drifted through the cabin.

2

Abruptly Lester jerked awake. His tee-shirt was damp with sweat. Bright coals radiated heat from the fireplace. A sharp pain shot down the left side of his neck. His back was stiff. *Damn!* He had not intended to doze off in that high-back rocker.

He had dreamed of an earlier time and place. He stood in line at the little walk-up hamburger stand across Bancroft Street from the law school. The bronze letters on the building's fortress wall were half obscured by branches. Beneath the trees students tossed a frisbee. Catching and throwing in long graceful arcs. The afternoon sun shone hot. He was waiting for someone. He had always been waiting for her.

Lester buried his face in the crook of his arm. He stood up and stretched. Rolled his head on his shoulders. He turned to consider the cabin door. Something had awakened him. Had someone knocked on the thick plank door? Or was it only a part of his dream? He had not heard a motor. Nor a car door slam. Yet still . . . it would be easy enough to tug it open and check outside.

What was that sound? It was more than fog drip from the cedars. Suddenly an unfamiliar hope rose in his chest. Hope for who might be out there. An irrational hope, yes, yet time's slow passage, which left him untouched in the cabin, would have altered things *outside*. Rearranged the possible. And had he not stayed up late into the night quietly waiting for just such a gentle knocking at the cabin door? There was another sound. Lester heard footsteps crunching up the gravel path. They stopped. He held his breath. There was a soft knock at the door.

Lester sprang to the door. Paused. Gripped the smooth carved handle with both fists and tugged. It squealed open.

Before him in the cold and miserable night stood a visitor. A small figure in an oversized parka. The one he had been waiting for. She was actually there before him. For a long time Lester stood still, not daring to move for fear that she might evaporate into the mist.

Softly she spoke, "Hello Les. Guess you weren't expecting me."

Ah, but he had been.

"May I come in?"

"Yes. Of course. Please. Come in." He swung the door wide. "You must be cold. Sit by the fire."

He took her heavy parka, the fur collar shining with droplets of moisture, and hung it on a nail by the fire to dry. Turned to look at her. She was lean and tan with long black hair flowing down her back. The fire, blazing more brightly for her, cast yellow highlights onto her raven hair. He had never seen a more lovely vision. She was just as he remembered her, seated in the rocker by the fire. Gazing eagerly up at him.

Lester poked at the fire, tossed on another log, then pulled the desk chair close beside her. "I was hoping you would come," he said.

"I wanted to talk to you." She turned her face to the fire. "I felt I *had* to come talk with you."

"I'm so glad you did. I have much to say to you, too."

But neither of them spoke for a long time. They sat side by side and imbibed the peace of the small cabin. They were in no hurry to begin. After all, they had all the time in the world out there.

"Les?" she whispered at last.

"Yes, my darling?"

Fright glinted in her dark eyes. "There's something not right . . . about this . . ."

"Shush." He put his arm around her. Held her close.

"What *is* it?" she insisted, squirming. She lifted her fingers to the side of her face. "What's *wrong?*"

"Let it be," he spoke too quickly. Drew a breath. "Try not to think about it . . .," he tried to whisper her name. To comfort her. His mouth hung open. Lester could not remember her name, though it was engraved upon his soul. His eye caught a name tag clipped above her left breast. Like the nurses had all worn at the hospital. Large black letters carved into white plastic. But try as he might, he could not make sense of them. He could not read the words that were written there.

As in a dream, he thought.

Lester knew something had gone terribly wrong. The more he tried not to think about it, the more he found himself swimming away, upward toward the light. Toward the hellish red glare above. Away from the dark thing that tried to hold him in the depths below.

3

Lester's eyes fluttered open to the bright burning embers of the hearth. "Mariah," he whispered out loud. *Mariah was her name.*

His tee-shirt clung damply to his chest. He was slouched in his rocker, his head canted painfully to the side. His back ached. *Damn!* He had never intended to doze off like that.

He had been dreaming something beautiful. Something that left him warm inside. Relaxed. Fulfilled. He was waiting for someone. *Mariah.* He had always been waiting for her. She had come, rapping on the cabin door. She had come inside. Sat with him silently by the fire. A silly dream perhaps, but one that filled his heart in that uncompromising way that only a dream can.

Until it all began to unravel.

Lester ground his knuckles into his eyes. Slowly he stood, a bit dreamy still. A bit unsteady. Lightheaded. *Mariah is gone.* In that unholy hospital bed, sprouting tubes and tags and electrical wires, she had wasted away and died. He had been holding her hand. Her fingers were cold and limp. Unfeeling. Unconscious. Her body was shutting down. She drew in a gulp of air. Seemed to stop breathing. He waited, summoning no one. She took another quick gulp. He waited. Then another. The pauses grew longer. The gulps shallower. Then one final gulp of breath. And never again. Bathed in the unforgiving fluorescent light of that strange morning stillness, he welcomed her release from suffering. From the horror. Yet he had wept. Oh he had wept.

He had buried her beside a new white azalea in the little pocket meadow beyond the cedars. The "family plot," the paperwork had called it.

He turned to consider the door. Had he heard a faint rapping on the thick planks? A tap, tap, tapping at his chamber door? Or had that only been a part of his dream? No one was out there, of course. Not Mariah. Not Lenore. Not anyone. It was an absurd notion. Yet still . . . what would it hurt to tug open the door and check? Open it and step out into the darkness.

Ah, but what evil might such darkness bring? Suddenly he was afraid. Afraid of what might be out there. Afraid to welcome what he had been waiting for. Afraid of again finding nothing at all. Heads or tails, he was bound to lose if he were to open that door.

In stocking feet Lester padded unsteadily to the door. Paused. Placed one palm on the smooth carved handle and the other against the rough planks, trying to feel what might be on the other side. A vibration? A radiance? An aura? He felt nothing but the dead wood.

Something scratched on the door, and Lester lurched backward, almost falling over his empty boots. His heart leaped. His pulse triphammered. His breath was caught somewhere deep in his chest. It had sounded like a bony knuckle on the door, though it might have been just a branch clawing against the cabin wall, driven by the soughing, moaning wind. But when he breathed again, he drew in a faint aroma of rotting flesh. The sulphurous smell of something long dead.

From beyond the door came an ugly sound. The sound of something being dragged through the duff. Grating and whisking across the gravel path. He did not go to the window to look. The night outside was as black as an empty grave. Lester stood there trembling, rooted with fear, until the dragging sound receded, moving away toward that little pocket meadow and the long-dead azalea.

He did not open the door. He squeezed shut his eyes.

4

Lester awoke in his rocking chair to the hot glow of the fireplace. His tee-shirt was clammy with sweat. A sharp pain shot down the left side of his neck. His back was stiff. *Damn!* He had not intended to doze off. His heart was pounding. *What a dream!* An intense, convoluted dream had left him unsettled. A dream nested within another dream. And another. A recursion of dreams. He could no longer remember the details, but he was trembling.

He rubbed his face in calloused palms to clear the cobwebs. Stood up and stretched. Rolled his neck. His spine crackled. The pain eased a bit. He turned to consider the cabin door. Something about the door. No one was out there, of course. It was an absurd notion. *Mariah?* What the hell *had* he been dreaming?

Yet still . . . it would be easy enough to tug it open and check outside.

The door squealed open. He stepped out into a night as black as an empty grave. Pinpricks of moisture still rode the drifting mist. But it was not really raining. There was nothing out there. As he had known in his rational mind. Nothing at all.

And what will happen, he wondered, *when I awake from* this *dream?*

5

Lester awoke.

Nor Iron Bars a Cage

The suspension of the maximum-security prison experiment at Piedra, California, can without question be attributed more to the unexplained disappearance of Warden E. W. MacLeash than to any other single factor. With the death last month of inmate Jasper Riggins, due, a thorough autopsy has disclosed, to natural causes, many feel that the fate of Warden MacLeash will remain forever a mystery, and prison reform has suffered a devastating setback.

I was the last person on earth to see Warden MacLeash. My name is Robert Inglewood, and I was associate warden of Piedra at the time the warden vanished. I accompanied him to the threshold of Riggins' cell that night and watched him enter, as I have testified before the Governor's Commission. But some things I left out of my testimony, because no one asked about them, because I feared no one would believe me, perhaps because I was not sure myself what should be believed, and because I was terrified beyond all reason by the strange events I had witnessed. With Riggins death I have at last come to accept my responsibility for chronicling those events, whatever the consequences might prove to be. The Piedra experiment is too important to be abandoned for the wrong reasons. Riggins death must not be viewed as the disappearance of all hope for a final explanation, but rather as the removal of the last impediment to the success of the project.

Piedra was an experimental prison, isolated from the rest of California by the dense mixed-conifer forests of the northern Coastal Range. Its purpose was to rehabilitate and reeducate long-term prisoners who displayed aptitude and incentive though they might lack formal education. In addition to the more customary institutional amenities, inmates were provided with classrooms, an extensive library complex, and optional tutorial instruction. Prison regulations encouraged trust and self-reliance. The cells were designed to each house but a single inmate and were so constructed that no one, not even other prisoners, could observe from outside the activities within a cell. Except under specified emergency procedures, the solid steel cell doors were not to be opened without the consent of the cell's inhabitant. The new facility was built without guard towers, without walls or barbed wire, and without bars, creating an atmosphere more like that of a hospital or modern school than a penitentiary.

In an examination specially prepared and administered to neutralize cultural bias, inmate Jasper Riggins obtained the highest score of any candidate seeking admission to Piedra. He was sixty-seven years old at the time, and his snow-white hair blazed against weathered, tar-black skin. While serving a life sentence for murder, Riggins had taught himself to read and write. Educators nonetheless quickly recognized in him a mental power of comprehension, which could only be categorized as genius. In light of his latent ability, the extraordinary depth of his cultural and educational deprivation, and his desire to participate, the venerable old Negro was the very first inmate selected for Piedra. In his progress many saw a barometer for the success or failure of the entire project.

In light of later developments, this was unfortunate, for without a doubt Riggins and his strange mental powers lie coiled at the heart of the mystery surrounding the disappearance of Warden MacLeash. The Governor's Commission Report, relying principally on my testimony, traced the warden's last-known steps to the cell of Jasper Riggins. The paucity of tangible evidence and other peculiar circumstances enveloping the entire affair prevented formal charges from being brought against Riggins, and when the elderly inmate passed away last month, the only tongue which might have explained the disappearance was forever stilled.

When Piedra received its first inmates on September 1, 1975, E. W. MacLeash held the position of warden. Hindsight persuades me that his selection for that post was the most uncanny and fateful accident to befall the experiment, if, indeed, it was no more than an accident. He was a wiry little man with bushy gray eyebrows and sideburns that framed a glistening, hairless pate. Meticulously neat in personal appearance and brusque in manner, what little humor he suffered himself was dry and crackling. He bore a passion for order in everything he did. At an age when other men grow mellow, the new warden refused to brook any nonsense in his administration of the otherwise progressive institution.

MacLeash had been chosen by conservatives as the result of the complex political compromise that provided the funding for the Piedra project. He was a hard-nosed retired army major of the old school who had built his military career during the Viet Nam War. After his retirement he had established a reputation for aggressiveness and cunning in a prosperous real estate investment practice. I recently inspected the legislative history of his appointment, and it all appears to be obvious and even inevitable. And yet I cannot help believing that other, more obscure forces, perhaps at a level and by a means that our petty sciences have not yet begun to suspect, played a powerful hand in his selection.

For a time I too had been on the list of candidates for the warden's position. My Ph.D. thesis in criminology at USC had proposed just the sort of experimental rehabilitation that Piedra came to represent. I was not surprised, however, when an older man received the appointment, and contrary to the malicious innuendoes that surfaced at the commission hearings, I bore MacLeash no ill will because of it. Indeed, when the offer of second-in-command came, I didn't have to think twice about leaving my work at Atascadero State Hospital and moving my family to the remote north coast. Not even the specter of toiling under "Bulldog MacLeash," as some of my colleagues called him, dampened my spirits.

I learned from MacLeash's personnel file that his parents had died in an airplane disaster when he was very young, and his only sibling, an older brother, had been lost at sea during the Second World War. He was a lifelong bachelor. Knowledge of these personal hardships helped me accept the warden's lack of customary social graces. It must be said that, despite our diametrically opposed views on the purpose and function of the prison, we somehow managed to pull together to get the program off the ground. By surmounting the numberless difficulties which plagued those first years of the experiment, a tentative friendship and, I might even say, admiration, began to grow between us.

It is undoubtedly true that, as in all things, MacLeash bore a certain mistrust for those in his command. It is generally agreed that his unyielding self-reliance and determination to solve problems in his own way drove him later to assume solitary command of the investigation of the unusual occurrences which began to surround Jasper Riggins. But more than that, I believe he perceived those incidents as personal affronts.

The first official mention of anything out of the ordinary concerning Jasper Riggins came on the night of August 12, 1979, in a brief memorandum submitted to the warden by Captain Oscar Medinger, chief guard in charge of the night detail in Block A. In the account, handwritten and stapled to the usual eight-by-ten shift report required for security and statistical purposes, Medinger relates that at 12:50 a.m. he was summoned by the third floor duty guard who complained that as he was passing Riggins' cell, he had heard a sound like the howl of a wolf emanating from behind the closed door. He described it as a lonely, plaintive cry. It chilled his blood. At first he thought that Riggins was making the sound. As he continued to listen, however, the howling was repeated, and a moment later a second similar cry overrode the first in such a manner that it would have been quite impossible for a single man to produce both sounds simultaneously. Thereupon the guard summoned Medinger, as he was required to do by prison regulations.

Medinger himself heard nothing when he arrived, but the duty guard was so adamant and agitated that Medinger knocked and requested admission to the cell. Riggins appeared to have been awakened from a sound sleep when the door was opened. The two guards found the outside window tightly closed, producing a stuffy, musty atmosphere inside like an overcrowded animal cage at a circus. A quick investigation revealed nothing to be out of the ordinary, and Riggins disclaimed any misconduct. Scrawled at the bottom of Medinger's report in his own handwriting, apparently added as an afterthought sometime later, were the words, "Subject was reading London's *Call of the Wild*," as if this statement could somehow be fitted into the causal sequence of events, and as if, in Medinger's reluctant mind, it needed to be included for a complete understanding of the incident.

Warden MacLeash took a special interest in the incident from the first. On the afternoon following his receipt of Captain Medinger's report, he summoned the two guards into his office for a lengthy interrogation. Perhaps, as some have speculated, the warden was concerned only with the reliability of his subordinates, for it is true that within six weeks Medinger had been transferred to Folsom prison. My own opinion, however, is that he believed the guards' story utterly. The records of the prison library show that the lone copy of *Call of the Wild* was checked out two days later in the name of Warden E. W. MacLeash.

On the morning of August 23, the maintenance trustees found in the cell of Jasper Riggins a primitive figurine of a tiger or a horse carved from a porous stone the color of ash. Its appearance was completely inexplicable, and Riggins refused to discuss the matter. No one else had set foot in his cell since the final cleaning of the previous day, and Riggins had spent most of the intervening day reading in the prison library. The rough totem was hauled away to the maintenance building, and a short report was made out which found its way into the hands of Warden MacLeash.

MacLeash seemed extremely agitated by the discovery. It struck me as peculiar at the time, but the warden immediately set about interrogating the library staff, trying to ascertain the names of the books Riggins had been reading. His search bore little fruit. Most of the shelves were open to the inmate community, and apart from the voluntary tutorial program, no records were kept of such matters. The following day the warden prepared and circulated a directive to all personnel that any further incidents involving Riggins should be promptly brought to his personal attention. He instructed me to drop whatever I was doing, assemble all available information on Jasper Riggins, and be prepared to discuss the matter in depth at our conference the following Friday.

I spent the next three days poring over rap sheets, court reports, psychological profiles, parole evaluations, and anything else I could find on Riggins in the prison files and CII and Adult Authority records in Sacramento. With increasing gloom I traced the hopeless plight of a poor Southern black man. Riggins had been born in Coopersville, Alabama, in 1912, the fifth of nine children. His father, a poor sharecropper, had been unable to provide adequately for his family, and Riggins had been needed to help on the farm rather than attend school. At the age of fourteen he drifted to Montgomery, where he was promptly arrested, convicted of loitering, and sentenced to six month's hard labor on a county road gang. Arrest and conviction records spanning 1927 to 1945 followed Riggins in and out of the jails of Montgomery, Elmore, and Jefferson Counties for a variety of minor charges from expectorating in public to petty larceny. He spent two terms in the Alabama State

Penitentiary, for attempted rape in 1934 and assault and battery in 1940. When not incarcerated, Riggins hired out as a seasonal farm hand and, later, worked off and on in the steel mills of Birmingham. When the war ended, so did his chances for a good job, and his search for employment carried him to California. He possessed few skills and was pitifully uneducated, so he soon found himself again behind bars in the Contra Costa County jail, convicted of a theft in Richmond. On October 24, 1948, three days after his release from jail, a black man named Thomas Edward Washington was stabbed to death during a brawl in a bar in the Negro section of Richmond. Seven months later Jasper Riggins was convicted of first degree murder and sentenced to life imprisonment.

During his first two decades of incarceration in the California prison system, the Adult Authority reports labeled Riggins "incorrigible." He had served several lengthy periods of solitary confinement. Following the last and longest period, a remarkable change was recorded. In 1969 Riggins swiftly taught himself to read and write and began to display a voracity for literature, science, and scholarly treatises on almost every subject. It was as if he had decided to make up in a few years for a lifetime of illiteracy.

Late Wednesday morning I came across correspondence indicating that Jasper Riggins had been one of three prison inmates selected in 1973 for a special federally funded sociological study. The subjects had been chosen on the basis of their scores on the Piedra experiment admission test and some other rather obscure sociological criteria I didn't really care to understand. The research was to be conducted by a Dr. Sylvia Richardson of the University of California at Davis. I couldn't find a copy of the study anywhere, so I telephoned Dr. Richardson to see if the work had ever been completed. Indeed it had, she assured me, and it included a fascinating in-depth investigation into the ancestry and social background of Jasper Riggins. She promised to send me a copy by express mail. The report arrived an hour before my meeting with Warden MacLeash.

Those Friday conferences always made me uncomfortable. Not that MacLeash was personally formidable. Quite the contrary. He often looked to me like a frail child lost in the folds of an old man's skin. But the plush leather and gleaming mahogany of his inner sanctum, the meticulous order, the dustless, odorless, soundless precision of everything standing just in its proper place kept me balanced uneasily on the edge of my chair.

I distinctly remember the morning of that first conference concerning Jasper Riggins. I had never before seen the warden so upset, so frightened, and I couldn't understand why the petty occurrences disturbed him so. At the time I attributed his reaction to an abhorrence for the anomalous and his insatiable appetite for order. I now suspect that he had already begun to dimly perceive on some non-rational or unconscious level, perhaps on some genetic level, the threat Riggins posed to him.

"There is something going on here out of the ordinary," the warden pronounced as soon as I had pushed the heavy door closed. He slapped shut the file he had been working on. "I shall not tolerate it, whatever it is, as long as I'm warden of this prison!"

I nodded and assumed my usual chair, a stack of files balanced on my knee.

He cleared a neat space in front of him. "Now, show me what we've got on this Riggins character."

One by one I lay the reports, files, records, profiles, photographs, and folders before the warden, giving him a short synopsis of each. He would leaf listlessly through a few pages, then look up at me for the next item, like a child waiting for just the right Christmas present, though I am certain he could not have said quite what he was expecting. I offered my own evaluation of Riggins based upon the sparse contacts I had with the prisoner and the several psychological profiles I had reviewed. He seemed to be only half listening. The guards who knew him better than I described Riggins as charismatic and extremely bright. The warden yawned. When I got to the California Adult Authority reports, his interest brightened. Riggins' abrupt transformation from an incorrigible ruffian to a cooperative, intelligent, studious model prisoner fascinated him.

Because I had only had time to glance briefly through Dr. Richardson's study, I did not mention it until last. Warden MacLeash snatched it from my hands. It was a thin volume of perhaps fifty pages bound in a clear plastic cover. He skimmed hurriedly through the document, then dismissed me with a preemptive wave of his arm. He took it home with him that night.

The following morning, a Saturday, Warden MacLeash burst into my office while I was still sipping my first cup of coffee, threw open the Richardson study, and without further introduction or explanation, began reading. In tones solemn, yet excited, he read several pages that I had basically discounted the previous day because they seemed to me to represent inadequately documented sociological pseudo-science of the worse kind. The warden obviously felt otherwise. Later when I found the study locked in his desk after his disappearance, I had no difficulty locating the paragraphs he read to me that morning.

Dr. Richardson asserts in those passages that the paternal great-grandfather of Jasper Riggins was a man of high prestige among his own people in Africa before being captured and sold into slavery in America. She relies principally upon a bill of sale dated June 3, 1814, between a Captain Bartholomew Horn, a slave trader, and one Essau Anderson, who operated a large tobacco plantation in South Carolina, for the sale and transfer of a slave named Adam Riggings for a sum of money ten times what was customarily paid for the highest quality slave. According to Dr. Richardson, Captain Horn enjoyed a reputation for guile and ruthlessness among his contemporaries, arising chiefly from a well-publicized incident reported to have taken place in 1813. On that occasion Captain Horn had been anchored off the Gold Coast concluding the purchase of slaves from a powerful tribal nation which had taken prisoners in a battle over territorial boundaries. Because the transaction was large, the slave trader negotiated directly with the chief of the victorious nation, a man highly venerated among his people and said to possess unusual spiritual powers. After the slaves had been herded aboard ship, but before final payment had been secured, Horn deceitfully protested that he had received ten fewer slaves than he had bargained for. The chief was invited aboard to count for himself the number of slaves delivered. Once aboard, he and his party were overpowered by the crew and themselves bound into slavery. Captain Horn's ship weighed anchor and easily outran the primitive dugouts that pursued.

Dr. Richardson contends that the betrayed tribal chieftain was the same person as Adam Riggings, sold to Essau Anderson the year following Captain Horn's notorious deception, and Jasper Riggins' paternal ancestor. I have reviewed two articles published recently in respectable sociology journals challenging her conclusions. Both regard the entire betrayal report as apocryphal and point out that while her conclusions are statistically possible, the probability is marginal. At the time the warden read to me from Dr. Richardson's report, I would have sympathized wholeheartedly with her critics' more scientific skepticism.

The warden, on the other hand, spoke with certitude and awe as he read the passages in which Dr. Richardson reexamines long- forgotten bills of sale and dusty estate inventories, purporting to trace the lineage of Jasper Riggins. The documents, she claimed, indicate that only the highest prices had been paid for members of Riggins' paternal line, and more than one contained a reference to some vague power possessed by those ancestors, often chilling in effect because the power itself remains unnamed.

Finally, as if concluding a ceremony of imponderable significance, Warden MacLeash replaced his marker, closed the manuscript, and awaited my judgment.

I was rather embarrassed by the whole situation, to say the least. At first I found a few nice things to say about Dr. Richardson's dedication and energy. The warden was not to be put off so easily. I suggested that Dr. Richardson's research may be somewhat deficient, and, in any event, even if the tribal chief was indeed Riggins' ancestor, his particular genetic makeup would have been so diluted over the subsequent generations as to be inconsequential. Distant ancestry ordinarily has little bearing upon present behavior and ability.

"Ordinarily," he replied, parrying my intent.

I had no alternative but to tell him point blank what he seemed to be ignoring, that Dr. Richardson's suggestions were tantamount to attributing supernatural powers to Riggins. "I feel bound to point out," I concluded, "that many people would consider such an approach unscientific, based upon incredible evidence, and considering your position and responsibilities here at Piedra, dangerous."

"Ah, yes, dangerous." His voice bore a quiet resolve. "Whatever it is that Riggins is doing, it is my responsibility as head of this institution to put a stop to it." My comments had evidently not shaken his conviction. For a moment longer he studied the binding of the volume from which he had read, softly repeated, "whatever it is," and returned to his office.

Three days later another interview was conducted in the warden's private chambers. This meeting lasted forty-five minutes, according to the administrative calendar for that day, and was attended alone by Warden MacLeash and inmate Jasper Riggins. No official record was kept, which was just one more of the myriad minor violations of prison regulations that never much seemed to bother the warden. It is generally accepted that nothing of substance was discussed, that the warden merely wished to become better acquainted with the inmate who had come to occupy so much of his attention. I am personally convinced, however, that a significant bargain was struck between the two men at that mysterious meeting, though I will not speculate upon its nature or purpose. Thereafter, the affair lay dormant for nearly six months.

In the first week of October the Parole Review Board convened at Piedra for its regularly scheduled hearings. Among the petitions on the agenda that day was a special application submitted at the last minute by Jasper Riggins requesting that the board make a complete review of his prison record and set an early release date. Incredibly, the sole character reference listed in the inmate's petition was Warden E. W. MacLeash. When the staff summaries arrived the morning of the hearing, I brought Riggins' petition to the warden's attention.

"He's pushing this thing too goddamned far!" the warden bellowed, snatching the summary from my hands and retreating into his office.

At the hearing, Warden MacLeash launched into a soliloquy of unprecedented venom, insinuation, and, it seemed to me, paranoia, charging Riggins with repeated attempts to undermine the administration of his prison by unspecified subversive acts. With an intensity that made most of the members uneasy, he urged the board never to release such a man, lest the board itself be held accountable for unleashing a devastating scourge upon an innocent free society. Riggins sat as inscrutable as a stone Buddha at the end of the long table and spoke not a word in his own behalf. His petition was summarily denied.

In the weeks following the Parole Board hearings, everyone commented on the warden's vigor and high spirits. I actually saw him laugh on more than one occasion. While I occupied myself with securing the funding for three new staff positions, preparing the fiscal year reports, and trying to complete the east ballfield before the autumn rains began, Warden MacLeash managed to get in eighteen holes of golf almost every afternoon. Jasper Riggins was no longer mentioned at our weekly conferences.

Early one fine mid-October morning, the warden and I left the administration building a few minutes early on our way to a meeting with the recreation staff at the new field house. It was his idea to walk the long way through the central quadrangle to enjoy the sunshine. We were intercepted by an anxious young inmate dispatched as a messenger from the guard station in Block A. Something very odd had been discovered, he explained, and the warden's presence was urgently requested.

On the third floor of Block A, two trustees stood with mops and buckets containing a trickle of clear water running from under the door of Jasper Riggins' cell. All the residents of the floor, including Riggins, had been sent to the classroom complex pending further orders from the warden. Lining the east wall inside the cell and clinging to the inmate's shoes, which lay against the far wall, the last clumps of snow and ice, the remnants of an inexplicable drift, melted in the autumn warmth.

Warden MacLeash was infuriated. "I'll not have this! Who's in charge here?"

A lieutenant who looked much too young stepped forward and saluted crisply.

"Search this cell immediately, Lieutenant!" the warden commanded.

"Yes, sir, but prison regula–"

"To hell with prison regulations! Wait a minute. Inglewood!" He waived me over. "How do we get around these goddamned regulations that keep us from doing what's got to be done here?"

Fundamental principles of rehabilitation theory, methodology, and technique were being assailed by the warden's question, not to mention thorny Fifth Amendment search and seizure issues, but I could see he was in no mood for an academic argument. "There is a Regulation 34E," I reminded him, "which temporarily suspends prisoners' rights under the Piedra special program charter, but it was intended for use only in the case of–"

"How do I do it?"

"It can be invoked by a declaration of emergency."

"Who does that?"

"You do, sir."

"How?"

I looked into Riggins' cell and back down at the warden. His face was flushed, his jaw set, and veins stood out on his glistening forehead. I decided not to flirt with the inevitable. "A simple statement ought to suffice. We can let the paperwork catch up later."

"All right, then, I declare this here to be an emergency situation, and I hereby invoke . . . " He glared at me.

"Regulation 34E."

". . . Regulation 34E, or whatever the hell it is. Is that all?"

I nodded.

"Good. Now, Lieutenant, will you search this goddamned cell!"

Among the unusual objects found as a result of the search, presided over personally by Warden MacLeash, nothing could be characterized as violating the California Penal Code or the rules and regulations of the prison. Lying on its side beneath Riggins' bunk was another of the curious figurines of a tiger or horse, identical to the one discovered several months earlier. A small quantity of sand and microscopic sea shells were found beneath the bottom book shelf, and two stains in the corner farthest from the door were later determined to have been made from horse manure. Certain long hairs which had been caught on a nail protruding from the edge of Riggins' desk were thought to have come from a large mammal, not human, probably either a dog or a wolf. The crime laboratory in Sacramento concluded that the unexplained snow and ice formations were pure, as might occur naturally in freshly fallen snow, with no trace of chlorine or other additives customary used in domestic water treatment.

The warden spent the rest of the day with an agent flown in from the state crime laboratory going over the clothing and personal possessions of Jasper Riggins with meticulous care. They found nothing particularly out of the ordinary, nothing that would substantiate the need for disciplinary action. In the late afternoon, Warden MacLeash rescinded his emergency declaration and suspension of prisoners' rights, and by evening the prison was ostensibly back to normal. Below the surface, however, the inmate community buzzed with curious rumors and awesome conjectures, and long into the night the institution lay awake in a superstitious unquiet.

Next morning the warden asked me to step into his office. He was pacing back and forth, and his eyes wore the uneasy dread of a man whose worst suspicions had been confirmed. "He was reading this," he said, thrusting out a heavy volume bearing the mark of the prison library.

I took the book and perched myself on the arm of the leather chair beside his desk. It was Pasternak's *Dr. Zhivago*.

"And this is the only book Riggins owns." He handed me a well-thumbed copy of Thoreau's *On Civil Disobedience*. "Read what he's got marked."

I opened it to the page where a worn leather book marker protruded. One passage had been heavily underscored in pencil, presumably by Riggins. It read as follows:

> ". . . and as I stood considering the walls of solid stone, two or three feet thick, the door of wood and iron, a foot thick, and the iron grating which strained the light, I could not help being struck with the foolishness of that institution which treated me as if I were mere flesh and blood and bones, to be locked up."

"Now you see why this man is so dangerous!" the warden demanded even before I had finished reading. It was not a question. He assumed I saw. "I want you to keep an eye on this situation for me, Inglewood. We're going to have to be very careful here, maintain absolutely complete records, document everything, you understand. When the time comes for action, we don't want those bleeding-heart ACLU lawyers dragging out any weak links in our chain of paperwork, right?"

I told him I really didn't understand what he was driving at.

He smiled as if he could not quite believe I was so naive. "Think about it, Inglewood," he said as he took both volumes from my hands. He stacked them neatly on the corner of his desk. "Think about it for a while." He opened the office door for me.

I reread the report of the third floor guard who had been on duty the night of the incident. As early as two o'clock that morning he had felt a cold draft in the vicinity of Riggins' cell, but at the time it seemed to him a matter of no great importance. In addition, twice during the night he had heard the faint, but distinct sound of whinnying horses from somewhere on the third floor. He could not locate the origin of the sounds, and because it was late and his mind was tired, the guard concluded he had imagined the sounds and paid them no more heed. In fact he would not have included them in his report at all, he explained, had not the warden brought them to light in his questioning and insisted that they be fully documented. Toward morning the chill draft from Riggins' cell increased, and then diminished abruptly at daybreak. A pool of water began forming under the door about an hour later.

I believe it is significant that Warden MacLeash did not personally interview Riggins following the search of his cell. It indicates to me that whatever bargain had existed between warden and prisoner had been broken so irreconcilably that further negotiations were impossible. The warden appeared unwilling to confront Riggins again until he had prepared himself thoroughly for the encounter. Instead he had me schedule a series of interviews for him with each guard who had worked the third floor of Block A at any time during the preceding six months. He apparently believed that others, like the guard who would have omitted the whinnying of horses from his report, may have experienced oddities, which they failed to document.

When he had concluded his interviews, the warden asked me to get him reservations on a flight to Salt Lake City as soon as possible. The cost of the tickets was to come from the prison administrative contingency fund, but he refused to tell me the purpose of his trip when I attempted to make the disbursement entry. He said he would take care of it himself when he got back. He never did. The warden was gone for four days.

At our usual Friday conference in the second week of November, Warden MacLeash informed me that he had gathered an extensive amount of evidence against Jasper Riggins from his interviews with the night guards, and from other sources he was not yet prepared to divulge. He seemed satisfied with whatever he had uncovered, though he refused to discuss with me the nature of the evidence.

"I intend to undertake decisive action in the near future," he confided rather ominously and winked at me.

Something in his manner suddenly alarmed me. All at once I

perceived his obsession with Jasper Riggins to be something more than the mere onset of a benign senility as I had previously supposed, something beyond the bounds of harmless eccentricity. For the first time it occurred to me that perhaps the warden was dangerously disturbed, that prison regulations might not be sufficient to contain his madness, and that he might do something to upset the delicate balance of the entire Piedra experiment. I managed to ask him, "What action do you have in mind, sir?"

"You shall see," he said, leaning back, smiling. "You shall see."

"Can I do anything to help."

"Yes, you can, Inglewood. I'd like you to keep a close watch on Riggins and keep me informed of his actions at all times. Don't let him know he's being watched. Particularly, I want to know what books he's reading. Do you think you can do that for me?"

"Yes, of course." The request seemed strange, but no stranger than the rest of the warden's increasingly bizarre fascination. "I'd like to be present when your 'decisive action' takes place, if I might. You'll have to admit, sir, that I'm a little more familiar than you are with the maze of prison regulations governing us here. Perhaps I can be of some help. Will you promise to call me before you do anything?"

"You realize it might come in the middle of the night?"

I nodded.

"Very well. I'll call you."

I didn't like spying on an inmate, but I couldn't see what harm could come of it. So I made arrangements for the chief trustee at the library to covertly watch Riggins and give me a report each afternoon on his activities and the books he was reading.

In the early hours of the following Monday morning I was awakened from a sound sleep by a jangling telephone. My wife handed me the phone. In hushed and somber tones Warden MacLeash instructed me to come as quickly as I could to the main guard station of Block A. Mystified and benumbed by sleep, I dressed hurriedly. When I arrived at the guard station, the warden was pacing nervously before the night captain and two uneasy duty guards.

Warden MacLeash took me aside. "It's Riggins again. Trouble on the third floor. What's he been reading, Inglewood?"

I thought for a moment. *"Heart of Darkness*," I told him.

His eyes were blank.

"It's a short novel by Joseph Conrad."

"Well? Damn it! What's it about?"

"It's about a man in tribal Africa, seduced by–"

"Exactly!" the warden exclaimed, smacking one hand against the other. His eyes narrowed as if he had just received some last bit of information to confirm a monstrous suspicion. "I'm going in, Inglewood." He grabbed my sleeve. "I want you to be my witness."

"In where, sir?"

"Into Riggins' cell. I'm forcing an entry. You act as my observer, just in case something happens."

One look into his fevered eyes and I knew it was no use arguing about prison regulations. "Are you declaring an emergency, sir? Are you invoking Reg–"

"Whatever has to be done, Inglewood. Do it. You take care of that end of things, okay? We're on the same side, aren't we?" He smiled and let go of my arm. "Okay. I'm going in there. This is my prison. Riggins is threatening my administration. I'll not have it!"

As the warden turned away, I thought I caught a glimpse of a shoulder holster, but I couldn't see whether it held his service revolver. Under the circumstances I was reluctant to confront him on yet another violation of prison regulations.

The warden's plan was for the duty guards to station themselves at each end of the third-floor corridor. I was to accompany the warden and wait outside Riggins' cell as he let himself in with an emergency key. The night captain would remain at the main guard post for communications and backup.

Perhaps it was because I had so recently awakened from a sound sleep, but I couldn't clear my mind. I was overwhelmed by what I can only describe as a lucid unreality, not so much like dreaming as like stepping into someone else's dream. From the moment I first entered the cellblock the feeling engulfed me, and it increased as I mounted the concrete stairway to the cells above. When the guard at last opened the hallway door, I heard the sound that faintly pervaded the entire third floor, as if coming from a great distance: the steady, hollow throb of drums. The warden still seemed highly agitated, but he delayed our advance until we saw the door at the opposite end of the sleeping corridor open and the second guard take up his station.

I clearly recall walking down that narrow corridor, numb, side by side with Warden MacLeash, as if in slow motion, or under water, with the light from the hidden neon tubes not dim, but dull, and the sound of our footsteps and breathing strangely muffled. We stopped before the cell of Jasper Riggins. The pulse of the steady drumbeat had grown only slightly louder, but it was now somehow all-pervasive, as if sounding from afar and resounding in rhythm to my own heart's quickened beat. I saw the warden step to the cell door with his key thrust awkwardly before him, shrunken and incredibly aged, and seeing him as from a great distance, I wondered if this was really happening, and I was afraid beyond all reason.

The drums grew louder as Warden MacLeash pushed open the cell door just wide enough to slip through. I stood transfixed outside. There sat Jasper Riggins cross-legged and Buddha-like on his bunk, his tar black skin testifying to unalloyed genes and glistening in the flickering light of a naked flame unseen somewhere behind the door, his eyes staring sightlessly ahead of him, unaware of what by contrast seemed an irrelevant intrusion. He seemed not to breathe at all.

The warden raised his trembling hand and seemed about to touch the prisoner on the shoulder when, in response to something behind him, he turned, and his eyes, lit now by the same uncanny flickering light, appeared to fix on something both marvelous and terrible, towards which he was drawn, out of sight, into the depths of the empty cell. For what seemed an endlessly long moment I watched in awe the godlike, powerful inmate who never moved and awaited the reappearance of the warden in the hypnotically flickering chamber. As the moment wore on, my concern for the warden faded, and forgetting the orders strictly forbidding me to follow, I was drawn by some primordial instinct to enter the cell. But before I had taken a single step, I was shaken by what sounded like pistol shots in rapid succession amidst the untiring drum beats, though the reports seemed to come from a very great distance, far beyond the confines of the tiny prison cell. Then there followed an unholy scream, a far-off, whining shriek, twisted and horribly frightened, perhaps that of the warden himself. It seemed for an unreal moment that the par-tially-closed cell door led into a jungle of limitless distances.

Abruptly the drum beats stopped, and I was gripped by a freezing terror that wrenched my heart. Without planning it, I heard my own voice screaming, "Riggins! In the name of God, man, wake up!"

Although I did not perceive the actual transition, the lighting was again normal, and again the ordinary prison sounds were everywhere. Jasper Riggins blinked, then stretched, and then stared incredulously at my ashen face through the open cell door.

Warden MacLeash was never seen again by me, by the bewildered night guards, nor by any of the authorities and investigators who converged on the scene the following morning. The inexplicable pool of human blood found at the base of the rear wall of the cell was determined to be of a type different from that of either Riggins or the warden. Riggins disclaimed any knowledge of the disappearance, and the intensive investigation conducted by the Governor's Commission turned up no evidence incriminating him, or even supporting the conjecture that a crime had been committed at all. Within six months the Preliminary Report of the Commission was released, recommending suspension of the Piedra experiment, and shortly thereafter the inmates began returning to the prisons whence they had first come.

I found the Commission hearings arduous, coming as they did just at the time of my divorce and at the time I was forced to take my first medical leave of absence for a nervous condition. The doctor advised me to try to forget about what I had seen. But the Commission would not let me forget. I was called back three times to testify. Each time I answered the questions which were put to me with the facts as I recalled them, but beyond that I refused to speculate. I volunteered nothing.

Shortly after the publication of the Commission's Final Report last year, I made a trip to San Quentin, where Jasper Riggins had been returned. At first Riggins refused to talk to me, but when I assured him that the official investigation was closed and I was simply trying to sort out my own recollection of events, he consented.

Riggins leaned heavily on a cane as he shuffled slowly into the interview room and painfully lowered himself onto a chair. He seemed so very old and withered, so unlike the powerful warrior I had perceived through the doorway of his cell that night. Quick to laugh, loose and friendly, he projected a sharpness of mind. I couldn't help liking him. Curiously, I had never before sat down and talked with him face to face. I did most of the talking, actually. He claimed to know nothing more than what he had testified before the Governor's Commission.

Yet it seemed to me he did know something more than he was admitting, and I told him so.

He laughed disarmingly. "You got all the facts, Warden. You gonna haf' to make up your own min'. The'ain't nothin' I could say you don' already know. Nothin'd change your way o' thinkin' 'bout it."

"But you understand what happened," I said.

"I do believe I un'erstan's 'nough. Wouldn't hardly suit you, though, way I sees it."

"Try me."

He was quiet for a while. "They say a man like me who's done spent half o' his life in prison, in an' out o' solitary, gets a perty damn good fantasy life agoin' in his head."

I waited, but he seemed to have finished. "I'm afraid I don't get your point."

"Let's jus' leave it at this." His big, friendly grin was belied for an instant by the menace in his eyes. "If'n a man is gonna go messin' 'roun' in 'nothe' fella's dreams, he damn well better watch out he don' get caught out when the othe' fella wakes hisself up."

Late last year I drafted a brief report summarizing and analyzing what I knew of the disappearance. I went beyond my oral testimony before the Commission and drew certain conclusions. I suggested that perhaps Warden MacLeash was in some manner being held a captive by the inmate he had intended to undo. I enumerated accounts of terrible rumors whispered among the inmates of San Quentin of unholy conjurings in Riggins' cell in the blackness of the night. The apparitions were always the same: the vague figure of a white man, bound and gagged and supported between two naked black men, lit by an eerie, flickering light, while the dull, staccato pulse of drums filled the cell block. Unscientific as my position was, the Governor's Commission Report, as an alternative, proved to be no better, offering neither conclusions nor an explanation for the disappearance.

I never found the nerve to submit that report.

With the death of Jasper Riggins even my slim hopes for Warden MacLeash have evaporated. For even if the warden had somehow survived until the inmate's death, at best he has lost the only bridge linking this world with the imaginary one into which he wandered, and at worst he has perished with the dream that can no longer be dreamed.

A thousand times my mind has traced the sweeping curve laid down by the evidence, much of which for me is beyond question, since I witnessed it myself. Yet the only explanations are not reasonable. My scientific sensitivities refuse to allow me that blind leap Warden MacLeash appeared all too ready to make, concluding that supernatural forces are at work here. But just as I am prepared to foreclose the paranormal absolutely, I stumble once again over the persisting question: where in the name of hell is Warden MacLeash? Thus for me the circle refuses to close, and I fear for my own sanity if I do not lay the matter aside once and for all.

I recently followed up a single remaining thread of evidence. Locked in the warden's top desk drawer next to Dr. Richardson's report was a name and Salt Lake City address. The address turned out to be the National Genealogy Center, and the name that of one of the staff researchers. I telephoned the man. Warden MacLeash had met with him and paid for the research and preparation of a genealogical chart. Before he had done his research, however, he had heard of the warden's disappearance on the news and so never completed the project. I asked him to finish the chart and send it to me.

Since that conversation, a new and unsettling train of thought has troubled my sleep. Who really knows what we may yet discover behind the phenomena we now refer to as ESP, faith healing, voodoo, and the soul? Our petty science has only scratched the surface. The mind's depths have scarcely been sounded, and yet the conscious mind is itself merely a belated creation of the truly powerful force underlying life: the DNA. The mind is but one of many tools conjured and conceived by four billion years of relentless natural selection. What other tools do those immortal spiral strands also wield to accomplish their blind, or at best undeciphered, purposes? Have the unconscious thoughts in our minds a master we have never met?

I think we may have witnessed more than a mere skirmish between Riggins and MacLeash. They were pawns. I doubt if either had any idea why he was struggling at all, or what his role was in the overall conflict. For all we know, natural selection has fashioned for us minds incapable of understanding, so that we may not tamper with the only thing in the universe which is truly sacred. I believe we may have just dimly perceived the worldly reflection of a total war being waged at a level and by a means that we cannot even begin to suspect. Undoubtedly we are all unwitting soldiers.

I recently received in the mail an additional piece of information which has quite unnerved me and made it clear that my sanity requires I write this report and then drop the matter forever. The genealogical chart arrived from Salt Lake City shortly after Riggins' death, and traces the ancestry of Warden E. W. MacLeash. The diagram shows the warden to be the last surviving male issue descended from a notorious Nineteenth Century slave trader by the name of Bartholomew Horn.

Tommy
or
The Day Patrick Sean McBurney Found Jesus

The morning was unseasonably balmy for that time of year. A radiant sun blazed in the cloudless blue sky, brazing Tommy and his mother as they lazed on the worn patch of an army blanket spread out on the grassy bluff overlooking the New England ocean beach. The bright sands below were already dotted with early Sunday bathers and sun-worshipers who, from Tommy's lofty viewpoint, looked for all the world like ants converging on the sweetness of a sugar sea.

Tommy watched his mother's eyelids flutter as she fought the tug of drowsiness, saw her yield to the overpowering force, her eyes closing at last, and heard her regular breathing deepen. She lay peacefully, the storybook she had been reading to him resting in the crook of her left arm, her auburn hair in whisps across her face. He loved his mother, Tommy did, slumbering there amid the rich fragrance of Spring wild flowers. But he was six years old and growing restless.

Slowly Tommy stood up and shuffled closer to the bluff's edge. He shielded his eyes with his small hand and squinted out across the endless expanse of gleaming waves. A curious disturbance troubled the waters about a hundred yards out, just beyond the breakers. Its shape was odd. Briefly Tommy imagined he saw in the darkness beneath the glistening surface the angular, scaly haunch of a hideous sea monster.

A retired sailor named Ben Brewster sat on one of the higher dunes puffing a favorite pipe, his tattered blue sweater draped like a shroud over his thin shoulders. He was the first to observe the creature rising from the churning waters. Old Brewster leaped to his feet and screamed "*Run for your blessed lives!*" at his neighbors nearer the shore. Pandemonium erupted on the beach. Alarmed cries and frightened replies wafted up to Tommy on the gentle offshore breeze, but softly, without the force that might waken his mother.

There was really plenty of time to flee the hideous *thing* as it pushed through the thick foam and waded toward the beach, towering ever higher as it came. Most of the bathers were safely away by the time it emerged with thunderous clawing feet upon the dry sand. But a few people, like Walter Gray in his pinstriped walking shorts and white canvass deck shoes, were just too astonished to feel a proper fear. Oh, they got out of its path, of course, but circled around behind to see just what the hell it was.

The creature was peculiar. Most of the witnesses swore they had seen it somewhere before, in a comic book or the fantastic conjurings of some B-grade horror movie. Whatever forces formed those fearful, scaly sinews had studied Godzilla, Rodin, and the Creature from the Black Lagoon, but not much vertebrate biology or physics.

Walter Gray must have believe it to be some sort of Hollywood publicity stunt, for once he'd had a chance to view the improbable beast from every side, he began to laugh so hard he fell to the sand and rolled about clutching his sides. His unexpected contempt threw Tommy into an unaccountable fit of rage as he watched from his distant vantage.

Suddenly the monster wheeled on Walter, plucking him from the sands with lightning dexterity, and bit off his head. Any further thought of frivolity drained away as quickly as did Walter Gray's life blood. The remaining curious, suddenly sobered and far from safety, stampeded from the bristling beach, but for some the realization came too late. With incredible agility the monster sped back and forth across the blazing sands, biting off heads, twisting limbs from bodies, ripping torsos open with horny claws, and devouring others in a single gulp.

The leviathan lumbered away from the shore, ascending the fragile dunes, and at sand's end, began scaling the nearly-vertical rock cliff that lead up to the meadow where Tommy watched with growing alarm. When he lost sight of the beast under a rocky overhang, the boy hurried back from the brink to the refuge of his mother's blanket. On the edge of that threadbare fortress he made his stand, a comic book hero, feet planted, a last line of defense between his mother and the menace that approached.

Suddenly a massive forearm reached over the rim not ten feet from where he had sat, dug foot-long claws into the crumbling soil, and pulled the sea monster's horrible bulk up after it. Terrible yellow eyes blinked sideways and leered down at the minuscule warrior and his supine mother stranded on their pitiful life-raft blanket amid a sea of churning wild flowers. A gore-coated tongue flicked through hideous, dripping jaws. The monster started forward.

Tommy raised a tiny, trembling fist and challenged in a piping whisper, "You'd better leave my mommy alone!"

Tommy's mother stirred at the harsh sound. She stretched, the storybook falling from her arm, but she did not awaken.

The massive, scaly tail quivered with indecision. The monster snorted, pawed the ground, grunted and hissed, then it *winked* at Tommy, spun around, and loped up the trail that led to the county access road.

Two summer cottages front on the short stub of two-lane linking the beach with the Village of Swainsport. Both were totally demolished. The Edwards' cedar-built cabin looked like it had been picked up and smashed against the ancient oaks which stood behind it. Higgins' home was more substantial. Jose Villalobos, crouched behind his pickup, saw the monster burst in through the north wall and out again through the south side, leaving the shattered shell to collapse behind it. Fortunately, neither was occupied.

Ed Rummidge, the village butcher, was the first to see the creature lumbering down Main Street from the east. He began shouting and waiving his arms, but it was too late for the shoppers in Lytton's Grocery. The scaly nightmare burst through the plate glass window, trapping seven inside. It toyed with them (like Tommy had once watched his cat Amanda torturing a cornered field mouse) and finally, one after another, chewed off their heads.

Tommy's mother awoke abruptly, as if from a troubled dream. A cloud had passed in front of the sun, and she shivered in the fresh ocean breeze. She looked at Tommy and smiled, but the boy seemed to be lost in daydreams of his own.

Martin Coulter's old '51 Buick skidded into the monster's left flank. With Mr. and Mrs. Coulter inside, the beast picked up the antique automobile like a child's plaything, clamping it under its left forearm, and poked its right through the windshield, slicing the scaly flesh on fragments of broken glass. The cuts seemed to infuriate the creature. Long after the Coulters had been torn to pieces by the groping claws, the monster seemed intent on tearing the automobile's insides out.

Tommy's mother sat up and pulled her sweater close about her shoulders. She looked out to sea, then down at the beach. Her brow furrowed. "Tommy, where are all the bathers?" she asked.

Maurice Evans sneaked out the side door of the firehouse, right up behind the hideous creature as it troubled over Coulters' broken automobile, and emptied both barrels of his twelve-gage into the back of the bobbing head, without apparent effect. From across the street Patrolman Bud Simington fired six rounds from his service revolver point blank into the hulking beast as it tore Maurice Evans limb from limb.

"They all left," said Tommy as the sun reappeared.

His mother squinted into the bright sunlight. Something appeared peculiar about the way the few remaining bathers were strewn about the beach.

"A sea monster scared 'em away," Tommy volunteered.

"Oh, Tommy!" His mother turned to confront him. "You *know* there's no such things as sea monsters."

The primordial beast hesitated for just an instant, but it was time enough to let Bud Simington escape with his life.

"Sure there is, Mommy. I saw it myself. It climbed right up here." Tommy pointed to the freshly turned soil near the cliff.

The nineteenth and final fatality of that grisly morning was Billy Bunderson, the local paperboy. Poor Billy was legally blind from birth and supplemented his SSI income with Sunday morning newspaper deliveries. Returning home from his route on his chrome-plated bicycle, he never saw the thing coming. He was stomped to pulp beneath the massive lizard feet on the sidewalk outside Livingston's barbershop.

"I knew I shouldn't let you watch those old monster movies on tv," Tommy's mother remonstrated.

"But I *saw* it . . . ." Tommy was near tears.

Patrick Sean McBurney was beating the shirt off old Everett "Doc" Livingston at their traditional Sunday morning checkers match when they heard the commotion outside the barbershop. Doc threw open the front door, and that caught the monster's attention.

"What the hell is *that thing*?" Doc screamed and dove back inside.

With a single crunching swat the front wall was gone. The roof shuddered, but held. Doc grabbed McBurney and dragged him to the back wall.

The beast crouched down on its stubby forelegs and poked its snout into the rubble, leering, ready to finish them off. McBurney and Doc were trapped.

"Tommy! Shush! There are no sea monsters, and you know it!"

The monster stopped, as if undecided. It stood up, poking its head through the old skylight.

To this day McBurney can't say what made him think of it. He'll shrug and claim it was divine inspiration. He snatched those long barber shears and Doc's pearl-handled comb off the counter next to him and held them up in front of his face to form a cross.

"Well, maybe it was some kind of giant octopus," said Tommy.

Before their eyes the monster began to melt, to shrink, to evaporate. It lost its dark umber hue, contracted into a massive sand-colored lump with protruding tentacles radiating regularly from the center, each pocked with exaggerated hissing suction cups.

"No, Tommy," replied his mother with a gentle firmness. "Octopuses don't come out of the water. Ever. You really didn't see anything, now, did you?"

"Yes I did, Mommy! It came right up here! Maybe it was a crocodile."

The thing on the floor of the barbershop darkened in color, elongated. Its surface grew quilted. Two enormous, tooth-lined jaws formed and yawned menacingly.

"Tommy!" his mother insisted. "I want the truth! You didn't see anything, did you? You made it all up."

Tommy paused in thought.

The thing in Livingston's barbershop shrank before the eyes of the astonished onlookers.

"No, Mommy, you're right. I'm sorry. I didn't see anything."

It disappeared without a trace, evaporated into thin air. McBurney cradled the scissors and greasy comb in his trembling hands like relics of the True Cross. Doc Livingston just stared at him from across the devastated barbershop.

"That's a good boy, Tommy." His mother gave him a big hug, then brushed the hair back from his ruddy face with a reassuring hand. "I'm happy you've finally grown up enough to admit to telling a fib. But heaven knows what's going to happen if you don't learn to control that imagination of yours."

Only a Matter of Time

The following are clippings from The Northern Advocate *newspaper, Blue Lake, California, circa 1979:*

SCIENTISTS REVEAL CREATION OF 'TIME MACHINE'

BLUE LAKE, Ca. (API) Nobel scientist Dr. Christian Mason today announced that his experiments in the field of teleportation--the science of transporting objects by non-physical means--have succeeded in sending an object from the present into the past.

At a special news conference called at the Blue Lake City Hall to accommodate news cameramen and reporters, the graying scientist, seated with his associate, Dr. Malcolm Edwards, and his son, Christian, Jr., 20, told newsmen that the new time travel process, which he calls "temportation", may be "the scientific breakthrough of the century."

Dr. Mason won the Nobel Prize four years ago for his work with the atomic transformation of high-energy particles, and he pres-ently heads a team of scientists at the Mad River Radiation Laboratory located at Blue Lake in the redwood-covered hills 250 miles north of San Francisco. This small logging town seems an unlikely setting for one of the world's most sophisticated high- energy research laboratories.

Dr. Mason explained how temportation works: small quantities of silver, lead, and other elements are placed beneath a device which directs a high-energy beam and "scans" the object on a principle similar to that used in the ordinary television set. The beam disintegrates the object, and the escaping particles are converted into an electric current.

The electric current then modulates a beam of tachyons (from the Greek word meaning fast), which are recently-discovered subatomic particles traveling faster than the speed of light, and, consequently, having retrograde deterioration. This means, Mason explained, they go backwards in time, as a school of fish might swim upstream.

The tachyon beam, focused upon a high-energy field, supplies the structure, and the energy field provides the material, or electrical building blocks, so that the process is reversed, and the object materializes exactly as it had been, but at a moment earlier in time.

"There is a short period of overlap, when the same object exists simultaneously with itself, in the modes of before and after," Mason told reporters.

"We have not, however, either increased or decreased the total time-presence of the object. We have merely rearranged it," he said.

Several weeks ago Mason and his son completed a series of tests using a precise atomic clock, capable of measuring time to within billionths of a second, the scientist said. The preliminary results indicated that the appearance of the output object preceded the disappearance of the input object by a few thousandths of a second.

By carefully adjusting and modifying the device, the scientists managed to increase the time-lag between appearance and disappearance to about one-third of a second.

"It is a question of capacitance," explained Mason. "By increasing the capacitance of the circuit, we increase the time-lag. With a large capacitance and a small object, the time-lag could theoretically be increased to months or even years.

"Using the maximum capacitance available, that of the earth itself, and an object weighing, say, seventy-five kilograms, the computed time-lag would be approximately one billion seconds, or almost thirty- five years. In other words, the output object would appear thirty-five years before the input.

"This is, of course, all theoretical, and it assumes the existence of a satisfactory electric field thirty-five years ago upon which to focus the tachyon beam."

Mason revealed that construction of a new, enlarged version of the device is almost complete at the Blue Lake laboratory. It will increase the input capacity of the present mechanism a thousandfold.

Mason said that materialization of the output object takes place outside the physical limitations of the machinery and any high- voltage field will suffice. "There are probably a hundred particle accelerators in this country right now that produce a satisfactory field," he said.

Although the temportation process is complex, it takes place so fast that it appears to be instantaneous, the nuclear scientist told newsmen.

In response to reporter's questions, Mason pointed out that the experiments were not "time travel" in the strictest sense of the words, since the original object does not move, but is annihilated, and a new object is formed from new particles.

"But from a scientific point of view, the two objects are identical," Mason said. "The atoms which are the building blocks of each object are absolutely interchangeable, so that the new object, while built of totally new material, is identical with the original object by every known test of science and observation"

When asked if it were possible that animals and even men could someday be transported through time, Mason said that there was no way of knowing until further experimentation was completed. He did not rule out the possibility, however.

Preliminary reports indicate that a substantial segment of the scientific community disputes Mason's method of experimentation and the conclusions he has drawn.

Professor Gilbert Newman, recently retired from his faculty position with the University of California and until then working as a liaison for the Blue Lake project, said it was "preposterous" for Mason to reach such radical conclusions at this early stage. Newman said he would reserve final judgment until after Mason has published his results.

In a related development, the administration of Harvard University confirmed reports that Dr. Charles Aicher, noted molecular biologist, has left his faculty post in Cambridge to join Dr. Mason in Blue Lake.

Aicher, 57, a pioneer in the work of synthesizing amino and nucleic acids, the building blocks of life, announced illness as his reason for abruptly leaving his lecture position.

Today's announcement fueled speculation that the Blue Lake team of scientists is attempting to subject living matter to the temportation process.

MILITARY INTERESTED IN TEMPORTATION

WASHINGTON (API) The Defense Department today announced it will participate in further research and development of the temportation experiments successfully completed at the Mad River Radiation Laboratory in Blue Lake, California, by a team of scientists headed by Nobel Prize winner Dr. Christian Mason.

According to a spokesman for the Army, which will handle the project, further development of the methods of temportation is necessary before it will have any practical application.

Reporters were told that the military significance of these experiments should not be underrated. "The ability to move weapons and equipment, and even men, instantly from one part of the globe to any other, before trouble develops, could revolutionize modern warfare."

The Army is also interested in the possibility of mass-producing weapons and ammunition by the temportation process.

A sizable allocation of the upcoming defense budget has reportedly been ear-marked for the research and development of strategic applications, it was disclosed.

FATHER OF TIME MACHINE UNDER INVESTIGATION

BLUE LAKE, CA (API) Nobel Prize winning scientist Dr. Christian Mason, who last month announced successful experimentation in the field of time travel--deemed to be a national security matter--is under investigation for falsifying information in his application for a federal research grant of $20,000 and on numerous other documents, a reliable source in the Defense Department reported.

The official source said that in requesting the grant, Mason gave information concerning his birth, parents, schooling, and other aspects of his life prior to 1945 which is "unverifiable and certainly false".

In the grant application Mason stated that he was born in Richmond, California, in 1924, to parents named George and Martha Mason. The Contra Costa County California records show no such birth and a thorough investigation by government agents has uncovered no trace whatever of Mason's parents, it was disclosed.

Mason also stated that he attended Richmond High School from 1939 until his graduation in 1944, another assertion that could not be substantiated.

The misinformation was also used by Mason in his applications for admission to the University of Chicago in 1946, and the University of California in 1951.

"What is most alarming is the fact that he seems to have appeared out of thin air at Stagg Field in the spring of 1945 with an interest in nuclear physics," said one high Army official. It was at the University of Chicago's Stagg Field that the preliminary work was done which made possible the development of the atomic bomb.

There is speculation that Mason may have been planted as a spy for the German or Soviet governments during the Second World War, and quietly defected to the West.

The earliest verifiable records show that Mason rented a basement apartment on 56th Street near Chicago's south side campus in March of 1945.

During the following year Mason became acquainted with several members of the university scientific community, the most notable being the late Dr. Howard Dixon, who was then working with Enrico Fermi in achieving the first controlled sustained nuclear reaction.

It was principally on Dixon's strong recommendation that Mason was admitted to the University as an undergraduate in the fall of 1946. Apparently no one at that time checked the accuracy of the information in Mason's admissions application. Mason received his B.S. in physics in 1950, and that same year was admitted to the University of California at Berkeley for graduate study. He received his Ph.D. in nuclear physics in 1955.

Mason's Ph.D. thesis, based on his research with atomic particles accelerated to within ninety-nine per cent of the speed of light--a study related to Einstein's relativity theory and quantum mechanics--was received as a major contribution by scholars. However, Mason was reportedly much criticized for hypothetical constructions in which he demonstrated the mathematical possibility of retrograde deterioration, or reverse time, of particles accelerated beyond the theoretical limit of the speed of light.

The foundations for Mason's later experiments with tachyons and time travel were reportedly laid in his Ph.D. thesis.

In 1955 Mason became a lecturer in the physics department at Berkeley, and in 1960 was appointed full professor. He gave up teaching entirely in 1975 to direct the prestigious Mad River Radiation Laboratory located here at Blue Lake, where the scientist devotes himself to further development of the time travel process.

Records show that Mason married one of his students in 1958, the former Beverly Phillips. The Mason's have a son, Christian, Jr., 20, who strongly resembles the graying scientist, and a daughter, Michelle, 17. The family resides within walking distance of the Radiation Laboratory in this quaint, secluded logging town 15 miles northeast of Eureka.

Christian, Jr., is an honor student at Humboldt State University in nearby Arcata, studying physics, and most of his time is taken up assisting his father at the laboratory. Mason's daughter plans to enter Humboldt State in the fall.

Professor Maurice Bloomgarten, who worked closely with Mason prior to suffering a heart attack two years ago, said in a private interview that he felt Mason was the only one who really understands the time-travel project. "If Mason were lost, it would take ten years just to find out what had already been accomplished," he said.

Bloomgarten, perhaps Mason's closest friend outside the laboratory, expressed great respect for the scientist. "He is undoubtedly the brightest and strangest man I've ever known," he said.

"Mason works as if he knows what the results are going to be, and his only interest is in verifying his equations. I've never known him to be wrong."

The key to all of Mason's work is apparently written in two red notebooks which the scientist keeps rigorously up-to-date. Even Mason's closest associates are uncertain of the overall significance of the work they are doing, and the scientific community looks forward to the publication of the notebooks, Bloomgarten said.

When asked about the current government investigation, Bloomgarten expressed amusement at the allegations that Mason might have ever been a spy. "And if he was, he was a very poor one. He has certainly contributed more new scientific knowledge to this country than he possibly could have stolen."

Mason reportedly has refused to answer questions put by Army officials investigating the alleged falsifications. No formal charges have as yet been brought, due to the urgent and sensitive nature of the scientist's work.

According to a Defense Department spokesman, Mason continues with his research here under the scrutiny of military police. Due to tight security, none of Mason's associates currently working on the project have been available for comment.

BLUE LAKE SCIENTIST SLAYS SON

Mason Sacrifices Son for Science as Army Watches

EUREKA, Ca. (API) Controversial scientist and Nobel laureate Dr. Christian Mason has been in the custody of the Humboldt County Sheriff's Department since early yesterday morning, charged with the bizarre slaying of his son, Christian, Jr., who was twenty years old.

On a closed-circuit television system installed without the knowledge of Mason, horrified security police watched as the scientist directed a high-voltage beam of atomic particles at his cooperative son and incinerated him instantaneously.

Military police at the Mad River Radiation Laboratory located in Blue Lake notified the Sheriff's Department. Humboldt County provides police services because Blue Lake is too small to have its own police force.

Mason appeared ashen and confused as he was escorted into Municipal Court by sheriff's deputies late yesterday for arraignment.

Accompanied by prominent San Francisco attorney James Whitcomb, Mason entered his plea of innocent to charges of the first degree murder of his son.

Deputy District Attorney Frank Oldsteiner, upon emerging from a viewing of the video tape provided by the Army, told reporters that both father and son seemed to be aware of the consequences of the experiment they were performing, and they solemnly said goodbye to each other just before the deadly power was switched on.

Oldsteiner was appalled that the Army had not intervened and stopped the tragic experiment. "For at least ten minutes before the boy died, it was obvious what they intended to do," he said.

At approximately 7:30 p.m. (Monday) evening Mason and his son entered the private section at the Mad River Radiation Laboratory set aside for temportation research -- the study of time travel -- and they began preparing new and untested equipment for the experiment, Oldsteiner reported.

Security officers routinely activated the closed-circuit television and recording equipment, secretly installed last month when it was discovered that Mason had falsified his early identity. There has been speculation that Mason may have been planted in this country during the Second World War for espionage purposes.

Shortly after 10:00 p.m. Mason told his son that they were ready and the boy abruptly left the room, returning some fifteen minutes later, changed from his laboratory clothes into a pair of brown slacks and a wide-lapel jacket.

A few minutes later Christian, Jr., with the help of his father, positioned himself in the receiving chamber of the new device, which is designed to hurl an object into the past. While his son lay waiting in the machine, Mason carefully rechecked the equipment and handed the fated boy a small leather suitcase.

The two said goodbye to each other, and Mason walked directly to the power switch and administered the lethal beam. In an instant the boy, his clothes, and the suitcase "just disappeared," Oldsteiner said.

Following the tragedy, Mason sat motionless for nearly ten minutes while bewildered security guards notified the sheriff's department. Mason then set about disassembling the apparatus. When sheriff's deputies arrived more than an hour later, the new equipment had been virtually dismantled.

Dr. Malcolm Edwards, allowed by military police to talk to reporters after viewing the video tape of the incident, said that he felt Mason had gone mad. The entire mechanism had been set up in a way totally strange to him, and he had worked closely with Mason over a period of years, he said.

When asked if he felt Mason was trying to send his son back in time, as Mason had done with other non-organic materials, Edwards thought it was "highly unlikely."

Edwards explained that the tempor-tation process involves the destruction of an object and its simultaneous reconstitution at an earlier time. Particles emanating from the destroyed object are projected upon a high-energy field in the past by means of a tachyon beam, which travels backwards in time like a fish swimming upstream. The new, but identical object is created at the place and time the tachyon beam intersects the field.

But last night Mason failed to activate the high-energy electrical field used in all previous temportation experiments, Edwards told reporters.

Early Trial Date
Agreed Upon

Yesterday morning a lengthy conference took place in the chambers of assigned Municipal Court Judge Stanley S. Cooper involving Mason's attorney Whitcomb, deputy Oldsteiner, and officials of the Army and Defense Departments. There has been speculation that the federal government might take steps to prevent Mason from being brought to trial due to the tight security that has been clamped upon the entire project.

Just before noon a compromise appeared to have been reached, and Mason was brought into court to enter his plea of not guilty and to waive his right to a preliminary examination before being bound over to the Superior Court for trial.

Mason was immediately taken for arraignment before specially assigned Superior Court Judge LeRoy Clayton, where he again pleaded not guilty and

waived his right to be tried by a jury. Judge Clayton set bail at $100,000, despite pleas by Whitcomb for a lower amount.

Trial has been set for next month before Superior Court Judge David Nomellini, who is to be brought in specially from Butte County. The selection of Nomellini and the early trial date appear to be the result of a complex behind-the-scenes agreement between prosecuting attorneys, Whitcomb, and representatives of the Army, who are interested in expediting the trial so that Mason can return to head further development of the temportation project.

Judge Nomellini was reportedly chosen because prior to his study of law he obtained a Ph.D in physics from I.I.T. and is conversant with sophisticated modern developments in that field. It is anticipated that Mason's trial will involve issues in the area of nuclear physics. Judge Nomellini could not be reached for comment.

Following his second court hearing of the day, Mason appeared briefly with his wife Beverly and his seventeen-year-old daughter, Michelle. At the insistence of his attorney, Mason refused to answer questions directly relating to the slaying. When asked how he was feeling, Mason responded that he was afraid. "I suddenly don't know what is going to happen to me," he said.

Mason also stated that he would not be able to raise the bail set by Judge Clayton.

In a related development, a Defense Department spokesman in Washington today announced that the temportation project would be continued without delay by the other scientists involved, and he named Dr. Malcolm Edwards nominal head of the team until Mason's return.

Dr. Edwards was later contacted and explained that Mason's notebooks, which alone contain the key to the project, have disappeared. Edwards speculated that the notebooks may have been inside a suitcase which was destroyed at the time the younger Mason was killed.

Due to tight security, Edwards has been unable to communicate with Mason, and it is reported that Mason refuses to talk to anyone, including Army scientists, about his work. Edwards expressed serious doubts about the ability of the research team to continue in Mason's absence.

Mason is expected to remain in custody pending the trial. He is being guarded by Army security police in a separate section of the Humboldt County jail specially set aside for that purpose.

MASON: SON AND I ARE ONE

Scientist Testifies Under Oath He Sent Son Back to 1945

EUREKA, Ca. (API) In the most unusual murder trial of the century, "Dr. Christian Mason testified under oath in his own defense here yesterday that on the evening of August 10 he sent his twenty-year- old son, Christian, Jr., on a trip back in time to Chicago, 1945, where he was to become the elder Christian Mason himself.

In response to his attorney's question, "What did you do to your son?" Mason testified without interruption for nearly an hour before Superior Court Judge David Nomellini at his own trial in which he is charged with the first-degree murder of his son.

"My entire life since 1945 has been devoted to this single task," Mason testified. He told the Court that he had lived through the past three decades twice, first as the son, and then as the father.

"I owe my very existence here today to the success of the experiment on August 10th, and the fact that I am here today is proof that it succeeded, that Christian did not die, because I am still alive today," he testified.

Mason further testified that this was the reason why he had been required to falsify certain records and applications concerning his childhood--presently being investigated by the Defense Department--because he had not in fact lived his childhood "before" his adult life, in terms of calendar years, but simultaneously with it. "To me, though, it all went along in one straight line," he said.

Likening himself to a modern-day Oedipus, Mason testified that in 1957 he sought out his own mother, the former Beverly Phillips, who at the time was one of his students at the University of California at Berkeley, and married her the following year.

Two years later she gave birth to a son, who Mason claims was he himself, and who is the alleged victim at the murder trial.

Mason's wife and seventeen-year-old daughter Michelle were conspicuously absent from the front-row seats specially reserved for them, and they could not be contacted later at the Mason home in nearby Blue Lake.

Responding to a list of questions read to him by his attorney, James Whitcomb, Mason substantiated the technical testimony given the previous day by prosecution witness and former colleague Dr. Malcolm Edwards, but expanded in detail on what actually occurred on the evening of August 10th at the Mad River Radiation Laboratory in Blue Lake.

The younger Mason, together with his clothes, his suitcase, and books, was converted into a beam of faster-than-light tachyons, tiny subatomic particles which go backwards in time, and the beam was focused upon the high-energy field produced by the early atomic scientists at Stagg Field at the University of Chicago in 1945.

Hitting the field with the beam was easy, Mason testified, comparing the task to that of throwing metal darts at a powerful magnet. Precisely where the beam would intersect the field, however, he could not be certain. "It could well have been 1944 or 1946. As a matter of fact it just happened to be February 17, 1945. That's the date I first appeared at Stagg Field," he testified.

Following Mason's direct testimony, the Court called a recess at the request of deputy district attorney Frank Oldsteiner.

Oldsteiner and Whitcomb retired to chambers with Judge Nomellini for a lengthy off-record discussion.

On cross-examination, Oldsteiner, who later told reporters he felt that Mason's testimony was the most absurd he had ever heard, asked Mason why he had never revealed his story before now. Mason replied that he had not wanted to do so even now, but he was forced to by the exigencies of his criminal defense.

On further cross-examination, Mason admitted that in the process of converting his son into the beam of tachyons, the "total material and substance" of the youth were "destroyed, annihilated, and disintegrated," so that if it were not for his being sent back in time, it could be said that the boy had ceased to exist.

Prosecution Case Brief

Mason's startling testimony followed what may have been the briefest murder prosecution of modern times. Deputy district attorney Oldsteiner rested his case the previous day after only four witnesses and a closed-door viewing by Judge Nomellini of a video tape of the August 10th slaying.

Starting at 9 a.m. sharp, Oldsteiner made a brief opening

statement and called Dr. Malcolm Edwards--one of Mason's colleagues and his successor as project head--to the witness stand to establish that Mason and his son had been working for several years with the high-energy equipment at the Mad River Radiation Laboratory.

On cross-examination, Attorney Whitcomb, with frequent assistance from Mason, questioned Edwards in depth about the technical nature of the equipment being used, and the nature of the experiments being conducted.

Edwards testified under questioning that the younger Mason disappeared as the subject of an experiment which in theory would have sent him back in time, although no preparations had been made for retrieving him.

Oldsteiner also called as witnesses the two Army security officers who watched the slaying live on closed-circuit television, and the Humboldt County sheriff's deputy who made the initial arrest of Mason following the incident. On cross-examination Whitcomb limited his questions to whether any of the witnesses had seen any evidence that the young Mason was in fact dead, to which all witnesses answered in the negative.

Following a late recess, the courtroom was cleared of all but Judge Nomellini, counsel, the defendant, three of the witnesses, and the court reporter, for a viewing of the video tape made by Army security officers of Mason's activities on the evening of the slaying. Due to its security classification, reporters were not allowed to view the tape.

Following the viewing, Oldsteiner rested his case.

Defense Testimony Limited by Court

After Mason's three hours of testimony and a lunch recess, Whitcomb attempted to call a fingerprint expert to testify that the fingerprints of the elder and the younger Mason were identical, but the prosecution objected on the ground that such testimony was irrelevant and immaterial. Following a brief but heated discussion between counsel at the bench, Judge Nomellini sustained the objection, adding that in the present posture of legal and physical science, he was "foreclosed from hearing testimony that two distinct persons existing at the same time are one and the same person."

The same objection, raised later when Mason's attorney attempted to call a dental technician to compare x-rays taken from the mouths of both Masons, was again sustained, with Judge Nomellini commenting: "I'm afraid I cannot allow proof that two different people are one and the same person, because the law unequivocally holds otherwise. If you wish to change the law, you will have to take that up with a higher court or the legislature."

Whitcomb then called biologist Dr. Charles Aicher, who had recently worked with Mason, but his testimony was limited by the Court to the actual effect of the scientific apparatus on living matter. On cross-examination, Aicher admitted that, but for the possibility of a reappearance of the young Mason in the past, the young man was biologically dead.

Apparently frustrated by Judge Nomellini's rulings, Whitcomb surprised the entire courtroom by resting his case, promising to appeal the Court's decision in the event that the judgment should go against Mason.

In his closing argument, Oldsteiner told the Court that as to premeditation--an element that the prosecution must prove for a murder to be first degree--he had never heard of a crime that was more premeditated. By his own testimony, Mason had been planning the act for the past thirty-four years.

The evidentiary phase of the unusual trial was completed, but Judge Nomellini allowed Whitcomb time to research the obscure legal issues and submit a brief of points and authorities to the Court. Oldsteiner will be given additional time to file his reply brief on behalf of the prosecution.

Following yesterday's court session, Gilber Newman, retired colleague and strong critic of Mason who was standing-by as a possible rebuttal witness for the prosecution, said that Mason was in his opinion "either insane, or thinks the Court is full of fools. I honestly don't know which."

A verdict is not expected for several weeks while briefs are being prepared. Mason will apparently remain in custody pending the Court's decision.

In Washington, a Defense Department spokesman admitted earlier that scientists were unable to proceed with Mason's work in his absence.

MASON GUILTY!

**Court Verdict of First-Degree Murder;
Sentencing Delayed**

EUREKA, Ca. (API) Dr. Christian Mason sat pale and trembling as Superior Court Judge David Nomellini pronounced him guilty as charged of the first-degree murder of his son during an experiment at the Mad River Radiation Laboratory in Blue Lake on August 10, 1979.

The Court's judgment followed last month's short, but bizarre trial in which Mason denied killing the twenty-year-old boy, testifying that he had instead sent the youth back in time to Chicago, 1945, where the boy was to become the elder Christian Mason himself, later marrying his own mother and siring himself as a son.

In briefs and oral argument held last week Mason's attorney James Whitcomb had urged the Court to recognize a legal distinction between "an atomic temportation" and a homicide and requested the Court to reopen the evidence to allow proof that Mason and his son were one and the same person. Whitcomb had unsuccessfully attempted to introduce expert testimony comparing fingerprints and dental records at the time of trial. The Court was not persuaded by the attorney's arguments.

Judge Nomellini's verdict was contained in a lengthy opinion delivered from the bench, in which he explained that he had no choice in the matter because the law as it stands requires a finding of guilty.

"Considering the evidence in the light most favorable to the defendant, we have a case in which this boy, young Mason, entered the laboratory as a warm, living, breathing human being, and through the instrumentality of the defendant, he left, if at all, as no more than a pattern of electrical impulses modulating a collection of atomic particles that are not even universally agreed to exist," Judge Nomellini said. From the biological standpoint, the boy is dead, and from the legal perspective, the boy was killed by Mason, the Judge said.

**Philosophical
Considerations**

The Court's opinion did not limit itself to strictly legal matters. Judge Nomellini stated he was "deeply troubled by the philosophical consequences" of Mason's defense: "If the defendant's account is true, whence came Mason's own genetic material? Who are his biological ancestors? And the red notebooks containing the project notes, allegedly sent back with the boy, caught in a time eddy, forever circling between 1945 and 1979--what of their origin? To accept the defendant's formulation would require us to rethink our most basic understanding of time and the universe, cast out Newton and Einstein, and confront a paradox coiled like a worm at the core of existence. This the Court is not prepared to do."

Agreeing with the prosecution's arguments on premeditation, Judge Nomellini observed that Mason knew, perhaps better than any other living person, the consequences of turning his apparatus upon a living human subject. The Judge therefore felt he could not consider second-degree murder or manslaughter, which would otherwise be proper as lesser included offenses.

Judge Nomellini said that if Mason or his attorney felt wronged by his decision, they should certainly exercise their right of appeal, for the appellate courts have greater freedom in areas of new law.

Finally, the Judge set an appeal bail at $250,000 and delayed sentencing for 30 days. Under California's new determinate sentencing law, Mason could be sentenced to a prison term of twenty-five years to life, unless the prosecution is able to prove special circumstances, in which case he could receive the death penalty or life imprisonment without possibility of parole.

Whitcomb Angry

Defense Attorney Whitcomb was visibly angry following the verdict. "You can bet your life we're going to appeal this one," he later told reporters. "We offered him (Judge Nomellini) positive proof that the victim of the alleged murder was in fact still very much alive, and he refused to consider the evidence or even allow it into the record."

Whitcomb also felt the appeal bond set by the Judge was too high. "If he knows that Mason can't make $100,000, how can he expect him to be able to come up with a quarter of a million?" he said.

Asked whether he had considered insanity as a defense, Whitcomb told reporters that Mason would not permit it. Whitcomb feels the defense used is an adequate one, and he hopes to be vindicated on appeal.

Mason's wife and daughter were again absent from the courtroom, and reporters have been unable to contact them or learn their whereabouts for more than a month.

The Defense Department, which has been awaiting Mason's release to resume command of the temportation project in Blue Lake, had no comment today concerning recent developments. Reliable sources say the Army is considering abandonment of the project, which has come to a standstill in the scientist's absence.

Mason will be returned to court next month for sentencing.

MASON ESCAPES

FBI Searching for Mason and Mysterious Accomplice

EUREKA, Ca. (API) Humboldt County sheriff's deputies and FBI agents here have mobilized a massive manhunt for convicted murderer Dr. Christian Mason and a mysterious, elderly man, estimated to be in his eighties, who calls himself Mason's father, and who engineered a daring daylight escape yesterday from the maximum security jail located on the top floors of the Humboldt County courthouse where Mason was in custody awaiting sentencing.

The elderly accomplice managed the jailbreak by burning a two-by-three-foot hole in a solid, inch-thick steel door located at the third-floor entrance to the jail. The man held three sheriff's deputies at gunpoint while he convinced Mason, over the objections of Mason's attorney, to accompany him.

The fugitives escaped from the building by descending only to the second floor by elevator, then calmly walking past the District Attorney's office to a seldom used stairwell leading to an exit on Fourth Street. They were last seen driving east in a late model blue-and-white Pinto that had been stolen earlier in the day from an Arcata man.

Despite immediate attempts by police to seal off the courthouse and then to head off the fleeing automobile, Mason and his companion avoided capture, and the escape vehicle was later found abandoned on West End Road near Blue Lake.

Authorities reportedly do not know the present whereabouts of the fugitives, and Mason's wife and seventeen-year-old daughter, both missing since last Tuesday, are suspected of aiding Mason in his flight.

Deputy District Attorney Frank Oldsteiner, who had handled the prosecution of Mason on murder charges, charged that the CIA had a hand in the escape, so that Mason could resume his secret research in time travel for the Army. Late this morning, however, both the CIA and the Army issued statements denying any knowledge of the matter.

Witnesses reported that at approximately 9:20 a.m. yesterday

Mason was interviewing with his attorney James Whitcomb in one of the two unlocked interview cells located just off the front desk on the third floor of the jail. The interview cells are under direct view of a desk sergeant and his two deputies, all armed, and the entire jail is cut off from the elevators and stairs to the street level by a heavy steel door which is kept locked at all times.

According to desk sergeant Clifford Boyles, there was a tremendous roar, which sounded like a prolonged explosion. When he looked up, an elderly man stepped through the smoke and pointed a large-caliber revolver at him and his two deputies.

Boyles described the man as about the same height and appearance as Mason himself, but older by at least twenty-five years. Under his left arm he held a device Boyles did not recognize which was apparently used to burn the hole in the door.

The armed man announced that he had come for Mason, who had emerged with his attorney from the interview cell at the sound of the explosion.

Boyles and the deputies were in agreement that Mason and Whitcomb both seemed as sur-prised as they were at the incident. Authorities later questioned Whitcomb extensively, but they do not believe that the attorney had any prior knowledge of the escape plan.

Mason was at first reluctant to accompany the gunman. According to Deputy Dorothy Probosian, who was also held at gunpoint, Mason asked the man who he was, and he replied that he was Mason's father, and that he had "come back" to get him. Mason responded that he thought he understood.

Attorney Whitcomb tried to dissuade his client from accompanying the armed man, assuring Mason that the court would be lenient in sentencing, but that there would be severe repercussions if he attempted to escape.

Then, according to Probosian, Mason asked the man if they would be caught, and the gunman assured him that they would not. This seemed to satisfy Mason, and the two men departed.

By the time the deputies had recovered and pursued with guns drawn through the new hole in the jail door, the elevator was on its way down.

Witnesses said that after emerging from the building, Mason and his armed companion entered a late-model Pinto and drove east on Fourth Street, with the gunman driving. Although police pursued immediately and set up observation points along all possible routes of escape, the auto was not seen again until it was found an hour later abandoned on West End Road not far from the Mad River Radiation Laboratory in Blue Lake.

The FBI was then called in to assist local authorities, who presumed that the fugitives would be in interstate flight.

Federal authorities seem particularly concerned that Mason may flee the country.

An FBI explosives expert examined the damaged door at the jail and later told newsmen that he had never seen anything like it in all his years of work. The only mechanism he knows that could have quickly burned such a clean hole in the thick steel door was a type of laser gun now undergoing development for the steel industry.

"But it will be years before it has any practical use, and twenty years before it could be made portable enough for a job like this," he said.

In an attempt to learn the identity of the mysterious gunman, investigators have dusted the escape automobile for fingerprints. In another strange development it was learned early this afternoon that although the gunman was seen to enter the driver's side of the auto and drive it away, the only fingerprints to be found on either door handle, or on the steering wheel (besides those of the owner) were unmistakably those of Dr. Christian Mason himself. Experts have not as yet been able to account for this.

When asked whether authorities possessed information which will lead to an early apprehension of the fugitives, a reliable FBI source said that it was only a matter of time.

About the Author

Richard S. Platz maintained a solo law practice in Humboldt County, California, for 35 years. He served as City Attorney for the City of Blue Lake for 32 of those years before retiring there in 2009. In addition to these short stories, the author has written another book of short stories entitled *Memories and other Fictions* and the novels *Appointment At Angahuan* (with James A. Kline), *Of Magic and Delusion*, and *Project Divine Wind*. He has also written short stories, poetry, and articles on various topics, including *Backpacking in Jefferson*, which can be read on his website: www.richardplatz.com.

www.ingramcontent.com/pod-product-compliance
Lightning Source LLC
Chambersburg PA
CBHW071502170626
46811CB00007B/2686